THE SEEKERS | BOOK THREE

THE LIGHT OF REASON

DAVID LITWACK

Litwack

THELIGHT OF REASON
Copyright © 2016 David Litwack
Cover Art Copyright © 2016 Mallory Rock

FIRST EDITION SOFTCOVER
ISBN: 1622534387
ISBN-13: 9781622534388

Editor: Lane Diamond
Interior layout & design by Mallory Rock

Printed in the U.S.A.
www.EvolvedPub.com
Evolved Publishing LLC
Cartersville, Georgia

What Others Are Saying About David Litwack's Books:

The Daughter of the Sea and the Sky:

"...a fully imagined, gripping read...."

~ Kirkus Reviews

"Author David Litwack gracefully weaves together his message with alternating threads of the fantastic and the realistic.... The reader will find wisdom and grace in this beautifully written story...."

~ San Francisco Review Book Review

"...an enthralling look at an alternative world... thought-provoking, beautifully written and highly entertaining."

~ Jack Magnus for Readers' Favorite

"David Litwack's sweeping novel *The Daughter of the Sea and the Sky* is a powerful story that follows the journey of a mysterious but charming little girl whose mere presence seems to have changed the lives of those people around her... Superbly imagined with a tense plot which makes it difficult to put down...."

~ the GreatReads!

~~~

The Children of Darkness:

"A tightly executed first fantasy installment that champions the exploratory spirit."

~ Kirkus Reviews

"The plot unfolds easily, swiftly, and never lets the readers' attention wane.... After reading this one, it will be a real hardship to have to wait to see what happens next."

~ Feathered Quill Book Reviews

"The quality of its intelligence, imagination, and prose raises *The Children of Darkness* to the level of literature."

~ *Awesome Indies*

"...a fantastic tale of a world that seeks a utopian existence, well ordered, safe and fair for everyone... also an adventure, a coming-of-age story of three young people as they become the seekers, travelers in search of a hidden treasure — in this case, a treasure of knowledge and answers. A tale of futuristic probabilities... on a par with Huxley's *Brave New World*."

~ *Emily-Jane Hills Orford, Readers' Favorite Book Awards*

~~~

The Stuff of Stars:

"...an excellent book about what it means to be human, what humanity can strive for, and ultimately the balance between technology and nature, dreams and reality... a great page turner and a ton of fun to read... one of my new favorites."

~ *Michael SciFan*

"...a thought-provoking and well-crafted tale - one that will delight lovers of dystopia, science fiction and fantasy. Its message will stay in your mind long after you've turned the last page."

~ *Hilary Hawkes for Readers' Favorite*

"...as unique, unpredictable and well-written as the first book... Another 5-star beauty from David Litwack."

~ *Awesome Indies*

"*The Stuff of Stars* is dystopian literature at its best."

~ *Feathered Quill Book Reviews*

"...a fantastic story that continues the plot initiated in the first Seekers book: a tale about a futuristic utopian world that is anything but perfect. There is only one word to truly define this novel: WOW!"

~ *Emily-Jane Hills Orford for Readers' Favorite*

For Amy, and for all the children yet to be born — for our hope for the future and for our dreams of a better world.

Part One

THE SMOLDERING FLAMES

"It's once I was free to go roaming in
The wind of the springtime mind
And once the clouds I sailed upon
Were sweet as lilac wine
Then why have the breezes of summer, dear
Enlaced with a grim design?"

- Richard Farina

Chapter 1

The Lighthouse

Near first light, I spotted a glimmer where the sun should rise, but it flickered too low on the horizon. If I trusted the dreamers' guidance—always precise until now—the red glow of dawn should be higher up, above the ragged peaks of the granite mountains. This light before me, though bright enough to cast sparkles across the waves, appeared more like a bonfire on the shore.

Perhaps weary from my four-hour watch, my eyes had deceived me. With the toe of my boot, I nudged Nathaniel awake and pointed to the east. "There. Do you see it?"

He rubbed the sleep from his eyes with the heel of his hands, and let out a lung-busting yawn before following my gesture. "A light, Orah, but too dim to be the dawn."

We both gazed until our eyes teared. Moments later, a second glow joined its lesser twin—the sun rising over the familiar saw-toothed peaks.

The dawn grew brighter now, letting us distinguish sea from land, and the source of the glimmer became clear. A wooden structure emerged from the fog, a tower on the beach where none had stood before. The modest tower tapered near its top, where a fire blazed, a flame too bright for torchlight alone—a beacon to welcome us home.

How fast our ship had flown. Its sleek hull, designed by the dreamers, had glided over the water when the sea lay calm, and sliced

1

through the waves when they rose to resist. The outbound voyage in our crude vessel had lasted nearly two months, but now our dreamer-designed boat had carried us back in less than half that time.

I clung to a spar of the mast as the breeze blew wisps of hair across my face, and relished the sound of seawater lapping the shore. The dreamers, so much wiser than the keepmasters, had plotted the most efficient course using maps that tracked the ocean currents, ancestral charts from a thousand years before.

And so, dreamer-guided and current-borne, we neared our destination.

Unlike our prior voyage, I felt well rested and in better spirits. With more than thirty souls aboard, no need to spend half of each night on watch, and this time I arrived not as a stranger to a new land, but as a wanderer returning home.

Ahead, what I'd learned to be a continent rose up from the mist, a shelf of dry sand followed by rocky cliffs rising steeply into the granite mountains. As I pondered the scene and the strange cargo in our hold, myth became reality — the explorers of legend bringing back treasures for their people.

Nathaniel led me to the bow for a better view. As our boat drew closer to the shore, the tower's peak came into focus — a flame reflecting off a polished mirror, and beside it a shadow, a figure standing alone.

Our eyes met, but the figure stood too far off to recognize. Then he turned away and raced down the stairs, hopefully a friend to greet us when we landed.

I donned the white bonnet with its winged flaps that seemed to mimic the sails, and adjusted the sensors around its brim so they fit snugly to my skull. At once my mind joined with our boat. I sensed the waves splashing against her bow, and gauged the depth beneath her keel. With a quick thought, I trimmed the sails to let her drift toward the shore.

Thanks to the genius of the dreamers and a gentler beach, we glided to a landing more peaceful than the year before, when the crash of wood on rock had destroyed our first boat. Not this time. Now our bow settled softly into the shallows.

Caleb rushed on deck, barking orders to the crew as he went. Those with tasks to fulfill scurried about, while the others lined the side rails, ogling as I had done when I first caught sight of the distant shore. Caleb lowered the ladder and insisted Nathaniel and I disembark first, a way to honor the seekers who had brought these two worlds together.

I scrambled down and waded through the knee-deep water. Once on dry sand, I dropped to my knees—another dream attained, one I'd believed impossible not so long ago. I turned to face the sea and formed a picture frame with my thumbs and fingers, imagining the world I'd left behind—a land of earth people and machine masters. How shocking to switch so quickly from one world to the next. What must it have been like in the time of the darkness to cross the ocean in flying machines, to complete such a journey in hours?

A seagull flitted aimlessly overhead across the clouded sky. Small waves broke against the shore at regular intervals, leaving behind a gentle curve and tiny bubbles on the beach.

With cupped hands, I scooped up some sand, so much like the sand where our boat had crashed the year before, but different. I let the grains trickle through my fingers like sand in an hourglass.

Yes, this sand is different — the sand of my home.

Nathaniel gasped beside me, a sudden intake of air.

I glanced up to catch the figure from the tower approaching. Despite the dim light, I recognized him at once by his gait, with his broad shoulders and jaw jutting out—Nathaniel's father, William Rush—but he appeared gaunter than I recalled, a shadow of the elder I knew.

His pace quickened, his face brightening with joy. "Nathaniel, Orah! My prayers answered. Thank the light you're alive."

We rushed to close the gap, and the three of us clutched in a long and silent embrace.

When we separated, his eyes widened as he took in our boat. How strange it must have been to gaze upon a boat so different from the one he'd helped us build the year before—no longer canvas sails, but wing-like sheets of the thinnest metal, with no hemp ropes or any other visible means to trim them.

How could I explain that these sails sensed the wind and adjusted for maximum speed on their own, or that if I wished to change their tilt, I had but to don a bonnet and think?

His amazement grew when dozens of strangers followed down the ladder, men and women from the far side of an ocean whose existence he'd once denied.

"So many," he said.

I nodded. "They've come to help."

He eyed the party as if counting heads, and then turned back to the base of the tower, where a flimsy lean-to sheltered supplies.

"For the past few months, I've kept a stock of provisions, thinking you'd arrive exhausted and starving. Our loyal neighbors brought enough for me to stay and stand watch, and if you arrived, to let you hide here until they made sure the village was safe. But with so many, these provisions won't last long."

"Hide?" Nathaniel blurted out the word before I could digest its meaning.

His father shook his head. "Things aren't as you left them. Better to wait here while those I trust survey the situation, before we risk the trek over the mountains. But with so many, we should return to Little Pond at once, especially with a storm on its way."

He tossed a nod to the horizon, and I followed his eyes. The sky behind me had darkened as if reflecting my change in mood—ominous clouds blowing in from the west.

"Why wouldn't we go straightaway?" I said. "We've been gone so long, and I'm eager to see my mother and Thomas again."

A shadow crossed his face, and he glanced away. "Your mother, yes."

A fluttering in my stomach made me wince, but I forced a smile, still happy to be back on my home shores. "And Thomas too."

Frown lines appeared between his eyebrows. He blinked and stared past me, with lips tight and eyes riveted on a point over my shoulders and out to sea.

I turned. The bank of clouds seemed closer, as if following us into shore.

"How long have you waited here?" I said, trying to regain his focus.

"Too long." He grasped Nathaniel's arm and squeezed as if to test the flesh was real. "Through all these months, I kept my faith and never believed the lies the vicars spread, but you come back to a sadder place. They punish folks who speak their minds, and deacons search for me." He took in a long draft of air and blew it out. "They've placed a bounty on my head. My good neighbors keep my whereabouts a secret and bring provisions as needed. Thank the light, the deacons believe demons of the darkness dwell on this side of the mountains. I'm safe as long as I stay here—safe but alone, with nothing but the lapping of the waves and the hope of your return." He eased into a grim smile. "And now at last you've come."

Nathaniel's lip curled into a sneer and his fists tightened. "How could they—"

His father waved him to silence and pointed at the encroaching clouds. "We can talk later. The storm will strike in a few hours, and this tower's too small to shelter so many. I've lived through such storms in the past. They can be violent, but never seem to go beyond the summit. Best we make the climb at once and clear the heights before the first gale hits." He glanced at Caleb's men as they started to unload provisions from the hold. "We should travel light. Though Little Pond's lot has worsened, we still have food and drink. Tell your crew to leave their cargo behind."

"Not all of our cargo," Nathaniel said. "Some of what we've brought must come with us." He signaled to Caleb. "Leave the provisions. We'll find plenty in the village, but fetch the machines."

Of those on board, only Nathaniel and I had gone to sea before. Now even Caleb's stout men struggled with the return to land, staggering across the uneven sand as they hauled the mending machine and the crate of spare parts Kara had insisted on bringing.

Nathaniel's father gaped at them. "What are those? Is it wise to haul so much over the mountain pass, when we need to travel fast?"

"It's wise and many times more," I said. "This cargo will bring a better life to our people."

His eyes widened when, last of all, the crew lowered the opaque black cube to the beach, its bits of lightning flashing inside like a captive storm. "What is that?"

I smiled my I-know-the-answer smile and patted the cube, causing a familiar tingling on my fingertips that traveled to the roots of my hair. I fought off the urge to don the white bonnet and commune with my wise friends, to share with them my excitement at returning home. "Too hard to explain, but you'll see I'm right, in time. What we've brought back from the distant shore will change our world."

"I hope you're right," he said. "We can use some good news."

Good news. An image flashed in my mind of a grinning Thomas sitting by the pond and playing his flute.

"But what of Thomas?" I said more insistently than before.

His chin dropped to his chest, and he stared at his boot tops. "We'll talk later, once you're safe and in your mother's arms. Then she and I will sip hot tea by the fireplace and share the sad news, as we once told you about the teaching your father and I endured."

I opened my mouth to speak, but before I uttered a word, distant thunder rumbled from the gathering storm. I spun around to look. The massive bank of clouds was rolling toward us from far across the sea, letting loose a flurry of lightning bolts, as if probing every nook and cranny of the waves, searching for our long-lost innocence. In a dozen seconds, their resulting claps boomed and dwindled to a faint but angry echo, followed by silence.

Without another word, Nathaniel's father trudged off, his shoulders hunched like one close to defeat, yet with some fire still burning inside. Seabirds scattered before him as he headed back across the cove to the start of the notch through the granite mountains, and beyond it, to Little Pond, my home.

Chapter 2

Over the Mountains

I'd forgotten how steeply the trail climbed, a heart-pumping trek over a mountain pass that no one before us had crossed for a thousand years. To prepare for our initial voyage, our neighbors had widened the path, removed prickly undergrowth, and carved steps into the rocks where the slope steepened, all to make way for supplies needed to build our boat and sustain us during the long passage. Now, after a year of neglect, winter snow had littered the path with debris, and the prickly bushes had re-grown, encroaching everywhere.

As we plodded along, hoping to beat the storm, those bearing our cargo struggled to navigate the trail, their legs weakened from the weeks at sea. After a while, Caleb took the lead, swinging his axe in wide arcs to clear the way.

Kara raced back and forth, from the black cube to the other machines we'd brought along, urging those entrusted with her treasures to take care.

The bearers grumbled despite her encouragement. Why shouldn't they? Though they'd experienced the miracle of the mending machine, as it had healed both greenie and techno alike, the contents of the cube remained a mystery to all but Kara, Caleb, Nathaniel and me. The others viewed the dreamers as objects of myth, and their container struck them with fear. No wonder. How could anyone fathom a device containing the disembodied minds of

7

geniuses? Even after the dozens of times I'd delved into the dream, the cube still struck me with awe.

The rest of their burden consisted of spare parts Kara had gathered in haste from the machine masters' city, choosing what might be needed in our more primitive world. Only she understood their possible use, and even then her choices were more guess than plan.

Jacob and Devorah lagged behind, craning their necks and gawking at the terrain to gauge how much this new world differed from their own. From their chatter, they seemed surprised it looked the same. They'd left the safety of the earth mother's village to follow us, hoping to learn new skills from our people. I could hardly wait to introduce them to our craftsmen, who'd lived far longer without machines.

Zachariah walked close by, as usual unwilling to leave my side. He eyed the granite peaks and said, "A nicer mountain."

"Nicer?"

"Than the mountain of fire that took the dreamers."

Despite the effort of the climb, I smiled, his presence lightening my mood almost as much as Nathaniel's. He'd celebrated his tenth birthday during our voyage, and seemed to have grown a hand since I met him on the beach a year ago.

"Who is that man," he said, "the one from the tower?"

"He's Nathaniel's father, and mine now as well by marriage."

"What makes his shoulders slump like that? Isn't he happy to see you?"

I gazed up to the top of the pass, still looming too far ahead. My breath came in short bursts, though Zachariah barely labored, and I answered between gulps of air. "Yes, of course."

"Then why does he wrinkle his brow and stare past you when he speaks?"

"It's nothing. Just your imagination after so much time at sea."

"Now you're wrinkling your brow as well."

I trudged along another dozen steps, until he stopped and tugged at my hand. "Will he protect the black cube?"

His never-ending questions reminded me of Thomas at the same age, and how he'd pester me, never letting an answer pass, but now I was the adult and Zachariah the child. All my experience, through pain and sorrow, had taught me the truth in the questions of a child. I ruffled his hair, much as the elders had once done to distract my friends and me.

I paused a step to catch my breath and sniff the air—the smell of salt had lessened, overwhelmed by the earthier scents of plants and soil. "You worry too much, Zachariah. All will be well."

He turned and confronted me with eyes too big for his head. "I worry because what's left of my parents lives in that cube, and all their memories too."

After a time, the slope became so challenging even Zachariah ceased to speak. Deep breathing replaced all chatter, along with the crunch of boots struggling for purchase —a sound much closer to silence.

Occasionally, a bird twittered, but soon it fled as well, as if seeking shelter ahead of the storm. The wind picked up speed every few minutes, until it howled as only a mountain wind could howl. The faster the wind, the quicker we walked, but my imagination came alive.

I imagined other sounds, evil portents I couldn't identify—a rustling in the surrounding brush, a trampling of fallen leaves, the occasional creak of tree limbs bowing in the breeze. These conspired in my mind, as they did when I'd lay awake at night as a little girl while a storm passed over our cottage. I'd imagine an army of creatures from the darkness clawing at my bedroom window, trying to get in.

At last we reached the height of land, and the trail switched downhill. Now our breathing eased just as the footing turned more treacherous. Kara and I raced back to warn the cargo bearers to narrow their stride and dig their heels into the hill, for fear of slipping on the loose scree.

An hour after we'd navigated the height of land, the wind calmed and the slope became less severe.

Nathaniel's father held up a hand to halt our parade and bid us rest at a rock ledge while he scanned the terrain below. After a moment, he cupped both hands around his lips and let out a call, which echoed down the mountain—two sharp notes, the first short and the second long—*hoo hooah.*

He turned back to us. "Now we wait."

After checking that everyone was doing well and our cargo remained secure, I brought out the water skins we'd taken from the lighthouse stash and passed them around. Then for the first time since we arrived, I sat down next to Nathaniel and took a moment to reflect.

The scents and sounds of the forest brought back kinder memories. As I stared out across the vista below, I drew in a quick breath, for in the distance lay my fondest dream come true—Little Pond.

Nathaniel pointed. "There! That patch of green is my family's farm, and beyond, you can make out the tower of the commons."

I gazed out with him and could almost hear the bell that night at festival, clanging sixteen times and signaling the vicar's arrival, an event that changed our lives.

Nathaniel went silent, regarding the place of our birth with a look more wistful than appropriate for one returning home.

I leaned close, forcing him to face me. "You've stopped at this spot before."

"I sat here that spring day I ran like a coward from the blessing of the light. Looking down at the village, I realized I was wrong to run. I dashed back but was too late. The vicar had gone, and he'd taken you with him for your teaching."

I brushed his cheek with my fingertips. "And if you'd arrived in time, we'd never have found the keep."

Our reverie was interrupted by a sequence of sounds from below.

Every child in Little Pond learned to mimic various birds, so perfectly that only those who practiced this skill could tell the difference. Now the air filled with such calls, mimicking that of Nathaniel's father—*hoo hooah, hoo hooah*. From down the mountain came a response. Then another a few hundred paces farther out, and another and another, each farther away, until the birdcalls stopped or were too far off to hear.

Nathaniel grabbed his father by the arm and faced him. "Why do you need to signal our arrival?"

William Rush crumpled his brow, gestured for quiet and listened. After a minute, a different sequence sounded in reply, three notes this time, repeated starting from afar—*hoo, hooah, hoo*.

He released the breath he'd been holding in, and the tension eased from his face. "We can go now."

"Why so much concern," I said. "We're going home."

"I'll explain in time, but for now, let's hurry down the slope, and get you and your strange cargo tucked away in neighboring farms while the village remains safe. The sooner we're out of the open, the better."

Nathaniel and I exchanged glances as the final birdcall faded away. I grasped his hand, and he squeezed back, but we said not a word. The thought passed unspoken between us, friends since birth: *This is not the world we left.*

Chapter 3

Little Pond

As we marched down the familiar path to my mother's cottage, the air filled with a shower of whistles. Birds flitted from branch to branch, calling out to each other in impassioned chirps, as if to show off their skill and humble their human imitators.

The storm had spent itself battering the far side of the mountain, and now noontime sunbeams streamed through breaks in the clouds, floating past like newly freed souls. Their light poured through the branches of the trees, brightening the clearing in front of my childhood home. With each breath I took, the fresh air pierced my lungs, and for the moment I understood how my people could worship the light, and how the greenies could give thanks to the earth.

I'm nearly home.

Word of our arrival had reached the villagers and many lined the road to greet us. From their midst burst a familiar face — my mother emerging to grasp me in a strong embrace.

When we separated, with both of our cheeks moist with tears, I scanned the crowd.

"Where's Thomas," I said.

She took in a quick breath, and the blood drained from her face. Her gaze retreated somewhere to the east, and when it came back, it settled on William Rush. "You haven't told them?"

He winced and looked away.

"Gone," she said. The word sounded hushed and hollow.

"Gone? To where? Has he traveled to the keep to find more music or to learn from the helpers how to make a new instrument?"

"Not to the keep. No one goes there anymore. He's gone to a darker place. But let's get you off the road and into your home, where we can conceal you for a while until we find a safer refuge."

My heart beat faster, a dull sound like somebody wearing mittens knocking at the door. "Conceal? But—"

My mother grasped my arms to steady me, as she'd done so often when I was a child. "Come home, Orah, to the cottage of your birth, where you can satisfy your hunger and quench your thirst, while William and I tell you what has befallen our side of the world."

I ached to find out more, but had a pressing task to do first. I glanced back at our weary crew, those who had followed Nathaniel and me from the distant shore, all strangers now in my land. I'd led them here and would be remiss to abandon them.

I turned to Nathaniel's father, and waved a hand to encompass Caleb and Jubal, Jacob and Devorah, Kara and Zachariah, and the rest of our crew. "What of them?"

My new father gazed to the bell tower of the commons, just visible over the treetops, and beyond to the east. "I've sent scouts ahead to watch for approaching danger, so we'll have ample warning. Just in case, we should disperse your fellow travelers into twos and threes, and tuck them away at neighboring farms. We'll swap out their strange clothing and dress them in local garb so they'd be indistinguishable from the villagers in the event the deacons come."

Kara slipped between us. "What about my machines? They should not be left out in the open. I won't leave them until you assure me they're safe."

So brash and impatient, as I was at her age.

I eased her aside. "Above all, our cargo must be protected."

His eyes narrowed. "Be reasonable, Orah. We need to protect your people first."

I grasped his arms, leaned close, and whispered in his ear with an urgency that took him aback. "Trust me, my new father. Whatever they seem, they're more vital to our future than the keep itself."

His brows rose, and he eyed me as if seeing me anew. "I trust you, new daughter. You've traveled to places beyond what I can imagine, and become more of an elder than me." He stroked his beard and considered a moment, then brightened. "I have an idea. Do you remember the grist mill at the outskirts of the village?"

"Yes, of course. The old stone building with the water wheel by the stream. Nathaniel, Thomas, and I used to play there as children."

"Since no one lives there, the deacons seldom search it, and now, in the harvest season, stacks of wheat pile high, waiting to be ground into grain. We can hide your treasures beneath the sheaves, at least until we make a better plan."

Nathaniel picked out Caleb and five of his stoutest men to accompany us and help carry the load, trusted men who would swear to silence and withstand a teaching if need be.

Kara insisted on coming as well, hovering over her machines like a mother over her young and making sure they were handled with care. Despite her youth, I'd watched her in time of trial and knew she'd defend these legacies of her forbearers with her life.

Zachariah, as usual, tried to follow, his big eyes staring at me as if worried Nathaniel and I, like his parents, would leave and never return.

My mind wandered to that dark place, my time in the teaching cell. Now that he'd found his voice, I couldn't risk him telling what he saw.

I knelt and enveloped him in my arms. "Go with these people, Zachariah. They're my family and friends and will keep you safe, just as you kept us safe in the earth mother's village. Go now. We'll be together in the morning."

A ten-minute walk down the road from the commons brought us to a side path, marked only by a gnarled dogwood that seemed to sprout out of a waist-high boulder. Everyone in Little Pond knew this tree as the signpost to the mill. The path led to a lovely spot with a windowless stone structure alongside a sparkling stream. An attached wooden wheel straddled the stream and turned with the flow of water.

To our neighbors, the site served a practical purpose, to grind grain into flour after the harvest, but for the older children, it provided a pleasant place to get away from the adults and pass the time. On a sunny day, when the wind was light, we'd fill a basket with cheese and freshly baked bread, and a jug of apple cider in season, and sit on the grass by the stream. As we ate our meal and reveled in the sound of the water, we'd talk of our future lives and the way we'd change the world.

Older and less innocent now, we set down our load, and I drew Nathaniel to the water's edge. "Remember how we used to marvel at the sunlight dancing off the water as it splashed across the blades of the wheel? That is, until I peeked to the place behind, where the sun didn't reach. Moss covered the rocks, leaving a shadowed and brooding place."

He placed a hand at the small of my back and rubbed. "I remember. Thomas would make up stories about demons of the darkness hiding there and waiting to pounce, and you'd peek behind the wheel, but never go too close."

My mood turned grim. "Now we find demons in other places."

Caleb's crusty features relaxed when he entered the glade. "A place that would please the earth mother, like our hall of winds, but why the wheel in the water?"

"The wheel turns a millstone inside that grinds our wheat into flour, a device your people can use once the wheat you've planted has been harvested."

He eyed the structure, analyzing its details—how the wheel spun the driveshaft that engaged the gears that made the millstone turn. When he'd seen his fill, he looked at me and nodded. "A useful machine."

"Another benefit of our voyage," I said, trying to lighten what had been a somber day. "Our craftsman will show you how it works, so you can build one when you go home."

He broke into a reluctant smile that hardened to a scowl as he gazed back down the path from where we came. "That is *if* we ever go home."

***

We went back to a whirlwind of activity. Nathaniel's father had sent dozens of runners to the east, nimble climbers who would hide in trees and signal if deacons approached—a more primitive form of the temple trees that made words fly across the land.

"They'll stagger their locations," he said, "each five hundred paces apart, and will give us warning—at least four hours if the deacons come on foot, but only fifteen minutes if they ride in fast wagons. Thankfully, they're cowards and travel only on main roads and in large groups, fearful of the people they were meant to serve. In either case, we'll have time to hide you and your friends in the woods. Now, my son and new daughter, come with me to the Weber cottage. Your mother has baked a fine Little Pond dinner, and we'll answer all your questions."

14

Once inside, I was struck by how small my childhood home had become, as if the walls had shriveled in the sun, but something else had changed. My mother's hard-earned cleanliness remained—no furniture stained, no curtain soiled, and the floor showed not the barest speck of dust. Yet the air inside seemed smudged with unspoken thoughts, blemishes of hopes that had died.

My mother served my favorite meal of broiled mutton and yams, though she used neither honey nor her usual spices.

"Deacons intrude," she explained, "barging in to search our homes unannounced, so we avoid the few pleasures the vicars once overlooked." She stared down at her hands, knobbier and more veined than I recalled. "If they find you with forbidden food or your dress violates their standards, if your beard is not properly groomed or your hair grows too long, or light forbid, you possess an unauthorized book, you will be punished more harshly than before. Some have been taken to Temple City for the smallest of offenses." She looked up and sighed. "So we do without to be safe."

I longed to learn more, to find out the threat to my new friends who had risked crossing the ocean on my promise of a better life, but the manners instilled in me as a young girl took over. I gratefully partook of this long-awaited meal in silence.

Once we'd finished and had cleared the table, we settled around the fireplace with our hands wrapped around mugs of apple cinnamon tea. Nathanial and I waited, afraid to ask, while our parents seemed afraid to tell.

At last, Nathaniel's father rubbed his eyes red as he had that evening when he told me of my father's death from the teaching—a teaching caused by his betrayal. When he spoke, I struggled to catch his words over the crackle of the fire. "Our lives changed on a single day, one of the warmest of late winter, after the snow had nearly thawed, a day with a clear sky that belied the storm to come. Vicars and deacons spread out across the land, assembling the children of light in their villages, though not yet time for the spring blessing. In Little Pond, we gathered by the altar in the village commons, expecting good news. Instead, the voice from the sun icon announced that the light had ordained a new grand vicar who would replace your old adversary, the former arch vicar. To our surprise, the human embodiment of the light on this earth had been usurped by a man you might recall—the very vicar that brought you and Thomas to your teachings."

My stomach fluttered as I recalled my trip to Temple City four years earlier, with the small man with the black beads for eyes. "But he was... no more than a monsignor when we left."

"That's true. Most view him as an upstart, yet many follow him, those who prefer a return to simpler ways, to a time before the three of you discovered the keep. On that day, through the sun icon, he claimed that he'd received a vision from the light, temple magic that told him how your foolhardy quest had ended, with your boat sunk and the two of you drowned."

Nathaniel rose from his seat, his fists balled at his sides and his jaw clenched. "Our people should know better. We showed them the truth, that the sun icon was science, a communication device from the past."

My mother stood and stoked the fire, a way of not looking at us. "If we've learned nothing else, it's that old beliefs die hard. When people are hurting or confused, they revert to the beliefs of their youth. Even I have my doubts at times. What you found in the keep fails to explain all."

I thought of the earth mother, with her lined face and gravelly voice: *There remains mystery in this world, things we cannot explain.*

My new father continued, his voice softer now. "Some worried that the knowledge you'd found, true or not, had made our lives worse. The vicars fed their grumbling. Others spoke out against them, but fewer than I'd hoped. You see, the vicars feed on fear. It took courage to speak out, so only a few did." He glanced up, and his eyes met mine. "Thomas was one of them."

I waited, breathing in and out until I could wait no more. "What happened to him?"

"Thomas refused to believe you had drowned, claiming he sensed the presence of his friends since birth, a feeling stronger than magic. He rallied some of like mind to march on Temple City, to protest to the grand vicar that he'd violated the truce. Most returned battered and bruised. Some never returned. No word of what happened to Thomas."

"What of those who returned? They must have known."

He shook his head and sighed. "Of course they knew, but they were too cowed to tell."

***

After these revelations, we bid our parents goodnight and retreated to my bedchamber.

16

Once we'd closed the door and were alone, the vein along Nathaniel's temple pulsed, and his lips tightened into a thin and bloodless line, but he said not a word. He withdrew instead to a place within that I'd seldom seen, a dark corner of his soul where his passion for good turned into a smoldering anger, too hot to share with me.

As we readied for bed, my mood darkened as well, not with anger but sadness. As a little girl, I'd retreat to this room to hide from the world when bad times came. Now, once again I felt like a little girl fleeing a scolding. What harm had I inflicted on my people, what pain on my friend? I fled here now not to seethe but to mourn.

The window stood open, the evening breeze rustling the white lace curtain my mother had sewn when I was small. I pictured her sitting by the fire and sewing while my father hummed a song. They lived a life of limits but always hoped for more for their only daughter.

I recalled my father's words as he lay dying: *"Now, little Orah, don't cry. You have a wonderful life ahead of you. Study hard in school and don't let the vicars set your mind. Think your own thoughts, big thoughts based on grand ideas, and find someone to love."*

I'd studied hard and learned so much on our journey to seek the truth, more than he'd ever imagined. I never let the vicars set my mind, and I'd found someone to love.

While Nathaniel settled into a restless sleep, I lay awake beside him and wondered. Was it enough to seek the truth, or did we also have to battle those who denied it?

And where is Thomas? What have they done with my friend?

I glared out the window to the east, where the village commons loomed, and beyond it Temple City. The time for dreaming had ended, and a single thought raged in my mind, a vow taken without reason or plan.

I'm coming, Thomas, I swear.

Chapter 4

A Reservoir of Courage

I spent the night dreaming childish dreams in what should have been the safety of my childhood home. When I awoke to the glare of dawn, the reality of our situation returned. What good was passion without a plan? Yet how could I plan with so many unknowns?

In the keep, when faced with as difficult a choice, I'd turned to the helpers for wisdom. Though nothing but recordings from a thousand years before, they'd revealed to me how much had been lost—cures for disease, travel to the stars, an understanding of the universe beyond anything I'd imagined. They showed that foolish girl from the tiny village of Little Pond the extent of the possible, but when I asked for weapons to fight the vicars, they chastised me: *"The abuse of knowledge brought the world to its current state.... The Temple of Light needed only ignorance to overturn our world. Let knowledge be your weapon to reverse the damage."*

They taught me instead more peaceful ways to spread the truth. I learned how to disrupt the vicars' communication by disabling the temple trees, print hundreds of messages, and make Nathaniel's voice boom forth from the sun icon, interrupting the grand vicar and starting our revolution.

Now the keep lay beyond my reach, but better advisors awaited nearby, perhaps the wisest who'd ever lived—the reason we'd borne the black cube from the distant shore. Though I could no longer join with the dreamers, I could consult with them by using the bonnet Kara had designed, and hear their response in my mind.

Let knowledge be your weapon....

I waited until the dawn's early light leaked around the edges of our bedchamber curtain, making Nathaniel's still form stir, and then grasped him in my arms and pressed my lips to his.

When we separated, he eyed me, knowing me so well. "What are you scheming now?"

"Will you come with me to the grist mill, as you did when we were little?"

"Of course, but what are you afraid of now? We've long since learned the folly of believing in demons from the darkness."

"The darkness hides in places other than the shadows behind a water wheel. It hides in the corners of our hearts. I'm so angry now, I'm afraid to ask the dreamers for help, worried what they might empower me to do, but I need them if we're to...." My eyes teared and my voice broke.

He finished my thought. "...to find a way to save Thomas. But only you and Kara can speak to the dreamers."

Kara had offered to make Nathaniel a hat with sensors like the one her grandfather, the mentor, had worn, but he'd claimed my bonnet would suffice since he and I were as one. I knew the real reason—since his first aborted encounter, he'd been uncomfortable communing with those disembodied minds. He'd always preferred passion and action to logic and reason, and so he'd declined the offer.

I held out a hand. "Come with me. In my anger at the vicars, I once asked the keepmasters for weapons. With Thomas taken, who knows what demons I might now find in the corners of my heart."

He gaped at me a moment and nodded. Not another word need be spoken for friends since birth.

Hand in hand, we hiked to the mill. Once there, we brushed away the sheaves of wheat and exposed the black cube. I donned my bonnet, much like Kara's with flaps on the sides like wings, but without the flowers the greenies had embroidered for her. This simple device, tuned to my mind, let me speak to the dreamers.

I reached out and touched the surface of the cube, though I knew it was unnecessary—this cap could commune with the dreamers from several paces away. The million bolts of lightning flickered faster inside, sensing my presence, and I felt the familiar tingling on my fingertips.

The dreamers dwelled in a world of pure thought, beyond the realm of language. Speaking with them required no words, as concepts arrived whole into my mind.

***

A stirring of minds, a buzzing like a beehive aroused, and then the myriad of thoughts settled into a series of snippets distinct enough to understand.

"Orah...."

"Has the boat sailed yet?"

"Or are you still on our side of the ocean?"

"We have no sense of time or place...."

"You and Kara must be our eyes and ears...."

I calmed myself to organize my response. Communicating this way differed from joining them in the dream. With my mind separate from theirs, they had no access to my memories unless I directed them, one at a time, through the sensors in my bonnet, much like the way the machine masters sent commands to control their machines.

"We have arrived home. The boat you designed flew across the waves, much faster than our last voyage. The weather stayed fair but for a few squalls, and with the technology you provided, the ship rocked little when the seas grew high. I experienced nothing of the queasiness that had plagued me on our trip there, and our crew brimmed with hope."

Though they remained detached from the emotions of the physical world, I imagined a pride welling up among them. They valued competence, but their thoughts revealed nothing but logic, their purpose to accumulate data from their "eyes and ears."

"What of your home world? What did you find?"

"It's complicated...."

The buzzing rose and settled. The primary speaker took charge.

"Such a tedious way to communicate.... If only we could merge with your mind as before and know in an instant what you've learned. Now you must pass through to us in this primitive way what you've discovered, one thought at a time. We'll wait until you finish to respond."

I gave a shudder. How could I explain what I'd found, when so much remained unknown.

"When I at last sighted the granite cliffs in the dim light of pre-dawn, what a scene to behold — a fire flickering from the shore, guiding me home — but nothing was as I expected."

I went on to describe our plight — my neighbors afraid, a new grand vicar reasserting control, Thomas missing.

"Can you help?" I said.

"Insufficient data...."

"As our eyes and ears...."

"You and Kara must bring more information...."

"Only then will we be able to help...."

"But know this: the advice you seek is not a matter of logic...."

"This is how it always starts...."

"One side feels wronged. The other reacts...."

"Passions similar to these nearly led to our extinction...."

"Take care to avoid the downward slope...."

Their thoughts surged and silenced, a clear signal that they expected me to respond, but I remained confused. "I don't understand."

The buzzing rose and fell, a collective sigh.

"What we mean is beware the path to violence...."

"Or what your vicars might call...."

"...a return to the darkness...."

***

After I finished with the dreamers, Nathaniel and I wandered off to the pond that had given our village its name. We quickened our pace as we drew near, bursting through the trees to the spot we frequented so often in our childhood, a special refuge we sought out when we needed to reflect. Breaks in the branches let the sunlight filter through the leaves, dappling the water with stars. It was the kind of surprise you'd stumble upon after a long hike through the woods, a remote and secret place, so magical you believed you were the first ones to find it.

We settled on the bank and tried for the moment to forget the rest of the world. I followed the sparrows that flew overhead, fluttering from one tree to the next or gliding down to the water to bathe. How pleasant the moment's peace, with no wind howling through our metallic sails and no waves breaking across our bow. How wonderful to have no one to lead.

Oh, why can't we stay here forever?

I shook off the mood—the musings of a child—stood up and brushed away the stray bits of grass from my tunic. How I longed to linger, to pretend the world of my childhood remained, but then I thought of Thomas in the clutches of the vicars, and shivered.

Nathaniel grasped me by the arms and turned me toward him, as if he'd read my thoughts. "The seekers of truth have returned. We'll rally the people to our cause, and they'll march with us."

I glanced past him to the pond and shook my head. "We're not warriors. What do we know of fighting?"

"We'll learn if need be, and Caleb and his men will help."

I recalled the dreamers' warning—a return to the darkness. "We hoped to make a better world, and now we've found a world in shambles—and much of it of our own doing. What if we make it worse?"

He drew me close and lowered his chin until our foreheads touched. "Don't let despair drag you down. We've faced adversity before. This is our fight, and we'll overcome it again... together."

I pulled away and knelt by the water's edge, staring at my reflection. How weary I'd grown in the years since coming of age. A still, small voice whispered in my mind that we'd done enough, that our people were unworthy of our efforts.

Why, once more, must we risk so much to atone for the foibles of man?

I reached into the pond as if it were a reservoir of courage, and splashed the chill waters of hope on my cheeks.

The time had come. Though far wiser than the vicars, the dreamers had offered no magic to combat the Temple. No magic at all. Once, Thomas had saved us from a life in prison or, worse, a life apart. Now came our turn to rescue him. Nathaniel was right: the people would follow the seekers of truth, those who had miraculously arisen from the sea.

I dried my hands on my tunic and turned away from my childhood refuge without looking back. Then, arm in arm, I strode off with Nathaniel to confront our fate.

Chapter 5

A Gathering of Elders

People crammed the commons, more than ever before—neighbors from surrounding farms, representatives from Great Pond and other nearby villages, and of course our newest friends from across the sea. When all had settled inside, the elders closed the doors and shuttered the windows to keep out prying eyes. A lookout climbed the ladder to the bell tower to watch and listen for signals from afar.

As we waited for everyone to take their seats, an uneasy murmur filled the air, but loudest of all were the unsaid words, the silent fear that flitted among them, the unspoken question etched upon their upturned faces: *What will the seekers do?*

Nathaniel's father held up a calloused hand to call for quiet. When he spoke, he had no need to raise his voice. Not a whisper was heard, not so much as the scrape of a chair on the wooden floor.

"For these past months, we've lived beneath a dark cloud. Those of us who defied the Temple found ourselves outcasts, some like me driven into hiding with a price on our heads—and we're the fortunate ones who avoided capture.

"The vicars of the new order have dashed our hope for a rebirth using the knowledge of the keep. They insist that what we found is evil, a seductive remnant of the darkness. Those scholars who've delved into its mysteries know better, but most of them have been muzzled or have vanished from our midst. The winds from the east carry no word of their fate. Worst of all, we've been told those who led this change failed in their quest to find the far side of the ocean and drowned at sea."

He waved a hand toward Nathaniel and me. "Here you see with your own eyes the foremost of the vicars' lies. Much to my delight, my son and new daughter have returned to us alive, and brought back allies and wonders from the distant shore. What other lies have the vicars told to deceive us?"

A man from the last row raised a hand, a neighbor I recognized from his deep-set eyes and hollowed cheeks, the mark of one who'd been taken for a teaching. Some recovered from teachings in time. Others, like my father, were forever changed. This man bore the same look as when he first returned from Temple City years before—his dreams still ripped away.

The man stood. While he waited for Nathaniel's father to acknowledge him, he rubbed his hands together as if trying to scrub away the stains of the past. When he spoke at last, his voice quivered. "We're glad for their safe return, William, but they mustn't stay in Little Pond. They pose too much of a danger to our families. If they're discovered here, the vicars will punish us all."

William Rush narrowed his eyes and glared at him. "Then in addition to being slaves to the vicars, have we become cowards too?"

Shouts echoed from across the room, many people speaking at once, some with the voice of reason, but most with anger.

Nathaniel's father waved the crowd to silence, but before he could respond, Nathaniel stepped forward and rose to his full height, as he had that morning when the vicars assembled our neighbors for our stoning. His set his jaw and glared out at the assembled. "You needn't worry. We don't intend to stay here long. We plan to march on Temple City to confront the vicars."

I snapped around as he spoke, though I'd anticipated what he'd say. *Temple City!* My heart raced as nightmares of the teaching cell swirled in my mind. We'd always done what we thought right, regardless of the odds, but still....

The man at the back of the hall echoed my thoughts. "You've been to Temple City twice before and with the luck of the light walked away. Do you think you'll escape a third time?"

Nathaniel fixed the man with his gaze and measured his words. "We'll need no luck if we show our courage together."

The man who'd voiced his complaint stared open-mouthed.

24

I sensed a sickening odor, like leaves that had fallen in November and had since decayed into a brown mush that coated what remained of the flower beds, a stench I'd smelled before—the fear of having to choose between freedom and possible death.

I came to Nathaniel's side. "We ask you to march to Temple City with us. If we arrive in large enough numbers, the cowardly deacons will flee. We've seen it before. Now is the chance for a better life for you and your children." I paused and scanned the room from left to right and back, and then raised my voice, hoping to make it echo off the rafters. "Who will join us?"

The man from the back challenged me. "You ask us to join you on a fool's errand."

From among the crowd, Caleb strode forward, an imposing figure, as tall as Nathaniel but with shoulders half again as broad. He loomed beside us with feet spread wide, a mysterious stranger from a place beyond an ocean whose existence the villagers had once denied.

The crowd hushed.

"Who is the bigger fool?" he said. "The one who fights for what he believes in, or the one who cowers in these lovely cottages, hoping they'll protect you from the next storm? This is your chance. Do you want to go through the rest of your lives living in fear? Do you want to whimper in your old age, whining to your grandchildren about what might have been?

"We who have traveled from afar bring ideas and inventions that can enhance your lives, and you can offer much in return, but first, you must muster your courage to demand a change. My people and I stand with the seekers of truth. Who else stands with us?"

From the front rows, those who sailed with us arose: Devorah and Jacob, Kara and little Zachariah, Jubal and Caleb's other stout followers—thirty in all. Then others came: my mother, placing an arm around me and Nathaniel, elder John and elder Robert, Nathaniel's father, the blacksmith from Great Pond, the spinner and his wife.

Our neighbors stepped forward as well, one by one at first, and then by the dozens. We crowded together, looking down at the empty seats.

I scanned the faces. Practical as always, I knew not all should come. Some were too elderly or frail. Others needed to stay behind to care for them and their farms. I made a note to find a way to honor them for their willingness to sacrifice.

Last of all, the man from the back row—the one who years before had endured a teaching—took one halting step toward us and stopped. The blood had drained from his face, and his rigid muscles refused to move, as if resisting what his heart desired. After a moment, he gathered his will, shuffled to the front, and stood by my side.

My heart beat stronger as I regarded those around me.

Our newest quest was set.

Onward to Temple City.

Chapter 6

Shadows on the Moon

We marched in a column, four to a row, Nathaniel and I, some seventy volunteers from surrounding villages, and the thirty who'd sailed with us.

Despite their protests, I'd insisted my mother and new father stay behind—the village needed leaders to care for the old, the young, the sick, and the frail, and to look after the farms and the livestock. I'd handpicked for our expedition only the hardiest men and woman. Though I believed it unnecessary, Caleb encouraged them to bring farm implements for defense—axes and picks, rakes and hoes, anything with a sharp edge that could be swung with force.

I tried to convince Zachariah to remain with my mother, but he insisted on coming along. I agreed to let him go, but only if he obeyed my every word without question.

"If I say to stay in a village, you stay. Understood?"

He nodded.

"If I say hide, you hide without a word of argument, as silent as you were before you found your voice."

He parted his lips to respond, but I glared until he nodded again. I refrained from saying what I meant: *When I say run, you run.* I prayed to the light he'd have no need.

By the time we reached Great Pond, the word had spread—the seekers had returned. Others joined our parade, and our ranks swelled.

Our march took on an air of festival. With so many, there'd be no fight. When the vicars saw our numbers, now three hundred strong, they'd yield to our demands as they had that morning four years before in Little Pond.

When I was taken by the vicar for my teaching, our trip to Temple City took three days. Now, with such a large group, our progress slowed to a crawl. In addition to our cargo of precious machines, we had to carry provisions for everyone, and when we stopped for the night, we needed two hours to pitch camp.

Caleb insisted on organizing us into smaller groups, twenty to what he called a squad, with four squads to a troop. He appointed a leader for each squad, who reported to the elder in charge of the troop. In this way, we could give orders to a few leaders and have everyone else obey.

Nathaniel thought this a fine idea for dividing up the work. Why have each person gather their own water and firewood, or debate over where to sleep?

At the end of the second day, we camped in an open field by a stream, a minute's hike from the road. I laid out the campsite into quarters, one for each troop, and then divided each quarter into fours. Each squad had their place and was responsible for fetching water, making a fire, and distributing their own provisions.

Caleb also required each troop to set up a rotation, four men at a time, to keep watch while the others slept.

Kara, along with Jacob and Devorah, pitched a smaller camp of their own, separate from the troops and deeper in the woods, where they concealed the machines. No sense exposing these to curious gawkers — until needed — and then having to explain their purpose.

I myself had enough trouble understanding them.

After dinner, Nathaniel and I strolled among our followers, stopping at each squad and thanking its members for their support, but also gauging their mood.

Many had never traveled to Temple City, and most who had were, like me, dragged there for a teaching. As a result, an odd mix of excitement and apprehension pervaded the camp.

After visiting several squads, we diverted to Kara's hiding place. There we found the black cube of the dreamers and the mending machine hidden beneath mounds of leaves, but devices from the third container lay exposed on the ground.

Kara hovered over them with her bonnet on, so intent on communing with them that she hardly noticed our approach.

"What are you working on?" Nathaniel said.

She looked up and removed the bonnet so she could focus her thoughts on us. "Just trying to see if I can make things work, a holo here, a synthesis there. One never knows when we'll need a miracle."

I smiled at her joke but knew she spoke the truth. After a year living with machine masters and dreamers, I'd become accustomed to wonders a thousand years beyond the skill of the keepmasters. The people in the encampment behind me, those who'd followed us on little but faith and a shared hatred of the vicars, had no conception of such things. How would the children of light perceive these marvels when they were at last revealed?

From there, we continued on our tour. At the fourth troop, second squad, five of our neighbors from Little Pond approached us, shuffling their feet and with the pupils of their eyes drifting from corner to corner. It seemed there was some unease.

"We don't mean to question, but we wanted to know. Have you granted him authority over us?"

"Who?" Nathaniel said.

"The stranger from the far side of the sea."

"Caleb?"

"Yes."

I brushed the man who'd asked on the forearm. "It's only for a short time, until we reach Temple City. With so many, don't you think we need to be organized?"

"Organized? Yes, but why are all the leaders his men?"

Nathaniel stepped toward them, his face flushed. "*All* of them?"

A second man turned and pointed deeper into the woods. "Go ask him. He's gone with his friends to do light-knows-what."

Nathaniel spun around to follow the gesture, but I grasped his arm before he could leave. Now was no time for passion over reason. "Let me go. I'll talk with him."

Under the cloudless sky, a full moon lit the narrow path through the trees. I paused to gaze up at its pockmarked face. In the keep's observatory, I'd learned that the dark shadows on yellow were craters, deep scars made on the surface by rocks flying through space. I watched them with wonder through the eyepiece of the helper's instrument, the one called a telescope, but when I shared memories with the dreamers, I saw much more—startling images of a rocky wasteland from when their ancestors had flown there in ships and walked on the moon.

My reverie was interrupted by the crash of axes on wood. I followed the sounds until I came upon a smaller clearing, where several of Caleb's men cut branches and bound them with twine.

"What's this?" I said.

Caleb approached me, but signaled his men to keep working.

"A good leader should pray for the best but plan for the worst." He spread his arms wide to encompass the encampment. "These people are our responsibility. We build litters of the kind we used to take the boy up the mountain to the mending machine."

"Why do we—?"

"With so many in our party, we need to be prepared."

I thought of Zachariah, crumpled on the ground, his arm twisted at an odd angle and his face contorted in pain. The greenies kept a litter at the ready for such an event.

"I see. With so many, what if one trips and twists an ankle, or another falls ill. We can't leave them behind so we'd have to carry them."

Caleb came closer and rested his huge hand on my shoulder, but gently, and released a long sigh. "I wish that were the only reason. We need these litters for more than accidents."

"I don't—"

"Though I've never met your vicars and deacons, I've heard you and Nathaniel describe them—not a kindly lot. They subjected their people to teachings when their rule was secure. How much worse might they do now that their authority has been questioned?"

I squeezed my eyes shut. When I opened them again, I needed a moment to calm my breathing. Finally, I nodded. "I understand. For the wounded... just in case."

He stared down at me with weary eyes, like when he'd recounted the fate of his late wife. "Aye, Orah, for the wounded... or worse, for the dying."

***

As I trudged back to camp, the daylight waned, and flickering shadows cast by the branches overhead confounded my vision.

What should I do?

With a growing troop, I needed Caleb. I'd implore my people to be patient, to give our new enterprise time, and I'd urge him to temper his passions and share his lead with others.

Chapter 7

Memories of the Darkness

To my relief, Caleb's worries were unfounded. We'd needed neither litters nor guards, nor any other defenses. Our troops had plodded along without incident, and by noon of the fifth day, we stood on the hillside overlooking Temple City.

Though the day remained cool, a bright sun blessed our mission. With no threat apparent, we ordered everyone to take out their water skins and rest.

Nathaniel, Caleb, and I crept forward, crouched behind a moss-covered boulder, and assessed the situation below. From this vantage, the spires of the city loomed. Though an imposing sight, I knew what lay inside—a warren of dwellings more wretched than any we'd found in the machine masters' city; vicars spreading lies and punishing those who doubted them; a people filled with fear. Yet the question remained: how should we approach?

In the past, as the seekers, Nathaniel, Thomas, and I had slunk through the night from village to village, evading the deacons and nailing the truth onto posts normally reserved for temple bulletins. Now we were gathered more than three hundred strong.

Should we send in a scout to survey the city, or a delegation to negotiate with the vicars? Or should we enter in force?

I cupped a hand over my eyes to block out the glare. No guards stood at the open gate, and no activity showed within.

I turned to Nathaniel and wrinkled my brow. "How can they not see us by now? Why don't they respond? Why not bar the gates or muster the deacons to keep us from entering?"

He placed an arm around my shoulders and peered in. "What if they spotted us from their towers, saw our numbers, and fled?"

As we focused on the gate, Caleb rose to one knee, scanned the surrounding wall, and pointed.

No longer were we unseen. High along the ramparts, shapes scurried about, gaping over the fence and gesturing toward us, but none wore the uniforms of deacons. They were children, dressed in rags.

Caleb stepped out from behind the boulder and stood astride the crest of the hill, feet spread wide and axe on his shoulder. He must have appeared a fearsome figure from below.

When those on the wall saw him, they scampered away and vanished.

He gazed down at the city, grim and stone-faced for a minute or more before turning back. "We have no choice. Nothing more to learn here. Let's march in together. My men and I will take the lead."

I tapped my thumbnail against my teeth. As a child, I pretended to be the leader of my friends, a know-it-all making decisions in our make-believe adventures—games without consequence. Now, I turned and scanned our gathering, trying to read each face as they awaited my decision. I'd set out to seek truth, to make a better world, but never intended to hold the lives of others in my hands.

"All right," I said. "We'll go."

Caleb aligned the troops in order, one through four, with one exception. He and his men moved to the front, a sturdy vanguard with their picks and axes held high on their shoulders.

At my signal, we headed off to the gate.

The situation became clearer as we neared. No one raced out to meet us, and no one blocked our way. Now three hundred strong, we passed through the gates of Temple City unchallenged and triumphant.

My foolish heart swelled with pride.

Yet something seemed amiss. No deacons marched four abreast on patrol, with the stars on their chests flashing in the sunlight. No people appeared at all. The streets lay deserted until a few curious children ventured outside. These skipped along with our army, while their parents eyed us from behind soiled curtains and from around the door jambs of their hovels, peeking out and hissing for their offspring to come back inside.

We turned a corner past a cluster of wooden shacks, each in such disrepair that it appeared to be held up by its neighbor, and marched into the main square.

A bonfire blazed at its center, and all around it, a knot of older children huddled together, seeking warmth from the chill air. When they saw us, they dispersed to the far side of the fire, and all conversation stopped. The flickering light revealed somber faces, confused and frightened by our appearance, unsure whether to stay or run away. A dog barked at us, not with the growl of an angry beast, but rather a loyal pet protecting its master from harm. Its owner, a lanky boy only a few years older than Zachariah, grabbed him by the scruff of the neck and dragged him back. Once the animal calmed, the boy glanced up, and a look of recognition brightened his features.

He pointed at Nathaniel. "You! They said you had drowned."

He turned back and whispered to the others, and an excited murmur rose among them.

I stepped closer, hoping to hear what they said. One phrase stood out, spoken louder than the rest: *the seekers*.

Nathaniel grasped the boy by the shoulders and eyed him, taking a moment to reassess a memory from the past. "I know you. You're the one who told me about the deacons my first day in Temple City. You ran off before I could thank you and ask your name."

The boy beamed, as his friends viewed him with admiration—one known to the seekers. "I'm called Micah, and you—" He waved a hand at us and grinned. "—are the seekers of legend, the ones who discovered the keep and promised a better world." The grin faded, and he lowered his chin to his chest. "That is, until...."

I came to Nathaniel's side. "That's right, Micah, and our goal remains the same—a better world. You can help. Can you tell us where the vicars have gone?"

"The vicars? Fled, and their filthy deacons too."

"Fled where? Behind their fortress walls."

"No. Fled from Temple City. Their buildings stand empty. We play games in them now, and take what we please."

"Show us."

Micah led us through a maze of streets littered with debris, with his gang of youths from the bonfire parading alongside.

My blood rushed, eager to see Thomas again, but when we reached the main temple building, site of our imprisonment and my teaching, I froze in place, stunned at what I found.

The grand doors to the entrance had been cast aside. One hung askew from its upper hinge and the other lay in the dust on the ground. In the impressive hall that had once intimidated me with its grandeur, timbers had been plundered for firewood, and the statues had been ransacked, their arms and heads chopped off as if they were the vicars themselves.

Inside, I found the chamber where teachings were held and where Nathaniel and I stood trial for our apostasy. The tapestry on the back wall, which depicted the battle of darkness and light, had been torn down, with nothing but tatters of cloth at the corners left clinging to their attachments. The polished teak planks from the raised desk had been ripped away, taken presumably to enhance the dwellings of the city's inhabitants.

I stepped to the front, my boot steps clattering as I crossed the cover of the teaching cell. On a whim, I knelt down and lifted the wooden plank—such a tiny and dismal hole, but one that had caused so much pain. As I stared below, unable to tear my eyes away, Nathaniel came and rested a hand on my shoulder, with Zachariah and Kara at his side.

"What is it," Zachariah said.

Kara spoke before I could respond, her voice taut with rage. "I've seen this place when we shared memories in the dream, but I hoped it was imagined. Such cruelty. How could they do such a thing?"

When I shook my head, at a loss for words, Nathaniel answered for me. "Such punishments get justified when those in power believe they own the truth. We should remember this. Seek the truth, but be wary of what we find."

The truth so far was this: the vicars and their henchman had fled, but one place remained to explore. Despite my revulsion, I led the others down the narrow stairway to the prison below.

The oaken doors stood open now, their metal bolts hacked off. I passed from one to the next, stepping into each, searching the corners and under the cot in the vain hope of finding Thomas there. At last, I entered my old cell, the one in which I'd expected to waste away for the rest of my life, like the first keeper, Samuel, who'd given all to protect the secret of the keep. The scant furniture still lay there, and the peephole through which Nathaniel and I spoke remained, but nothing more. Only the memory and the stench lingered.

Nathaniel hesitated in the doorway, refusing at first to enter. His jaw tightened and his arms hung rigid at his side. Yet he gave me time, watched me brush the peephole with my fingertips, like greeting an old friend.

Finally, he crept up behind me, and for a moment, stood still in the dark. Then he edged closer, his breath warm on my neck as he said in the softest of whispers, "Time to go."

Once outside, I drew in a long draft of fresh air, as if the prison had constricted my lungs.

Caleb's men had gathered a few of the residents eager to speak, and brought them to us.

A kindly woman, who reminded me of my mother, told us of the day the vicars fled. "They sacked the town of anything of value, stripped our homes of food and provisions, and left us to rot."

An elderly man came forward next. "That upstart monsignor...." He paused to spit on the ground. "So high and mighty. Skipped all the tradition and declared himself the human embodiment of the light in this world. He proclaimed a new age and rallied all those of like mind to his cause, but not everyone accepted him. The coward and his followers fled to be with more of their own." The man squeezed my arm with his bony fingers and hissed into my ear. "To be closer to the keep, they say. To steal its magic as they did before."

"What of the prisoners?" I said.

"Taken in chains and marched to the east."

I stared to the east, though I could see no farther than the city walls. A question welled up inside of me, a question so big it plugged up my throat and made it hard to breathe. I swallowed once and forced out air, giving the question sound.

"Was there a young man among them, short with sand-colored hair?"

The man rubbed the stubble on his chin and consulted with the woman. She whispered in his ear while he nodded.

He turned to me. "We can't be sure. None dared come close and stare at those bruised and battered souls, but this woman believes one of them matched your description."

Blood rushed to my face, and my skin burned. I barked to Caleb, "Gather the troops. We follow them to the east."

35

The boy Micah grabbed me as I started to leave. "Let us come with you, me and my friends. There's nothing for us here."

"But you're too young, not even come of age."

He lifted his chin. "I'm almost fifteen, and have been beaten by the deacons three times. If each beating counts for a year, then I'm old enough."

I eyed him, so young, but not much younger than we were when we first set out to the keep. And with no less passion.

I checked with Nathaniel, and we both nodded.

Why not? Let all whom the vicars have wronged join our cause....

...though I have no hint of where that cause may lead.

Chapter 8

Adamsville

From Temple City, we marched to Adamsville, but with a more measured stride. Despite the rumors rippling throughout our troop, we could only guess how far east the vicars had fled or how large their numbers had grown. How I wished to do as Caleb urged, and send scouts ahead to spy, but if caught, their punishment would be swift and severe. Who would I ask to go?

Word spread before us like a spring breeze, and each village we passed drew more to our cause. With the crush of followers, Nathaniel and I became swamped with issues big and small: how much food and water to bring, how to deal with the injured or ill, and who should settle squabbles between groups vying for better sites at our encampments.

Thank the light for Caleb. With little effort, he designated more troops and squads, and made decisions that everyone rushed to obey — a natural leader. With so many people, he could no longer rely on his own men, and needed others who would command respect, and whom he in turn could trust. He possessed a gift for identifying a person's talents — those best suited to cook or gather wood, those with skill to fashion tools, or those born to lead. He required each squad to build a litter, to name one person responsible for caring for the sick or wounded, and to anoint another to run messages back and forth to his command.

He assigned Kara to form a special squad, one that would carry and protect the black cube and other machines. These elite few formed their own identity, and much like the grey friars, took to embellishing their tunics, this time with black armbands to designate their role. They called themselves the bearers of the cube, an honor guard of sorts.

On clear days, when the weather was mild and our progress steady, I'd climb a mound by the side of the road and beam at my people as they paraded past.

I'd given Zachariah a flute, one of several I brought for Thomas— knowing how they'd provide him solace once we found him, as I was sure we would. The once silent boy taught himself a simple tune with a beat appropriate for marching. He played this twelve-note tune as the troop marched by.

I found it cleansing, like rain washing over stepping stones in a garden. I brimmed with hope— my dream come alive, my faith at last fulfilled.

Until I learned about the weapons.

One evening, as Nathaniel and I prepared our bedding for the night, Devorah approached, with shoulders hunched as if bearing a heavy pack.

"May I speak with you," she said.

I set aside the bedding and faced her. "Of course, anytime. No need to ask."

She sniffed at the air and glanced away, staring at something unseen in the distance before turning back to me. "I sailed here along with Jacob to study your crafts, to learn to build better homes, to make sharper tools and feed ourselves from the land—new skills we could bring back to the people of the earth. But now I find these hands the good earth gave us are being asked to create tools to do others harm."

I glanced at Nathaniel but he only shrugged and gaped back at me. "I don't know what you mean."

"Caleb ordered every squad to assign one man to be their armorer. He insisted they provide at least one weapon to every member of the troop—the implements of war. I know little of your world, but from what I've heard, your children of the light, much like my people, have refrained from violence for hundreds of years. Yet I understand the challenges we face, so I will not judge.

"What pains me is that Caleb ordered Jacob to mentor this group, to teach them how to carve long sticks and sharpen their points, to modify tools of the farm so they may better maim and kill. Jacob does as he's told, but it tears him up inside."

"You must be mistaken," Nathaniel said. "We've given Caleb no such order."

She lowered her gaze to the ground. "Then he does it on his own, as he once defied the earth mother to tunnel through the mountain to the dreamers."

I reluctantly rose from the cushion of pine needles, gathered to provide a much-needed night's rest. Nathaniel jumped up with me, the blood rushing to his face, but I pressed a hand to his chest. "Let me go alone. Better to understand before we react. We have enough enemies." I turned to Devorah. "Where's Jacob now?"

"Follow me."

I followed Devorah to the edge of one of the camps, where Jacob had set up a makeshift workshop, stocked with tools accumulated from the villages we passed—a saw here, an awl or file there—anything that could enhance his significant skill in shaping wood or metal. Now the fruits of his efforts lay stacked against a waist-high rack, spears and knife blades, sharpened picks and hoes and axes, any implement of the farmer that might be converted for war.

Though Jacob surely sensed us coming, he kept his head down and focused on his work as if ashamed to be discovered at such a dishonorable task.

I thanked Devorah, promised to deal with this matter from here, and bid her goodnight.

When Jacob still refused to face me, I rested a hand on his arm. "I'm sorry you have to do this."

His eyes drooped at the corners. "I'm sorry as well, but no person has forced this upon me, only the circumstances. Rumors abound of evil done. If even half are true, this task I perform is necessary."

"You didn't follow us across the ocean for this."

He rubbed his salt and pepper beard and stared at his boot tops. "No, not for this." He set his tool down and shuffled over to a log. "Come sit with me."

After I settled on the log, he slid closer and fixed me with his eyes. "When the earth mother first came to us, she taught a harsh lesson about our existence—that we're wired to want purpose in our lives, but that we can never be certain what that purpose is, and so, we must trust in ourselves and each other and have faith. Did *you* choose to lead these people? Your nature and circumstances have brought you to this day. Why do I help them make weapons? It's what I was blessed to do, to work with my hands. With the evil we've found in your world, I can't say for certain that the making of these weapons is wrong."

"I'll talk to Caleb."

"Do as you wish, but what he asks is not on a whim. There's a need in the air."

"Do you know where he is?"

"Aye. As always at this time of day, with his men practicing. Whenever we camp for the night, they go off deeper into the woods to train and drill."

He directed me to the edge of the encampment, to the start of a narrow trail formed by the runoff of rain.

After a minute's walk, I spotted an opening in the trees. Before I reached the clearing, I shifted sideways and peered from behind the broad trunk of an ancient beech. What I saw made my eyes water.

A formation of Caleb's men stood before me, all those who had come with him from the distant shore, split into pairs and aligned in a row, each clutching a blunt stick with two hands. They wore tunics stuffed with straw to provide padding, making them appear larger than life in the dim light of dusk. All focused on the front, where Caleb stood astride a boulder, barking out instructions.

"Plant your feet wide and maintain your balance. To lose your balance may be to lose your life. Keep your eye on your enemy's chest. He may feint one way or waggle his head to the other, but his chest will always show his intent. Each of you has been assigned a number, one or two. On my command, one will thrust and two will parry. Then you'll switch. Remember to drive your front knee forward. Weapons at the ready."

Each man pointed his stick, aimed at his opponent.

Caleb's voice rang out in the night. "Attack."

Those on the left lunged with their sticks, while those on the right blocked them. The air filled with the crack of wood on wood and the grunts of straining men.

"Attack."

The roles reversed — a second thrust, a second parry.

"Attack, attack." Caleb repeated the command at an ever faster pace.

Here and there, someone missed a parry. The weapon of their opponent struck his padded chest and knocked him breathless to the ground, but Caleb gave no quarter. The fallen scrambled to their feet to fend off the next blow.

I gritted my teeth to keep from crying out. How could he practice such violence without our consent? I withdrew deeper into the woods, glad to have left Nathaniel and his temper behind, and glanced up to the heavens as if seeking guidance. Above me, the impending dusk cast a shadow on the branches, cloaking them in a dark green, but higher up the leaves glowed gold in the rays of the setting sun.

Darkness and light—always together, always shifting roles.

I sighed. What sense would it make to burst into their midst and scold him in front of his men? What good would it do?

From the precision of their movement, these protectors of the people of the earth had practiced this drill many times before, likely long before our boat had sailed. Why? To defend against the forces of darkness.

Perhaps Caleb was right and such training was necessary. Maintain your balance or die.

A good leader should pray for the best but plan for the worst.

We needed Jacob to continue his work, and I'd persuade Devorah to agree.

But as I turned to leave, I recalled the litters, imagined their purpose, and shuddered.

***

Our trek to Adamsville proceeded without incident. Why not? Who would challenge such a throng—as the vicars might say, the living embodiment of the will of the people?

How different this visit compared to our last, when we three young seekers slunk into town, skulking in doorways and peering around corners as the deacons nailed the vicars' edict to the temple post. How less tense than our escape, fleeing out a window like thieves in the night.

Not this time. We marched down the main street with heads held high, and everyone knew who we were. Small children lined the road, bearing baskets of braided rolls and cheese, which they offered to the brave souls who promised them a better future. Young girls rushed forward to hand us flowered wreaths.

Nathaniel leaned in and whispered to me, while keeping his eyes ahead. "Too much like festival, but we haven't won anything yet."

I nodded and forced a smile to keep up appearances. How could I appear worried to these people who waved at us, cheering and chanting *"The Seekers"*?

In the main square, by the post that once held temple bulletins, the spinner of Adamsville greeted us. No hesitation this time; he grasped Nathaniel and me with both arms in a tearful embrace.

As our troops filed into the town, in such numbers that not all could fit in the street, he climbed the front steps of his yarn store and gazed out over the sea of heads. "So many."

"And more each day," I said. "The vicars will have no choice but to yield."

He blinked and his smile turned to a frown. "May the light make it so, but I wouldn't be so sure. Come into my home, just the two of you and a few of your leaders. I'll make you my special tea and tell you what little I've learned."

We invited Caleb to join us, and Devorah, and Kara too, and waited around a table while the spinner warmed tea. Only when the scent of apples and cinnamon filled the air and we'd settled with cups in our hands did he begin.

"I'm sure you heard the grumblings before you left. The keep may contain wonders but they take effort to learn. Those who studied the history of the darkness returned to their villages with tales of horror, confirming what the vicars always claimed. Nevertheless, the grand vicar kept his word, banning all teachings and protecting those scholars in the keep. The clergy loyal to him preached patience. With their wise counsel and the blessing of the light, we prayed to someday master the wonders while avoiding its horrors."

He took a sip from his tea and set it down, then scrunched his nose as if he'd swallowed something sour.

"Many among the younger clergy had no such patience. They sought to restore the power they wielded over the children of light, before you discovered the keep. And not just the vicars. Many of our neighbors heeded their sermons.

"The grand vicar aged and became more frail, and his influence over the naysayers weakened. Then came a rebellion of sorts. A young vicar, some say no more than a monsignor, overthrew him and usurped control of the Temple, including the gray friars and deacons."

"We heard," Nathaniel said. "We know this man who once ministered to the Ponds. It was he who took Thomas and Orah for their teaching."

The spinner sighed. "Then you know of his character, a calculating man who uses the Temple to his own advantage. He came to Adamsville once, with his bootlicking followers, a slight man with black buttons for eyes. A cold man. Once he declared himself to be the human embodiment of the light in this world, most of the other vicars and their deacons fell in line. All had been trained to obey, and they were frightened by the change rushing toward them too fast. Some of our people followed as well, those longing for the comfort of the old ways. Many more were aghast at what happened but were too afraid to speak out.

"Now they've consolidated their power to the east, a better defensive posture with more vicars and deacons, in a smaller area and nearer the keep."

I slid to the edge of my chair. "What of the keep? Is it still in safe hands?"

The spinner grasped the table and winced as he pushed himself to standing. "Wait here. I'll fetch someone who can tell you more."

He limped off, leaning on his walking stick with the carving of a mallard's head on top, his gait stiffer than I recalled.

Moments later, he returned with a slightly built man with a face that seemed younger than his years. After so much time apart, I might have taken him for Thomas but for his shock of red hair. Though not much older than me, he walked with a limp, grimacing with each step, and the slanted sunlight filtering through the spinner's curtains revealed a face laced with scars.

He stopped an arm's length from where I sat. "Hello, Orah. Hello, Nathaniel. I'm glad to see you've returned."

I stared at that face, reassessing it without the wounds, and brightened. "I know you. A fellow scholar. We studied together in the keep."

The boy lowered himself into a chair, yelping in pain until he straightened his right knee with both hands.

The spinner hovered over him as if to protect him from further harm. "I see you remember Enoch, your former neighbor from Great Pond. Good. That will make it easier for you to believe his story, though I have to admit, I struggle to believe it myself. Like you, he went to the keep to learn from our past. One day, two weeks ago, we found Enoch by the side of the road to the west of town. He lay there half-dead, unable to walk another step or speak of what had happened. His body was broken, and he'd had no food for days. More than that, his eyes refused to focus, and he turned away and covered his face with his arms when anyone came near.

"As you can see, we've nursed him back to health, although he has a long way to go. Likely he'll never be the same. Now that Enoch can speak for himself, I'll let him tell his story."

I checked around the table. Nathaniel had set his jaw, and Caleb had folded his thick hands so tightly that his knuckles whitened. I pictured his men training with sticks and wanted to train myself.

Only Kara looked calm, staring at the boy as if assessing his wounds.

The wounded scholar accepted some tea from the spinner and, after taking a few sips, set the cup down and faced me, as if he intended his story for me alone.

"At the time you left the keep, all who stayed there worked in harmony. The gray friars used the helpers to better understand what made temple magic work. When parts of the keep ceased to function, they learned to repair them. The vicars pondered how the Temple came into being and where it might have gone wrong, and the scholars studied whatever piqued our curiosity. You introduced me to the observatory, and like you, I developed a love of the stars.

"One day, a new set of vicars arrived with a column of deacons in tow, and took over control of the keep. Whereas each of us had studied as we saw fit before, now they limited what we learned. Entire sections were closed off, some helpers silenced, and many subjects forbidden as apostasy. The scholars were offered a harsh choice — swear obedience to the new grand vicar, or be driven from the keep."

He lowered his eyes and stared into the golden liquid in his cup, as if searching for answers there.

I rested a hand on his arm, careful to find a spot with no bruise. "What happened?"

"I refused to leave. I told them the keepmasters built the keep to let free thought flow, and that its knowledge belonged to the people."

He breathed in and out. Twice he tried to continue but stopped himself.

"We're here to help you, Enoch. No one will hurt you."

He looked up, and his eyes met mine. They were moist with tears.

"They took me into one of the bedchambers the gray friars had modified so the door locked from the outside. I stayed there alone for two days without food or water. Then the deacons came...." He shuddered, but a sudden strength seemed to fill him, a gathering of will. "Some of my fellow scholars snuck in one night, those who'd faked allegiance to the Temple to save themselves from my fate. They helped me escape."

I waited for more, but Enoch had ceased to speak. It almost seemed he'd ceased to breathe. I drove my fingernails into the palms of my hands to stay under control. No need to upset him further. "Did they resume their teaching then, in violation of the truce?"

The young man stared at the surface of the table as if counting the knots in the wood.

"No teachings," he said in little more than a whisper. *"Nothing so benign."* He looked up at me with anguish in his eyes. *"Only old-fashioned, darkness-inspired pain."*

Chapter 9

Cudgels and Staves

For the next two days, we camped on the outskirts of Adamsville, restocking our supplies and resting our troops.

During that time, Kara pleaded with me to try her hand at mending. Through her winged bonnet, she'd controlled other machines, but this one required a special skill, appropriate for the complexity of the human body. She'd observed her grandfather use it many times and studied its workings in her lessons, but now she needed time to consult with the dreamers before attempting to heal Enoch's wounds.

On the evening of the second day, she came to Nathaniel and me, her hair matted from where the sensors in her bonnet had pressed it flat. "I explained about the boy's injuries as best I can without joining their minds in the dream, and they gave me instruction. I can gain no more from them in such a short time."

"Will you succeed?" Nathaniel said.

"I can't be sure. Even the mentor sometimes failed, but we hauled the mending machine from across the sea to serve a purpose. From the rumors floating about the camp, we might have need for it soon. Better to test it now. Please let me try."

I checked with Nathaniel. We'd crossed the ocean with a dream to bring back miracles to our people. How could we turn down this chance?

We both nodded.

Nathaniel narrowed his gaze so a wrinkle formed above the bridge of his nose. "You should make your first attempt away from curious

46

eyes. Our people have struggled with the knowledge of the keep. Who can say how they'll respond to the wonders of the dreamers? If you fail this first time, no need for them to watch."

I stepped forward and brushed her arm. "We'll wake before dawn. I'll alert the spinner to have Enoch ready. Pick the most loyal of the bearers of the cube to stand guard at that time, those who can be trusted to keep quiet no matter what they see. That way, only a few will know."

Before first light the next morning, while the troops still slept, Nathaniel placed Enoch on the spinner's two-wheeled cart, normally used to transport spools of yarn, and wheeled him to the clearing at the outskirts of town. The stars had all but gone out, and a glow spread on the horizon, welcomed by the first notes of birdsong emerging from the trees.

The four bearers, handpicked by Kara, snapped to attention as we entered. They'd concealed Kara's machines in the brush, covered by a thick blanket of spruce branches—all but the mending machine, which lay exposed at the ready.

On the way, I'd explained to Enoch what to expect. As a fellow scholar, he'd long since accepted the wonders made possible by science, yet his eyes widened when he took in the dreamers' creation.

A tube stood at the center of the clearing, made of a clear, glossy material like the keepers' scrolls and large enough to envelop a grown man. Before it lay a slab on wheels.

We placed Enoch on the slab, and Kara covered his eyes with a black cloth.

"Just relax," she said. "You'll feel some discomfort but nothing like the pain you've experienced until now."

I patted his hand. "Soon, light willing, all will be well."

Then I stepped away.

Kara donned her white bonnet with the flowered crest and the flaps like wings. She wiggled it around until the sensors properly set, and closed her eyes. A whirring filled the air, and the slab began to roll, inching Enoch head first into the tube.

A sound startled me from behind, the crack of a twig. I thought to turn, but the mending machine captured my eye. Just a squirrel, I told myself. Nothing more.

Though I'd witnessed a mending before, I held my breath.

Soon the tube surrounded Enoch, and a light flooded the space where he lay, brightening to an unbearable intensity and forcing me to look away. The stoic bearers fell back a step and raised their arms to shield their eyes.

A gasp rose behind me, or was it the breeze in the trees, muffled by the whirring of the machine? I cast a glance around to check, but half-blinded by the glow, I saw only shadows.

After a few minutes, the light dimmed and Enoch emerged from the tube. He glanced at me and took a trembling breath. Tears flowed down his cheeks, making them glisten, but the tension that had racked his body was gone.

Sweat beaded on Kara's forehead, but her eyes sparkled as she eased into a smile. "It worked." She took a step toward me, but stumbled and almost fell.

I caught her in my arms.

On the walk back to town, I wheeled the empty cart, while Nathaniel supported a weakened Kara with one arm and a recovering Enoch with the other. By the time we reached the spinner's home, the boy no longer needed help. The angry marks on his skin had faded, and he walked upright with a bounce in his step, appropriate for a man of his age.

When the spinner spotted us, his brows lifted, and he let out a silent whistle. "You said you crossed the ocean to find miracles beyond the keepmasters."

I nodded with a smile. "And we succeeded."

He prepared a hearty breakfast for us, with freshly baked bread, poached eggs and thick slices of ham. Nathaniel and I ate our fill, but Enoch and Kara devoured their meals and asked for more.

As I rose to clean the table, I heard a ruckus on the street outside and went to the door to check.

Micah, the boy from Temple City, stood in front grinning, surrounded by his friends. Behind him, dozens of troops had gathered in various stages of undress, wiping the sleep from their eyes, with more arriving by the second.

The boy crowed to the assembled. "I followed them to the place of miracles." He pointed at Kara. "That's the one. She donned a strange hat, closed her eyes, and prayed to the light. Then the power of the sun, giver of life, came down to the earth to heal the scholar."

When Enoch joined me at my side, everyone raised their arms in celebration and a chant spread: *"Praise the true light! Down with the vicars!"*

Yet a different phrase worried me more—a muted murmur whispered in fear and awe: *Seeker Magic*.

***

My time in Adamsville proved a salve for my spirit. The latter days of spring had arrived, with milder weather, a gentle breeze and blue skies that brightened my mood. Nathaniel and I passed quiet nights together as guests in the spinner's home, while our troop prepared for the next leg of our journey.

Enoch recovered from his abuse and became a prime spokesman for our cause. With his health restored, he spent his days mingling with the people and retelling his story. Their anger raged, just as their confidence in our leadership grew. The seekers brought miracles, they said, and under our banner, they'd vanquish their enemy and create a better life for all.

If only I had their faith.

Once I believed we had merely to reveal the truth and the people would rise up and change the world. Older now and bearing the scars of trials past, I knew better. Our future hovered like an indistinct thundercloud on the horizon, an impending storm. Light knew who or what would survive its fury.

How I longed to renounce the hard ground of the road, to stay in this soft bed with Nathaniel, freeze time and wish the world away. But no wish would rescue Thomas or save the keep.

On the third day, I convened the council to discuss our next move. We met in the town hall—Kara and Devorah, Caleb and the troop leaders, and Nathaniel and me.

I cleared the table, unrolled the map to the keep, and pointed to the spot marked Adamsville. "Here we sit. Rumors drifting our way say the vicars have concentrated their forces nearer the keep—for them, an obvious plan. We need to proceed on the road east with caution—at least until we learn more. Before the turn north to Bradford, we'll pass two roads to the south, each leading to a different Temple City. Enoch slipped through the nearest and said it looked abandoned, but the fate of the second remains a mystery."

I ran my finger along the paper, tracing the path to Bradford. "The trek to the crossroads takes six days for a small party traveling light, but will take our troop much longer. Since we know nothing of what awaits

49

at the second Temple City, we should avoid it until we're better prepared, heading north instead. Once in Bradford, we can rest and reorganize before facing our enemy for the first time. The town is remote but large enough to provide support. Moreover, its vicar is our friend, and will be a valuable adviser as we plan our next step. Agreed?"

Everyone nodded, all but Caleb.

He pulled the map closer and studied the terrain, following the road east until he stopped and lingered at the second Temple City. "If I understand you, our first encounter with the enemy may lie here. A horde such as ours cannot travel in stealth. We'll announce our presence far in advance. These well-intentioned neighbors of yours are not ready for what might come."

He folded his thick hands on the table and waited.

I recalled Thomas on our quest for the keep, constantly asking if we'd be safe. I kept reassuring him, but I turned out to be wrong. In the end, Nathaniel and I needed *his* help to save *us*.

I tempered my response. "That's why I'm proposing we stay clear of the vicars and go north to Bradford."

He shook his head and sighed. "You know this side of the ocean better than I do. I never met your vicars or deacons, but they seem a nasty lot. I'll agree to this plan on two conditions. Let me arm our troop without constraint. Then on our trek, grant me two hours out of each day to train them. Best to plan for the worst."

My mouth opened, but before I could respond, Nathaniel leaned in and whispered in my ear. "Think of the boy, Enoch. This is not the world we left."

I pressed my lips together, glared at the map, and agreed to the plan. We'd ready our troop for the march to Bradford and, if need be, for war.

***

When I awoke on the morning of the fourth day, Nathaniel had donned his travel tunic and was filling his pack. His face had turned grim.

I stretched my arms overhead in a yawn. "Do we have to be up so soon?"

He came to my side, rested a hand on my cheek, and kissed me. "Time to muster the troops. The usurper won't yield while we idle away here."

50

Our original trek from Adamsville to the crossroads had taken six days, but now took twice as long. With so many, we needed more time to gather provisions, eat meals, and layout our camps. The training of the troops also consumed more hours than expected. Caleb had too few instructors, and the children of the light, after a thousand years of temple-imposed peace, had proven less than adept students in the art of war.

When Zachariah saw the others arming, he begged for a weapon as well.

"Absolutely not," I said.

He glared at me and rocked on his toes to appear taller. "I'm ten years old now, big enough to fight the bad men."

I smiled at him, so impulsive... like a young Nathaniel. "Your flute does more than any weapon. A weapon strengthens only one, but your music strengthens all."

After that, he puffed out his chest and played his tune with such passion that the birds seemed to join in, adding their chirping to his marching song.

Nothing stopped Nathaniel from joining those who bore arms. He now carried a stave as tall as his chin and as thick as my wrist. Jacob had helped him carve handgrips in the center, complete with notches for each finger, so it would hold firm when swung with force or struck in return, but as a concession to me, he'd refrained from sharpening the point. With its dull tip, it remained a formidable weapon, but mainly for defense.

As we marched, I gaped in horror as he and the other would-be warriors adopted the look of revelers at festival, flaunting their staves and sharpened picks and axes, laughing and joking as they paraded along.

What had I wrought?

An unsettling foreboding came over me. I tossed and turned at night, haunted by nightmares: of a panel of vicars sitting in judgment on a high bench; of drab stone walls etched by decay and iron doors with deacons lurking on the far side; of my own neighbors gazing at me glassy-eyed in the dim light of dawn while the voice from the sun icon called for our stoning; of rocks the size of apples grasped in their hands.

I longed to share my fears with someone, but in whom could I confide? A leader leads alone, and must show nothing but confidence in the mission, so I maintained the mask and hid the doubting little girl who lurked behind, revealing her to no one — no one but my best friend who'd known me since birth.

Yet with so much to do, Nathaniel and I had little time together, each of us occupied with the tasks of guiding our would-be army. I spent my evenings wandering through the camp and spreading words of encouragement, while he went off to who-knows-where. In our few moments before sleep, I'd try to ask what he'd done.

He'd glare at me, tense and tight-lipped. "A bit of this and a bit of that. Anything to help the troops." Then his eyes drifted to the corners, and he turned away.

By day, when we marched, I took to eying the edge of the trail. At one point, past the first turn south, the road narrowed. Gnarly roots on either side crept inward, and the shadows of late afternoon cast a pall over our troop.

I froze in place, sniffing the air and glancing from side to side at the tree line. A gust kicked up, cutting through the branches and making the leaves around me tremble.

A crack in the brush startled me, and I stumbled back a step, bumping into Nathaniel.

He reached out to catch me and waved at the undergrowth. "Just a squirrel, Orah. Nothing more."

I turned to him and held on. "Ever since we rummaged through the ruins of Temple City, I've been dreaming of our prison stay."

His grin turned into a grimace, and he nodded. "I've been dreaming too."

I thought of Enoch in the deacons' hands, and shivered. "If we're caught again...."

He stared into the distance and tightened his grip on the stave. "Our new captors won't be so kind."

Two more days passed, and my mood brightened. According to the landmarks on my map, the road to Bradford lay only hours ahead. Once we turned north, we'd put distance between ourselves and temple power. I became encouraged this leg of our journey would end without incident, and looked forward to hearing the wisdom of the vicar of Bradford. I insisted we press on without rest, hoping to make camp at the crossroads before dark.

Our path, though muddy at times, remained flat and wide, and rarely took us out of the sunlight, until we reached the base of a familiar notch through the hills, the last obstacle before the turn north.

Almost safe.

As we started our ascent, the shadows deepened and the sky disappeared, the dimness of dusk widening its grip on the world. The slope climbed steadily, until we marched along a ridge with woodland encroaching on either side, and branches arching overhead, their leaves dense enough to create a tunnel. We wandered now in twilight, with the forest surrounding us like a prison.

As I gazed up, trying to pierce the thick canopy to the darkening sky, Nathaniel grabbed me by the elbow and pulled me aside.

"What is it?" I whispered.

He stared up at the still branches and listened. "The birds. They've stopped singing."

At once the leaves quaked, despite the absence of a breeze, and twilight turned to darkness. Men dashed from the trees, dressed in forest green and with faces streaked with black paint, making them hard to spot in the dim light. Each wielded a dagger in one hand and in the other, a cudgel with nails protruding from its top.

Our disciplined ranks dissolved, and the squads scattered. Once proud warriors let weapons thud to the ground and ran.

So much for the power of light over darkness.

The darkness had arrived in force, and the light was fleeing.

Three paces before me, a boy fell, struck in the forearm as he protected himself. Through the blood splattering his face, I recognized Micah.

A deacon approached him to strike a fatal blow.

I rushed forward and slammed my shoulder into his side, knocking him off balance.

He turned on me, his blade extended, but a rough hand stayed his arm.

A gruff voice barked an order. "Not that one. Take her alive."

They raced toward me, though I barely saw them moving. As I fell back, a stave as thick as my wrist swung past me and caught the lead deacon in the chest.

He dropped to one knee, clutching his ribs, but two more followed.

Now I understood how Nathaniel had spent his evenings—he'd been training with Caleb.

Nathaniel stood taller than his adversaries, and his long arms held them at bay, but he had trained for days, and they for years. Soon he too gave ground under their assault.

I scratched around and found a rock to throw and then another, and when no more rocks were found, I flung dirt in their faces.

They kept coming, five at once.

I winced at the crash of wood on wood, and Nathaniel's stave slipped from his hands. Undaunted, he stepped before me, his fingers curled into fists, but before he could engage, a hulking figure flashed from behind, as tall as Nathaniel and half again as broad.

Caleb!

Two swings of his axe, and two men fell. Then a third, and the others fled.

Nathaniel retrieved his stave, and I gathered up handfuls of stones, but when I spun around to confront the enemy again, my spirits rose. Yes, many of our supporters, so buoyant a moment before, had panicked in disarray and scattered back down the slope, but others stayed, led by Caleb and his men.

These strode forward now, shoulder to shoulder in a disciplined wedge, weapons gripped in calloused hands, protecting each other's flank. Axes flew, picks found their mark, and now the deacons bled.

Surprised by such a stout defense from what they believed to be the meek children of the light, the deacons fell back, dropped their cudgels and knives, and ran away.

After no more than minutes—but what seemed like days—the road quieted and the troops reformed. Those assigned to care for the wounded dashed in with their litters and performed their appointed tasks.

I slipped among them counting, the most painful tally of my life. I should have thanked the light—nine wounded, none dead—but as I followed the boy, Micah, to a litter and listened to him moan, the light was furthest from my mind.

When all was secure and we'd stationed our guards, I assembled our leaders in a tight circle around me. "No camp tonight. The full moon will let us travel in the dark, and if we push through without sleep, we can reach the safety of Bradford by dusk tomorrow." I turned to Caleb. "Pick your strongest and fastest men to go ahead and carry the wounded." Then to Kara. "You and your bearers of the cube go with them. Too dangerous to attempt a mending here. Wait for Bradford. The rest of us will form a rear guard."

As the leaders split up to follow their orders, Jubal, one of Caleb's men from across the sea, dragged a frightened and bleeding deacon to me.

"What shall we do with this one?"

Caleb grasped the man in his thick hands and shook him until he cried out.

"Perhaps now, we can find out what awaits us in Temple City," he said as the terrified deacon looked on. "And the rules of your teaching need not apply."

I grabbed his wrist, my hand too small to encircle his forearm, and glared at him. "Enough violence. I won't allow this man to be mistreated." I clasped a wide-eyed Devorah by the shoulders and squeezed to regain her focus. "Do what you can for his wounds, and fetch him something to eat."

After the others moved out of earshot, Caleb fumed at me. "You're a fine leader, Orah, and wise, but you're innocent in the ways of the world. Before this quest is done, you'll need to learn."

"Learn what?" I said.

"That no change comes without the shedding of blood."

Chapter 10

Bradford

By the time we arrived in Bradford, the litters had been laid out in a row on the village green. Some of their occupants moaned from pain, but others just stared out with vacant eyes.

Kara had secured the cube and other devices inside the rectory, and now worked with a singular focus to set up the mending machine. She barely acknowledged our arrival.

The vicar of Bradford flitted between the wounded bearing a tray with mugs of hot cider. The new warriors—all those able—wrapped their hands around its warmth and stared into the steam as if searching for redemption. As each took a first sip, the vicar rested a hand on their shoulder and whispered comforting words.

When he spotted us, he came over at once and greeted us with the same grace he'd shown three road-weary travelers four years before. Though he retained the sparkle in his eyes, more worry lines marked his face, and patches of gray streaked his hair and beard, making him appear older than the intervening years should warrant.

"Greetings, seekers," he said. "Thank the light you're alive."

Nathaniel and I stepped forward and embraced him, without the hesitation of our first meeting.

He waved an arm to encompass the wounded. "The deacons' work, I presume. I'd heard rumblings from the south, but this is the first proof of how deep they've descended into the darkness." He gestured to Kara. "Your young friend raced in after them, assuring me she worked for the light, and asked my help in caring for them. Of course, I obliged, but she's told me little other than that she sailed here with you from the far side of the sea."

Despite my exhaustion, I smiled at this man who'd first enlightened us about the wonders of the keep. While he remained committed to serving his people, we followed his dream—to find the truth and make a better world.

"We found wise men there," I said, "a thousand years more advanced than the keepmasters, but no time to explain now. Young Kara is their proper descendant. With the guidance of her forbearers, she knows how to heal them."

He crumpled his brow. "I pray it's so, but I have some skill at healing myself. For some of these, there will be no healing."

"We'll see."

I shuffled over to Kara as she knelt by the mending machine, fiddling with its controls. "Is everything all right?"

She stood, brushed the dust from her knees and faced me. "I hope so. You were smart to send me ahead. It's been jostled by the journey and setting it up has been harder than expected, but I'm ready now."

I glanced over at the wounded and caught sight of Micah. He reminded me of Zachariah after his fall from the carousel, one arm twisted at an odd angle, and his face contorted with pain.

I turned back to Kara. "Take the boy first."

She shook her head so hard her hair swished across her eyes. "With so many, I may lack the strength to heal them all tonight. I asked your friend, the vicar, to place them in order by the urgency of their injuries, so I can start with the most severe wounds."

She led me to the litter nearest the mending machine, which bore a man I recalled from Adamsville. At first, I'd refused his request to join us, declaring him too old for the trek, but he'd made up in passion what he lacked in youth. Now he lay still, eyes closed and the blood drained from his face. Someone had crossed his arms over his chest, and they rose and fell as he breathed in shallow bursts.

Nathaniel and two others lifted him onto the slab, doing their best to cause no further pain.

The time had come. Kara donned her bonnet, and we stood aside while she hovered over the injured man and closed her eyes. As before, the machine whirred and the slab rolled into the tube.

Out of the corner of my eye, I caught a number of our troops gathering behind us. Their silence was deafening.

The glow grew so bright, everyone covered their eyes or looked away. I sensed the tension in Kara as her mind joined with the miracle machine. Through it, she'd synthesize new bone, muscle, and skin to mend the damage.

When finished, she opened her eyes, and the man emerged from the glassy tube, his face calm and his breathing normal.

Muffled cries of "Praise the light" sounded from behind me, but with so many left to heal, the troop remained subdued.

Kara went through them, one by one, until none remained but Micah. The strain of mending showed on her face, and she staggered, so Nathaniel had to catch her.

"Can you do one more?" I said.

She smiled weakly. "One more, a simple broken arm, and then you'll need to carry me to bed."

The light flashed. The boy healed.

Only then did the silent troop erupt into cheers, chanting louder and louder: *"Seeker magic."*

I winced but was too exhausted to correct them.

After the crowd dispersed and we'd put Kara to bed, Nathaniel and I sat in the rectory with the vicar of Bradford and shared a meal in silence.

At last he spoke. "I raged when the usurper overthrew the grand vicar, and grieved when they said you had drowned. I feared dark times ahead. Those new to power would oppress the people and punish them for their disobedience, and the people would fight back. I counseled my flock to stay true to the light, to foreswear violence and live in peace. Now I'm less certain."

"Why is that?" I said, unsure what I believed myself.

"Because of what I just witnessed, so much more advanced than anything found in the keep. These miracles you've brought from across the sea are not miracles at all, but fruit from the tree of knowledge."

I waited, hoping for more.

That spark I recalled from when he learned we were seekers flared once more. "I understand better now. The wonders that freedom brings may indeed be worth fighting for."

***

The next morning, Devorah brought the captured deacon to the rectory for breakfast. No need for protection from Caleb's roughhewn men, no need for guards at all, as her kindness had transformed the man. The cuts and bruises suffered in the ambush had been cleansed and dressed, and the fury of combat had faded from his eyes.

She pressed a hand to the small of his back and nudged him forward to the head of the table. "This man's name is Jethro. He became a deacon five years ago, before you discovered the keep. He says the vicars never treated him this well."

The former deacon made a small bow. "Thank you, Miss Orah, for your kindness. From what they taught us, I expected you to kill me... or worse."

I tipped my head, my own bow of sorts. "I'm pleased to see you better and with no weapon in your hand. Are you willing to help us in return?"

Jethro stared out the window at the rays of sun streaming through the trees and making the dust motes dance in the air. "I was raised a good child of light, never questioning the Temple and always obeying its rules — no teaching necessary for me. When the vicar chose me to be a deacon, my parents beamed with pride. For the first couple of years, I performed my duties out of a belief in the light. Later, like most of the others, I became cynical and obeyed to avoid the vicars' wrath. The punishment for disobedience makes a teaching seem like a stroll through the woods on a spring day.

"Increasingly, I saw practices more like remnants of the darkness than the virtue demanded by the light. When the man you call the usurper took charge, some deacons became corrupted by the power he let them wield. Others, like me, grew uneasy, but we'd had discipline beaten into us."

"Why stay? Why not run away?"

"We were afraid. Afraid of being punished, yes, but they warned us of what you'd do to us if caught. They told stories of how you treat prisoners, horrors like skinning or burning alive."

I winced, knowing his words rang true—not the first time the vicars had lied. "I hope you now realize we're not demons of the darkness, but simple folk trying make a better world. If one day, when your wounds heal, you wish to join our cause, we would welcome you. All here are volunteers. For now, if you'd like to repay our kindness, perhaps you can tell us what you know of temple plans."

Jethro glanced at Devorah for guidance, and she nodded back.

He turned toward me, but his eyes avoided mine, tracing the wooden grain of the tabletop instead. "They ordered us to fortify the walls of Temple City, the one two days south from where we attacked, declaring it the westernmost boundary of their domain, the first barrier against their enemies, but when they received word of the size of your force, they feared you were headed their way. They sent us out to slow you down while they retreated in haste."

"So the city stands empty now."

His pupils flitted from side to side and settled at the corners, but he failed to answer.

"Is the city empty?" Nathaniel repeated.

He met Nathaniel's gaze. "No. They left a guard to protect their rear flank."

"How many?" I said.

"Not many. A couple of dozen, perhaps. They took the majority with them, leaving only enough to man the gates and give the appearance of strength, another delaying tactic. Not much lies behind them, only a few to guard and feed the prisoners."

I nearly jumped from my seat, but quelled my excitement and tempered my tone. "Prisoners?"

"Yes. They took the healthy ones, but left those too weak to travel behind, concerned they'd slow them down."

I began to speak, but the question stuck in my throat.

Nathaniel asked it for me. "Was there a young man among them, slight of build, with sand-colored hair."

"I don't know sir. They never let me near."

My shoulders slumped, and I blew out a stream of air. "Is there anything else you can tell us?"

Jethro looked up at Nathaniel and me. His eyes widened, and he shook his head. "So much new to digest, so many changes from what I'd been led to believe. Devorah says she comes from across an ocean I once thought to be a myth." He slid forward to the edge of his chair. "And she claims you are the seekers, the ones who found the keep and started the great change. Does she tell the truth?"

"Yes, but why does that matter?"

"Because of rumors, whispered among my fellow deacons in the dark of night."

"What did they say?" My question emerged with little air.

"That deep in the prisons of Temple City, a third seeker lies captive."

Chapter 11

Rescue

We lay on our bellies, assessing our objective from a hilltop that sloped down to an open plain. In the gray of pre-dawn, this Temple City appeared more forbidding than the other, its walls surrounded with poles stuck into the ground, spaced a foot apart and rising at an angle with sharpened points facing outward. This makeshift fence stood twice the height of a tall man, and to make scaling it more difficult, a trench encircled the outside. Only two entrances remained—one gate to the west and another to the east.

On Caleb's advice, we'd circled around to approach from the east, where the city's defenders would be less likely to expect an attack. If few deacons remained, as Jethro had claimed, they'd apply most of their force facing their enemy. In addition, the sun would soon be rising behind us, forcing the guards to gaze into its glare.

Nathaniel rose to one knee and peered between stalks of grass as high as my waist. "I count ten, each holding a spear. I'd be reluctant to attack through such a narrow passage, if not for the report from our friendly deacon."

I peeked out from behind him and eyed the guards. "Then let's pray he told us the truth."

As we watched, several more deacons arrived. The others saluted them and left—a changing of the guard at sunrise.

Caleb signaled our men to the ready. They organized in a well-practiced formation, tightening their grip on their weapons as they waited for the next command, but he hesitated, still assessing the situation.

"In two minutes," he said, "the sun will clear the horizon, shining in their eyes and making us nearly invisible. Those who have gone off duty will begin to relax after their long night, an assault the least on their minds. Now's the time...."

He held up a hand to hold the troop back, and turned to Nathaniel and me. "You're our leaders, and these are your people. Give me the word, and they'll obey."

I gaped at the newly arrived deacons as they busied themselves, backs to us, dowsing torches on either side of the gate and preparing for the day. Would our numbers be sufficient to make them abandon their post when we attacked?

We'd left many in Bradford—those less fit or not as well trained. The bearers of the black cube stayed behind to protect the device that housed the minds of the dreamers and the other wonders from across the sea. Kara remained with them, as I couldn't risk her well-being since, for now, only she could use the mending machine.

I'd urged Jacob and Devorah to stay back as well. Unlike Caleb and his men, they'd joined our voyage not to fight but to bring back new skills to the people of the earth. Let them work with the craftsman in Bradford, the blacksmith and the cooper, the carpenter, the spinner, and the farmer. Let them master the crafts of peace.

But I'd asked Devorah to acquire one additional skill, requiring Kara to make her a bonnet like mine, but one attuned to her brain.

At first, she'd declined. "I grew up hearing tales of the dreamers, and would dread merging with those disembodied minds."

"Not the dreamers," I said. "I want you to learn to work the mending machine. If something happened to Kara, we'd lose the skill to heal."

I'd neglected to say that if we took too many casualties, we'd need more than one healer, so the second might mend while the first recovered her strength. I prayed there'd be no need.

While I pondered the risk, the edge of the sun flared.

Nathaniel grasped me by the arms and squeezed to regain my focus.

I nodded.

"Attack," he said.

Caleb waved the troops forward.

Half crept to the left and half to the right, keeping in a crouch and sticking to the tree line until all stood no more than a hundred paces from the gate. When everyone was in place, Caleb cupped his hands around his mouth and mimicked the screech of a hawk, and the troops dashed forward from both sides at full sprint.

By the time we emerged from the shadows, the red orb had cleared the horizon, a bright ball of light that blinded any who glanced our way.

We were seconds away before one of the deacons caught our advance.

He cried out a warning, calling for help, but no help came. Panicked by the rush of so many, he and the others fled.

We poured through without a fight, and moments later stood in the deserted street, conquerors of another Temple City.

Most of the residents had escaped to the countryside, fleeing the expected battle. Once those who stayed grasped the size of our friendly force, they came out from their hovels, mostly the elderly and the lame. They were quick to show us where the deacons hid, and in minutes, we surrounded their barracks. Our friend Jethro had been right—no more than a couple of dozen remained. Faced with overwhelming numbers, these dropped their weapons and surrendered.

After we secured the deacons, Caleb handpicked twenty men, and with arms at the ready, followed Nathaniel and me to the city center, where the main temple building stood.

My heart raced, no longer fearing an attack but rather what I might find.

Ahead lay the base of the vicars' power, a building I once viewed with awe. In its chambers, the vicars had administered teachings to keep the people in line, teachings for those like Thomas and Nathaniel's father and me, a brutal ritual that left me fatherless as a seven-year-old.

But the teaching cell was least on my mind, for far below ground, in the bowels of this building, lay the place I sought—the prisons of Temple City.

***

Unlike the last Temple City, the vicars here had only recently fled. The main structure remained pristine and unblemished.

We strode through the arched corridor that formed its entrance under the stony eyes of marble statues depicting long dead clergy.

The layout seemed similar to that of other temple buildings, and I quickly located the judgment chamber. The raised desk of the panel of vicars loomed at its front, with the mural that had once frightened me hanging on the wall behind. I stepped to the center of the room, to the wooden cover that concealed the teaching cell, but when I thought to remove it, my hands stuck at my sides and my feet stayed welded to the floor. What if the vicars, in their rush to flee, had abandoned some poor soul to languish?

Nathaniel came to my side and raised the cover while I looked away.

"No one there," he said.

I shuffled to the edge of the hole, stared inside and shuddered, then gathered my will and glanced around. At the front of the chamber, to the right of the desk, gaped the passage I sought.

"This way," I said.

We strode through a narrow corridor and down the spiral staircase, as we had before, but this time without fear. With no windows below ground, I needed a moment for my eyes to adjust.

There stood a lone deacon with his back to the locked door and his arms extended, brandishing a spear. The light of a single torch flickered off his face—so young, and less stout than most. Of course, the vicars would take the best with them for protection, and leave the weaker ones to rot.

I inched closer, and he fell back until his shoulders struck the door. His eyes flitted from side to side as if seeking a way to escape.

I recalled the lies the clergy had told Jethro about demons of the darkness, and held my hands out to him, palms outward. "Put your weapon down. We won't harm you."

He shook his head and raised his spear higher, trying to act brave, but the trembling tip gave him away.

Caleb came to my side.

When the boy spied this man more than twice his size, he panicked and lunged.

Caleb parried with the shaft of his axe, an instinctive move, no more than a flick of the wrist, and the deacon's spear clattered to the floor.

The boy scrambled to his knees to retrieve the spear and stared up at us with eyes wide.

Caleb loomed over him. "Why do you defend this door? What lies behind it that you'd give your life for?"

"The grand vicar himself ordered me to—"

Caleb dismissed him with the wave of a hand and turned to me. "What shall I do with this one? Give me the word, and I'll dispatch him."

I extended an arm to brush Caleb aside and, despite Nathaniel's protests, stepped closer, until the tip of the boy's spear kissed the folds of my tunic.

"Your blood is too precious to waste, and spilling it does neither of us good. Leave the weapon and live. Join us and help make a better world."

I reached out to the boy, and his eyes met mine. After a moment, he dropped the spear and took my hand.

As the others led the boy away, Caleb leaned close and whispered in my ear. "I'm humbled. Your faith in your fellow creatures astounds me, but once again, you were right."

I turned to the roughhewn oaken door and released the bolt, but hesitated before opening it, glancing over my shoulder at Caleb. "I hope we both feel the same after we see what's inside."

***

On the far side, no torches burned, and no candlelight flickered from behind the doors, leaving the prison as dark as a teaching cell. Nathaniel grabbed the torch that hung in the sconce by the door and led me down the dank hallway. The nightmare unfolded again before my eyes—the stone walls etched with decay; the row of doors locked with a metal bolt from the outside; the slat covering a window for the guards to spy on the prisoners; the air thick with dust and the stench of human waste.

Those who followed us marched several paces behind, eyeing the cells with contempt. None of them said a word, the only sounds our measured breathing and the thud of our boots on the dirt floor.

We unlatched the bolt of the first cell and peered within, but when Nathaniel waved his torch across the cot, the small desk, and the shadowed corners, the firelight revealed no one inside. Perhaps no prisoners remained, but why then leave a guard at the door?

We searched a second cell, a third, and a fourth. Still no one. Then, as the light from our flame reached the next to the last door, I caught an odd sound, out of place in this circumstance. I raised a hand to hush the others and held my breath.

From the end of the hallway came a muted whistle, a haunting tune but vaguely familiar. We proceeded to the cell from which the sound came.

As soon as the firelight from our torch came close enough to filter beneath the door, the whistling stopped.

A voice emerged in its stead, raspy and raw, but one I knew so well. "Don't bother interrupting my music, unless you brought me something to eat."

Nathaniel and I looked at each other and spoke as one.

"Thomas!"

I raced to release the bolt as Thomas had once released it for me, my fingers fumbling with the latch.

The door creaked open, and my childhood friend lay slumped on the cot inside. His sand-colored hair and beard had grown scraggly and long, and his cheeks had sunk inward. Though he still looked young for his years, he'd aged since I saw him last, appearing older than the friend I recalled.

I broke into a long-suppressed smile. "Looks like you've got yourself into trouble again."

His cracked lips curled into a half-grin. "I dreamed you'd come. Since we were children, you've always come to save me. What took you so long?"

"Oh, Thomas." I rushed toward him and reached out in an embrace.

He struggled to his feet and collapsed in my arms. "Careful now. I'm not as limber as I used to be."

I signaled for Nathaniel's water skin.

Thomas grasped it in trembling hands and gulped the water down, wincing with each swallow and spilling some onto his soiled tunic.

When he'd drunk his fill, he turned to Nathaniel. "You don't have any extra food in that pack, do you?"

Nathaniel laughed. "The vicars and deacons are gone or captured. We have our own army now, with food to spare, but first let's get you away from this awful place."

I wrapped one of Thomas's arms around my shoulders, while Nathaniel supported the other.

He stopped us at the doorway. "What about the other prisoners?"

"Gone," I said, "taken away by the fleeing vicars, all but the weak and sickly."

He stuck his head into the corridor, marveling at our armed band, his eyes widening when he took in Caleb. "There has to be more. I heard moaning last night like an animal in pain. Did you check every cell?"

Only one remained, tucked away in the corner.

While I supported Thomas, Nathaniel unlocked the door and stepped inside. From his silence, I thought the cell must be empty, until he cried out.

"Samuel?"

I took a step closer. "It can't be Samuel."

He motioned to the cot with the torch. Upon it lay what barely seemed a man, with a discolored face blurred by wisps of gray hair, and a body shriveled from hunger and abuse so the skin hung off his bones. This prisoner matched how Nathaniel had once described the first keeper, who had anointed us seekers and launched us on our quest for the keep.

Yet Samuel was dead.

Perhaps I was confounded by the torch's flame, or the quivering shadow cast on the wall, but it seemed Nathaniel fixed on this prisoner with a peculiar intensity.

The man on the cot stirred. Eyes opened, though he remained too weak to sit. A frail hand extended, a bony finger pointed at me. The lips parted so his teeth showed, almost a smile, and muffled words emerged. "Orah... whose name means light."

I struggled to match that feeble sound to a voice that had long ago boomed those same words. I squinted to see in those clouded eyes the sparks that had burned like embers. I fought to find in that ravaged face the man I'd once feared.

Nathaniel moved the torch closer, and the face came into focus.

I gasped.

On the cot before me lay the deposed leader of the Temple of Light, our former enemy, the arch vicar.

Chapter 12

Retreat

We bore our rescued prisoners up the spiral staircase and outside to the fresh air—Thomas stumbling along with support from Nathaniel, and the arch vicar carried by Caleb. After so long in the dark, both had to shield their eyes from the glare and peek through spread fingers at their newfound freedom.

Within an hour—and after a much-needed meal—Thomas came alive, reviving enough to tease Nathaniel about how fierce he looked with his warrior's stave.

The arch vicar, however, suffered from the limited exertion. His neck seemed too weak to support his head, and his eyes kept rolling up into their lids.

For now, both would require a litter to travel.

The younger Thomas, with food, water, and loving care from his friends, would recover in time, and might find the strength to march into Bradford with head held high.

The arch vicar's only hope lay with Kara and her mending machine.

Dusk settled on a now peaceful Temple City. Caleb insisted on posting guards at the gates, while the rest of us sought lodging in the abandoned dwellings. Some of our troops built bonfires and clustered around them to eat their evening meal and celebrate our victory, but most stayed subdued as rumors spread about what we'd found. Perhaps they realized at last that this trek would be no festival. Our enemy lurked on the road ahead, clever and cruel, and our future remained fraught with risk.

After dinner, Nathaniel and I split up to do our rounds. Years before, after we'd revealed the lies of the Temple and the wonders of the keep, our neighbors expected us to guide them, disregarding that gangly boy who'd grown up among them with notions of becoming a knight, and the little girl who'd pretended to be the leader in adventure games. On the distant shore, the people of the earth had declared us a prince and princess who'd sailed across the sea to bring a better life. Now, as we embarked on more uncharted waters, the children of the light once again sought our guidance. All was pretense, but for the sake of keeping up their spirits, we maintained the illusion.

After I'd played my part, showing my steadfastness and congratulating the troops for their courage that day, I went back to check out the wellbeing of our patients. I tiptoed into the arch vicar's chamber, thinking him asleep, and settled by his side.

His breathing seemed more labored than before, and in the light cast by a nearby candle, his skin showed a sickly pallor.

As I sat watching his chest rise and fall, comforting myself that he still lived, his eyes opened a slit.

"Orah... is... that you?" His voice, soothed by food and drink, had strengthened, though the words still emerged one or two at a time. "I feared... it was... a dream. Come nearer, child."

I slid closer.

He grasped my hand and attempted to squeeze, though his grip lacked strength. "So many days I prayed to meet you one last time, to ask you to accept my penance. I lay in that cell, dwelling on the harm I'd done to you, Nathaniel, and Thomas. I was wrong. Thank the light for the chance to beg your forgiveness before I die."

I waited as a fit of coughing racked his frame. Then I squeezed back. "No need to beg. I forgive you. No matter now. We're all victims to the usurper."

He tried to sit, but lifted no more than a finger's width before dropping back to the litter. "The usurper!" His nose scrunched, and his mouth puckered like he would spit. "How foolish I was, insisting that the thirst for knowledge led back to the darkness. I misunderstood the nature of evil. Evil spawns not from the thirst for knowledge, but from the lust for power."

He coughed again and collapsed from the exertion, his breathing settling into a more regular rhythm as his eyes drifted closed. When he stayed silent, I rose and left him to rest.

Next I sought out Thomas in the abandoned cottage Nathaniel and I had commandeered for the night. How wonderful to be together again, the three of us as we once were, inseparable through childhood. If I blocked out the warlike chants coming from the bonfires outside, I could almost ignore our plight and imagine we played one of our adventure games at the NOT tree.

Thomas was in better shape than the arch vicar, sitting up and gobbling down a second meal.

"I'm glad to see you with a healthy appetite," I said.

He attempted his old grin, but blisters and bruises prevented his lips from widening, making his words emerge as a mumble. "The vicars came close to extinguishing my fire in the teaching, and more so in their accursed prison, but they never dampened my appetite. They only deprived me of food. Thanks to you, I now have plenty to eat."

"I owed you a rescue."

His eyed turned inward, seeming to burrow into someplace dark inside. "Consider the debt repaid, though you've done so much more for me than I ever did for you. Now I find you're the leader of an army, trying to do the same for the whole world. I pray you succeed."

A lump formed in my throat, quashing my response. I shrugged instead and shook my head. Then, remembering my gift from Little Pond, I rose and rummaged through my pack.

"Look what I brought you." I pulled out the flute he'd hand-carved and polished to replace the one the arch vicar had destroyed.

His crooked grin dissolved, and his chin wrinkled as he blinked back tears. Unable to utter a word, he caressed the instrument and slid his fingers along its surface, searching for its holes, but when he tried to play, no sound emerged. Determined to try again, he moistened his sore lips and blew. He managed a single note, but no more.

I rested a hand on his cheek, careful to not cause him further pain. "You'll play again in time."

He nodded. "After my lips heal, I'll play you the tune I composed as I lay in prison, a song of sadness, an ode to anger at what the vicars have stolen from us." His eyes flared. "A tune fitting for your troops as they march into battle."

I went to the window and searched through the tree branches for my old friends—the stars—seeking their guidance as they'd once guided our boat across the ocean. My fingertips brushed the glass as if reaching for the sky. "I pray there will be no battle. I hope the vicars take one look at the determination of our people and yield."

When I turned back, Thomas was staring at me, his eyes watery and his head shaking from side to side. "My Orah, always seeking the light, but since you left our shores, I've seen more cruelty than a child sent to bed hungry can conjure up in a nightmare, a throwback to the darkness. They'll never yield without a fight."

I brushed back a lock of hair that had fallen across my eye and blew out a stream of air. "Why did you leave Little Pond? You were never one to take risks. Why didn't you hide on the far side of the mountains like Nathaniel's father? Our neighbors would have kept you safe."

He set the flute down and stared out the window, not searching for stars but for a memory too painful to recall. "The vicar came to our village, gathered us around, and placed the sun icon on the altar. From it, the voice of the usurper announced new magic that allowed them to spy on happenings across the world. Do you think that's possible?"

I shook my head. "The astronomy helper told me they could watch anywhere using eyes in the sky, but I doubt the vicars could recreate such machines in so short a time, not even with a thousand gray friars."

"I suspected as much, given the lies they told before. They claimed this new magic, granted only to defenders of the light, revealed that you and Nathaniel had died, that your quest to cross the ocean had ended with your drowning. Our people, already discouraged, heard the sad news and lost heart, but I refused to believe it. I needed to witness this magic for myself, so I headed to the keep to find out for sure.

"On the way, I met fleeing scholars, who rallied around me as the last of the seekers. Our group gained strength and grew until word reached the vicars. They sent deacons to stop us, and I learned a bitter lesson."

"What lesson is that?"

"That being a leader is a heavy burden to bear."

***

The morning dawned with a dreary mist that wafted across the city in waves, as if the world was struggling to awaken from a bad dream. I checked on Nathaniel, still asleep with his stave tucked under his arm. Though we believed the vicars had fled to the west, one ambush should be warning enough.

"Keep weapons at the ready," Caleb had insisted, "and always be on guard."

With such a large group, we took until mid-morning to gather supplies and prepare to depart. The first blemish of our day came when Nathaniel and I caught several of our troops ransacking temple buildings and taking what they pleased. We chastised the men and took them before Caleb.

"What crime did they commit?" he said. "They risked their lives to come here, and take only from those who have stolen from them."

Before I could respond, Nathaniel shrugged and agreed. I turned to protest, but he grasped me by the arms and bent his head low until our foreheads touched "Think of the harm the vicars have done, men without virtue who've hurt so many. Now we seek to overwhelm them, to kill them if need be. How can we say stealing from them is wrong?"

I pressed my lips together and swallowed my response, not wanting to argue in front of the others. I thought of what Thomas had said — the burden of leadership.

When all was ready, the troops departed through the western gate.

I wandered among them as had become my custom, thanking and encouraging them. On this morning, I took the opportunity to visit our wounded as well. I found the grand vicar and Thomas carried in their litters, silent and uncomplaining.

A short way out of the city, a low moaning filtered our way.

"Do you hear that?" Nathaniel said.

I nodded. "It's coming from ahead, but our wounded lag behind."

With so many shuffling feet, we struggled to localize the sound, so I halted the march. A weak keening came from the woods to our right.

Nathaniel and I ventured further down the road and found a path, newly broken through the trees. Wary of escaped deacons, we collected Caleb and a dozen of his men to go with us.

We proceeded in single file, the passage remaining narrow, with a ceiling of dangling moss dipping lower and lower until even I had to stoop. Bits of torn cloth clung to branches and splatters of blood marked the way — some wounded soul stumbling in panic and making no effort to hide his tracks.

Fifty paces in, we discovered the source of the moaning.

A small circular clearing opened to the sky, except for the canopy of a single ancient beech. Beneath it and almost hidden in the folds of its sprawling roots, a solitary man sat with his back to the trunk and legs splayed out before him.

Through the shadow of leaves obscuring his face, I saw his cheek bore a spreading bruise, which had partially closed one eye.

"Declare yourself," Caleb shouted, brandishing his axe.

The man glanced over his shoulder, to his left and to his right as if afraid someone had snuck up from behind. He took a shallow breath and muttered to himself. "No... never... never ever. No matter what you do to me."

He pressed downward with his free elbow in an attempt to rise, but lifted only a hand's breadth before collapsing again. In that brief instant out of the shadow, I caught his tonture and red sash—a grey friar, one of the vicars' servants who maintained the technology pilfered from the past and disguised as temple magic.

As I leaned in, I realized something more. Though the tufts of white hair surrounding his ears had grown too long and his tunic was more tattered than the elements explained, his silk robe gave him away. Here lay not one of the brothers but their leader. Before me sat a prior.

I knelt beside him and offered my water skin.

He grasped it and gulped down its contents so fast some spilled, turning the dust in his beard to mud.

"I know you," I said. "You're the prior who led the gray friars in the keep. What are you doing here, and how did you come to this?"

His eyes refocused, and a grim smile crossed his battered features. "You're not one of them. You're Orah, a seeker of truth. But are you real or a vision conjured up by my mind through a mix of pain and phantom hope? They told me you drowned."

I brushed my fingers across his bruised cheek. "Your hope is real, and so are Nathaniel and I."

Nathaniel knelt down so the prior could see his face. "How have you come to be so far from the keep and abandoned in such a state? When we saw you last, you knew more than any of us."

"The keep is not as you left it. The usurper has taken over, declaring it the high temple, where only he and his followers may commune with the light. But they're too lazy to extract the keepmasters' knowledge themselves, so they asked me and the brothers to learn for them. What you see is the result."

74

"Why would they abuse *you*," I said, "a learned man and one who's served them so well?"

"They asked me to do that which my conscience denied, to go against what I'd believed my entire life. When I refused, they reserved their special treatment for me."

"How did you come to be here?"

"When they discovered I'd never yield, they sent me in a fast wagon to this furthest Temple City, where they encouraged the deacons to use me for sport. They hung me to a pole in the main square, a warning to those who would defy their edicts. Last night, when the chaos came, a kindly woman cut me down and helped me limp to the gate, but this was as far as my broken body could travel. I prayed to die here beneath this tree rather than be taken again, but now a miracle has occurred, beyond what a man of science should hope for—the seekers returned."

Nathaniel's fingers curled into fists, and the pulse in his temple throbbed. "What did they ask you to do?"

I held my breath, fearing the answer, but my heart knew what it would be.

The injured prior stared over my shoulder, through the trees and into the distance. "They demanded I use my learning to resurrect the sins of the past. They asked me to help them return our world to the darkness."

Chapter 13

Limits of the Dream

We arrived in Bradford three days later with our wounded in tow. Both the arch vicar and prior had worsened on the trek and lay lifeless in their litters, badly in need of the dreamers' mending ways.

As predicted, Thomas refused to be carried into his ancestral home. When we reached the outskirts of town, he staggered to his feet and insisted on marching in on his own, albeit at a slower pace than the rest. To be safe, Nathaniel and I stayed behind, trudging along with him, ready to catch him if he fell.

We reached the center of town by mid-afternoon.

I expected our road-weary troops to have scattered to their shelters, but was surprised to find large numbers of them gathered in a half-circle, backs to the rectory and facing the village green. I left Thomas in Nathaniel's care and maneuvered my way through the crowd. At the front, the black cube that housed the minds of the dreamers lay on the lawn alongside the other machines, exposed for all to see.

Kara and Devorah stood with eyes closed before the mending machine, both wearing matching white bonnets. The bright light shone through its tunnel though no patient lay within. From the strain on Devorah's face and the sweat on her brow, I could tell that she, not Kara, controlled it.

The vicar of Bradford spotted me and hastened to my side, waving his hand in their direction. "When you first arrived, you spoke of wonders. I never imagined...."

I glanced to my left and to my right, taking in the faces filled with awe. "I hoped she'd keep these wonders more... private... for now."

"Kara asked that we take them outside on the green. While they can store the power of the sun for days, she claimed increased exposure makes them stronger. How could I refuse? She was seeking access to the giver of life."

"Has she used them every day?"

The vicar of Bradford beamed. "Used and more. At first, she communed with the dreamers, seeking their wisdom to help Devorah. I watched in amazement as the bits of lightning in the black cube stirred and flashed. The next day, using the box of what she called spare parts, she made a vision of a new bonnet appear from nowhere and dance in mid-air. Then, with the aid of our seamstress and more parts, she created a second bonnet like her own, which Devorah dons each day as she learns to be a healer."

What could I say? Kara had seen the injuries the deacons had caused and wanted her apprentice to be as prepared as possible when we returned.

The bright light of the mending machine flashed one last time and faded. Kara and Devorah removed their bonnets and embraced.

Murmurs rippled through what had been a silent crowd, with those who'd stayed behind in Bradford describing what they'd witnessed to the newly arrived troops. "The human embodiment of the light in this world... not from the sun icon, but inside the black cube. Lightning flashed within. This priestess and her acolyte donned bonnets to commune with the light, and used its power to make miracles."

I winced at their words, but noted the two litters waiting at the front of the crowd, their occupants pale as chalk.

I strode to Kara. "We brought two in bad shape, prisoners of the vicars. I'm afraid our journey weakened them more. Do you have the strength to heal them now?"

She offered a half-smile. "I have strength enough. Devorah did most of the work today."

We lifted the nearly unconscious prior onto the slab. On our trek here, I debated with the others who should be healed first. My preferred choice was the arch vicar as the weaker of the two, but Caleb convinced me to take the prior first. He'd been to the keep and possessed knowledge of the vicars' plans, information we desperately needed. My heart longed to treat the arch vicar first, but my head knew better. I chose what was best for all.

After a brief examination, Kara worked her magic.

The light glowed... and the prior healed, after which strong hands bore him away in his litter to sleep and recover. We'd wait until morning to question him.

But the magic failed the arch vicar. The light flashed longer and brighter than ever before, and Kara grimaced with the effort. At the last, the glow dimmed, while the anguish on the arch vicar's face remained.

Kara bowed her head. "Broken bones, damage to internal organs.... How could anyone do a body such harm? I tried to repair his wounds, but synthesizing so much tissue and bone causes strain. He was too weak to bear it."

I regarded the old man's limp body, and my eyes misted. "That can't be."

A weary Kara grasped me by the arms. "I'm sorry. My forbearers were brilliant, but far from gods."

I knelt by the litter where my enemy-turned-friend wheezed in short gasps. I recognized that sound—a death rattle. I recalled waiting at my father's side, wondering which of those precious breaths we took for granted would be his last.

I cradled the arch vicar's hand in mine, and his eyes opened a slit.

"Do you have kin... someone we should tell?"

"No one," he said between gulps of air. "I've... given my life to the Temple."

"I'm so sorry. I hoped we could do more."

The pad of his thumb stroked the back of my hand. "Don't mourn for me. All men must die, and I've lived longer than most. After a lifetime of fighting the darkness, I have no wish to live... to see its return."

"Is there nothing more I can do?"

His eyes widened for an instant and his voice firmed as he mustered his remaining strength to deliver his final words. "Go forward and carry the banner. Restore... the light... to our world."

His thick brows wilted as he breathed in and gasped.

I waited.

Another breath, another gasp... then the heaving of his chest stopped, and the spark went out from his eyes.

I recalled that spring day before Thomas was taken for his teaching, sitting with Nathaniel by the pond and watching the reflection of the leaves off the water. How I longed for that life now. It had been so beautiful—so simply and terribly beautiful.

I reached out two fingers, as I'd done with the corpse of my father, and closed the old clergyman's eyes for the last time.

***

The vicar of Bradford urged me and Nathaniel to stay as his guests in the rectory, citing the first day we met, and how he regretted letting us leave so soon.

I accepted at once, eager to spend the night in a soft bed, but once I lay down, my mind denied me sleep.

A full moon rose, casting its pale beams through the branches of a willow that shaded the window of our bedchamber, leaving spidery shadows on the wall. As a breeze kicked up, making the ghostly web tremble, I fought off visions of the darkness and held Nathaniel close, burying my face in his arms and reveling in his breath against my skin.

When I was sure he was asleep, I rose, grabbed my own white bonnet, and padded to the chamber where the dreamers lay.

The bearers stood guard outside the closed door, so I faced the cube alone. With no windows and the candles burning low, the lightning within flashed brighter than ever. In the still of the night, as I donned the bonnet and pressed my eyes closed, a faint buzz filled the air.

As always, the exchange ensued as a stream of thoughts flitting across my mind.

"Welcome Orah," the speaker said. "Though we have no sense of time, we've visited with Kara on nine occasions since meeting you last. Were you away or ill?"

"We traveled with our troops to Temple City to learn more about the vicars' plans, and to search for prisoners."

"What did you find?"

"The vicars fled to the keep, but we found three prisoners alive. Two you know from my memories—the former arch vicar, and my friend Thomas."

The buzzing grew into a beehive of thoughts so intense I failed to follow, until the speaker brought them to order and they commented one at a time.

"The keep...."

"An obvious refuge...."

"Where the knowledge of your world resides...."

"And Thomas alive...."

"When we joined minds with you, you reserved a priority in the archive for him...."

"You must be relieved to find him...."

"Is he well?"

I adjusted the bonnet to slow them down and give me time to frame my thoughts. "Thomas is well, considering what he's been through, but the arch vicar passed to the light. Kara tried to heal him with the mending machine but failed."

More buzzing. The speaker responded. "The mending machine has limits."

"From your memories, this arch vicar lived long...."

"The machine's synthesizing circuits need careful tuning for one so frail...."

"If we controlled it ourselves...."

"We might have saved him...."

"Though we still could have failed...."

"The human body is a complex problem...."

"A poorly designed machine...."

They paused. The dreamers always seemed to pause when they realized they'd been spouting logic at an inappropriate time.

After a moment, their thoughts flowed in unison. "We're sorry."

I counted four of my breaths, something impossible to do when joined with them in the dream. I was pleased to remain attached to my body, imperfect machine though it may be.

Though once before they'd refused to advise me about our conflict, ill at ease with the folly of the living, the circumstances had worsened, and I needed to ask once more.

"I come to you seeking guidance. My people have witnessed the wrong the vicars have done, the suffering they've caused. Many cry out for vengeance, but if we march on the keep, more will be hurt, and some will die. They look to me for wisdom beyond what I possess. They place faith in the seekers based on nothing but illusion, wishing for magic. What should I tell them?"

The buzzing in my mind grew to such a level that I almost covered my ears, though the dreamers made no sound in the physical world.

I waited, praying to the light for guidance, but as Kara had said, her forbearers, though brilliant, were far from gods.

"We understand what you ask," the speaker finally said. "The more people dwell on illusions, the more these illusions take on a life of their own. In our archives, we store many such instances from our past, tales of concocted beliefs used more often than not to seize power or seek revenge, yet we can offer no advice. We've become creatures of pure logic, and logic has no place in the decision to go to war."

***

That night, I tossed and turned until shortly before first light, when at last I drifted into a deep and dreamless sleep. I awoke late to find the glare of mid-morning steaming through the window and Nathaniel gone. I scrambled out of bed and stumbled into the adjoining dining area.

Thomas lingered alone over his breakfast. Devorah's salves, gleaned from the earth mother, had soothed his blistered lips, and the color had returned to his cheeks.

"Where is everyone?" I said.

He glanced up from a heaping plate of cheese and ham, and managed a full grin. "You overslept. Nathaniel asked me to wake you, but I wanted to finish eating first—it's been so long since I relished a meal. The others are waiting for you."

The fog cleared from my mind, and I remembered the meeting I'd scheduled to discuss our next step, a duty I dreaded. Much as I wished to defer the decision, I hurried to wash and dress.

As I prepared to leave, Zachariah dashed in. He glared at Thomas, annoyed to find someone else with me.

"This is Thomas," I said, "an old and dear friend. He's the one who made the flute I gave you. Now why did you burst in here in such a rush?"

"A rumor's in the air. Everyone says you and Nathaniel will lead a big meeting today to decide to go to war. I want to go with you."

"Absolutely not. Only the leaders may attend, and no decision has been made."

"You've been away a week and spent no time with me since you returned. Please let me come."

"How about you stay here with Thomas, instead? I won't be far, only a few rooms away. In the meantime, maybe he'll teach you how to improve your marching tune."

I winked at Thomas.

He winked back and turned to Zachariah. "Let's listen to this tune I've heard so much about."

The boy put the flute to his lips and played his song, the twelve notes repeated again and again.

Thomas waited for him to finish and then ruffled his hair. "Not bad, better than I could do at your age, but I can help you add some spirit so we can inspire the troops even more." He pulled out his flute and tooted a note of his own. "Come sit by me and we'll see what we can do."

As Zachariah settled next to him, and the two began to play, I slipped away, leaving them to their music.

I entered the meeting room—the one with the long table on which the three wide-eyed seekers had first charted their course to Riverbend—to find everyone seated, hands folded before them, waiting: Nathaniel and the vicar of Bradford, Caleb and those he'd handpicked to lead the troop. At the head of the table sat the prior, back straight and hair no longer disheveled, looking more like the wise elder I once knew.

I took my seat at the opposite end, with Nathaniel by my side, and glanced around, gathering my thoughts.

Caleb rose before I could speak and leaned on the tabletop with one hand, while wielding a rolled-up map in the other. "The mending machine has worked its miracle, and with the blessing of the good earth, our new ally has regained his strength." He pointed the map at the prior. "Please, sir, tell the council your story as you told it to me."

The prior fidgeted in his chair, shifting sideways and glancing over his shoulder as if hoping someone new would enter the room and recount the events he shuddered to recall.

When no one appeared, he grasped the table's edge with both hands and, still wobbly from his mending, used it to boost himself to standing. After a long breath in and out, he began. "Thanks to Orah and Nathaniel, we gray friars went to the keep following the great change. I'd spent my life studying in temple archives, but never before had access to such astonishing knowledge. The inquisitive brothers, charged with maintaining the keep, eagerly explored whatever they chose. Yes, the vicars supervised us, but over the years they'd grown lazy. Most had stopped learning after they left the seminary, and were content to spout dogma from then on.

"Everything changed when the usurper stormed in with his army of deacons. Now vicars gazed over our shoulders and directed what we studied, interested less in knowledge than in ways to restore their power.

"Once they realized what the keep had to offer, capabilities far beyond temple magic, they insisted the gray friars relearn the dark skills from the past. Their demands grew more terrifying by the day. Their goal: to break the truce agreed with his holiness, the grand vicar, and take back the power ceded to the people—to seize it by force, if necessary."

After the prior finished, Caleb slapped the map on the table and urged everyone to gather around, but deferred when he caught me glaring. "With your permission, of course."

I bit down on my lower lip and nodded.

He unrolled the map I'd first seen four years before. "His eminence told me the vicars have withdrawn the bulk of their men beyond Riverbend with the goal of defending the keep, building a fortified encampment here."

He placed a thick finger where the river turned north, on the field behind the rock face where we'd first found the way to the keep. In the years since, our people had cleared and widened the passage, making the trek easier, but apparently the usurper had done much more.

Caleb slid his finger up the road, over the mountains to the ruined city, and then back again. "All along this way, they used forced labor and rudimentary machines, assembled from keepmaster knowledge, to build a better road, one wide enough to move large numbers of men and supplies. Why? The answer should be obvious. Now they grow stronger by the day."

Nathaniel stood beside him and gazed down at the map, replaying in his mind the path we'd traveled before. Then, he traced the way back from Riverbend, and stopped where our troops now camped at Bradford. "We grow stronger too."

Caleb stared where Nathaniel pointed and shook his head. "Yes, more people join our cause all the time, but we can ill afford to wait. I'll need two weeks to provision and arm our force, and properly train them, and then two more to reach Riverbend. We should move against these vicars as soon as possible."

I joined Nathaniel and waved a trembling hand at Caleb. "Do you realize the consequences of what you ask? We shouldn't take such a decision lightly."

He dipped his head, an acknowledgement of my authority. "Of course. Deliberate all you want. The decision is for the council, but know this: if we wait for them to come to us, they may have grown more powerful in ways we cannot foresee." He turned to the prior. "Your eminence, please tell them the usurper's plans."

The prior lowered his chin to his chest and stared at the map, the sadness of the world shadowing his features. "He insisted the brothers extract from the helpers what the keepmasters were loath to reveal — how to recreate weapons from the time of the darkness."

Murmurs of shock rumbled from the council.

I motioned for silence and glanced at the vicar of Bradford. "You've studied in their seminary and been an official of the Temple. Is it possible for them to stray so far from the precepts?"

He waited, gathering his thoughts. A last, he let out a sigh. "Possible? Yes. So many vicars learn nothing but to obey, to do as they're told without thought, and the usurper has already broken the most sacred precept, as evidenced by his treatment of this prior and his holiness, the late grand vicar. He's capable of anything."

Beneath the table, I reached for Nathaniel's hand and intertwined my fingers with his. He squeezed back, but I was unable to read his mood. We were treading on ground not trod on for a thousand years.

I turned again to the vicar of Bradford. "What do *you* think we should do?"

He tented his fingers, closed his eyes, and a moment later opened them. They showed a new determination, as if the time in the dark had helped him forge a decision.

His brows sloped downward, and his lips curled into a frown. "Forget I'm a vicar or keeper. I have no more answers than you, but here's what I believe. If the usurper obtains weapons from the darkness, he'll punish us all, and destroy these wonders brought from the distant shore, wonders that seem worth fighting for."

I glanced around, dwelling on each set of eyes — all but Nathaniel's. "Before we commit our people to such a perilous plan, let us vote." I took a deep breath. "Who... is for war?"

One by one the hands shot up.

I noted them all, turning to my right at the last — Nathaniel's hand was raised as well.

Caleb glared at me. "You haven't voted yet."

"No need," I said. "The council has spoken, and may the light protect us all."

When the meeting ended, I needed fresh air and some time alone, so I walked out from the rectory to the village green. As the sun climbed past noon in the western sky, I spotted Thomas and Zachariah on the steps of the gazebo, playing their new tune. A number of troops had gathered around to listen.

Now I understood what Thomas meant. On our way to the keep years before, only months after his teaching, he'd performed a song of sadness and hope as we camped high above the lake, between water and dark walls of pine. Now, after weeks in the usurper's prison, his tune had taken on a sharper tone, a note of anger.

I studied the faces of the surrounding troops.

Their eyes burned, and their feet marched in rhythm to the beat, as they tightened their grip on their weapons.

Unable to bear more, I glanced away, up to the steeple of the rectory.

A mourning dove nestled at the peak of the sun icon, and sang a more peaceful song, her coo echoing across the town. Hoo-ah, hoo, hoo. *After a minute, her mate answered back and joined her. The two stopped their cooing and surveyed the green below, with the flute players and the would-be warriors clustered around them. Then the birds took flight to the west, as if to flee the warlike tune.*

Chapter 14

The Darkness Descends

Whenever events threaten to overwhelm me, I seek out the comfort of my best friend since childhood, but when I returned to the meeting room, Nathaniel was gone. I searched in our bedchamber. Not there. I checked among the troops milling about on the village green. Not there either.

Finally, I interrupted Thomas and his music. "Have you seen Nathaniel?"

He nodded. "He came out of the rectory in a rush, clutching his stave and taking long strides with those big feet of his." He gestured with his flute. "I think he headed that way, to where the troops train."

A ten-minute walk to the west lay a large field, used to plant wheat. When I first arrived at the head of a column of more than a thousand, I asked the Bradford elders for a place where our troops could train. They'd recently tilled the land, preparing to seed the next day, but agreed to leave it fallow this year for the good of the cause.

Now, a dozen instructors drilled their squads, with shouts and grunts and the clash of weapons filling the air. With so many, Caleb had set up a rotation, assuring every volunteer two hours a day to practice, a complex problem with troops at varying levels of experience and skill, and with limited space.

Though troubled by where these efforts might lead, I thanked the light for Caleb on my side. None of us had chosen this battle, but if we had to fight, better to be prepared.

I searched around, but had no luck finding Nathaniel, until I caught a friendly face, a neighbor from Little Pond.

"Have you seen Nathaniel?" I said.

He wiped the sweat from his brow, and with little breath to answer, pointed with the blade of his axe to a storage shed at the edge of the clearing, a place that now served as the armorer's workshop.

I found Nathaniel sitting on a rock beneath the shade of a drooping elm, working on his stave. The once blunt end had been tapered down, and he grated away with a rasp, honing the tip to a deadly point.

When he noticed me, the corners of his eyes drooped to match the tree. "Time to sharpen my stave."

"I thought we agreed to leave it for defense only."

He turned back to the stave and continued his sharpening. "The days for defense have passed, of no more consequence than memories of our childhood. Maybe you should get a weapon as well."

I settled next to him on the narrow rock, but he slid away, creating a tiny gap that felt like a chasm. For a time, neither of us spoke, as he worked on his stave and the wood dust flew.

Then he set it down and faced me. "After your coming-of-age, you told me the meaning of becoming an adult—that from then on, we'd have to make choices without illusions. Four years ago, we had a choice—to live within the limits set by the vicars, or to start a revolution. We chose revolution, and now we reap what we sowed. We either lead these people to victory, or many of them will die, and those who survive will be enslaved."

"Is there no another choice? With this troop that Caleb's trained, can't we negotiate from strength as we did that morning in Little Pond? Shouldn't we at least try a path to peace?"

Nathaniel shook his head. "They once accused me of being a dreamer of dreams, but now you're the deluded one. Our enemies do evil, far worse than teachings. They hurt people. They kill to stay in power. It's an illusion to believe they'll yield without a fight."

He picked up his stave, blew the wood dust off its point, and tested it with his fingertip, drawing a tiny drop of blood.

Then, without another word, he strode off to the training field, leaving me sitting open-mouthed on the rock, staring up through the boughs of the elm.

***

The next few days trudged by like prisoners on their way to stoning. The troops trained, Nathaniel and I planned, but beyond that, we said little. The future stifled our words like an impending storm.

Each afternoon, as the sun sank low on the horizon, my personal demons descended on me. My mood darkened as if the problems of our land infested the air. I ignored the tactics, the logistics of moving so many so far, or the shape of our battle formations, or the details of how to reclaim the keep.... leaving such things to Caleb.

Instead, I became obsessed with why. Why can't these problems be resolved? Why can't those who resist change see the benefits change might bring? Why do we drift toward battle, knowing that many will die?

On the seventh day, I stayed outside until well after sunset, wandering about Bradford and chatting empty chatter with troops I hardly knew, not even going back to the rectory for dinner. My limbs grew heavy. I trudged along with the same weariness I bore when I first awoke in the machines masters' cocoon in the fortress of the dreamers. Seconds passed like minutes and minutes like hours, until night fell and I could close my eyes and pretend to sleep.

For the first time in my life, I was afraid to be alone with Nathaniel, terrified of what either of us might say. When I returned to our bedchamber, he lay on our bed, hands folded behind his neck, glaring at the ceiling. I found no words, and neither did he, so I blew out the candle and rested by his side.

Exhausted from the strain, I nodded off, but not for long. I awoke a short time later and dragged myself from bed, afraid my restlessness would wake him. I stumbled to the window and peeled back the edge of the curtain to check for hints of first light. When only gloom stared back, I slipped from our bedchamber, but not to the black cube—no help to be found there. Instead, I grabbed a candle from a sconce by the door and headed to the empty conference room.

Sitting at the long table, where once we'd plotted our approach to the keep and now laid out plans for battle, I set down these thoughts in my log:

> *Less than five years have passed since I left the comfort of Little Pond, but I've aged, it seems, five lifetimes. The world closes in on me even when I'm outdoors, compressing the air and making*

it difficult to breathe. Where has my stubborn will flown, my striving toward the light?

Always before, in the darkest of hours, I found a way forward. No matter how slight the possibility or how great the risk, I believed righteousness and good would prevail. Yet now, I stand at a crossroads. To yield to events is to abandon all we've strived for these past years, to accept stagnation, to never be more than we are. But to fight...?

I fear a return to the horrors the vicars once preached in their teachings. In my dreams, I see the mural of the riders that stood at the back of the hall of winds: desolation, despair, destruction, and death. I can almost hear their hoof beats.

I long to sleep, but I'll sleep no more this night, for at last I understand where our quest for truth has led. Now come the ghostly horsemen galloping our way, the much prophesied return of the darkness.

Now comes the time for war.

PART TWO

CONFLAGRATION

"For I am a wild and a lonely child
And the son of an angry man
And now with the high wars raging
I would offer you my hand
For we are the children of darkness
And the prey of a foul command"

- Richard Farina

Chapter 15

The Way of the World

More people poured into Bradford as rumors spread of vengeful vicars and increasingly aggressive deacons. Most sought refuge from the oppression, but many came to join our cause.

Caleb and his leaders spent three days traveling to nearby towns, going from house to house, and nailing our call to action on the posts once reserved for temple bulletins. After five days, he declared the recruitment complete, with insufficient time left to train any stragglers. He stressed the importance of discipline, of everyone knowing their role, and being prepared to follow orders in the chaos of battle.

Messengers went out to surrounding farms, imploring the farmers to donate food or carts for our journey, and any tools that might be forged into a weapon. Jacob now managed a team of craftsmen-turned-armorers, who sharpened the edges of hoes with whetstones and fixed knives to the ends of walking sticks. Their efforts reminded me of the age of the darkness, when inventions intended for good were corrupted to do harm.

When not training, Nathaniel followed Caleb around, a way of learning leadership, he said. One morning, he rushed off without his usual farewell kiss, giving no hint of where he was headed. He returned two hours later with a carved handle protruding from the belt of his tunic.

"What's that?" I said.

"My new weapon, one to supplement the stave."

I noted how his eyes shifted down and to the corners when he spoke. "May I see it?"

From its sheath, he pulled out a blade the length of my forearm, of the kind used to shear sheep. He whirled it around, showing off its balance and heft, his eyes ablaze as he tossed the handle from hand to hand. I imagined him replaying in his mind past wrongs: his father's teaching, my father's death; Thomas returning for festival with his dreams ripped away; the abuse of the scholar and the prior; the murder of the arch vicar. The soft texture of love he displayed whenever we met after being apart had given way to anger. The muscles around his jaw twitched and his lips curled, exposing teeth, and his eyes grew cold — the scowl of a warrior.

He caught my concern, and his features hardened. "This is no game, Orah. You've seen what they can do."

I opened my mouth to speak, but no words came. Nathaniel had become what the founders of the Temple had feared, no longer a crusader for the light but an angry man willing to kill. The man I loved, who always wanted nothing more than to change the world for the better, had succumbed to the darkness.

I drew back a step, and my heart wept.

***

For the next week, I attended endless meetings and pretended to be a sympathetic leader, wandering through the encampment and encouraging the troops. Yet whenever I found a spare moment, I sought solitude away from the people I led. A five-minute walk from the Bradford rectory, I'd discovered a refuge in the woods, a clearing not so different from the site of the NOT tree of my youth.

On this day, I crept along the narrow passage to the open space, and caught a figure hunched on my favorite rock with his head bowed as if praying.

A refugee from the vicars, perhaps, or another fleeing scholar — certainly not danger, for the cowardly deacons never traveled alone.

I spread the branches that blocked the entrance and stepped through.

A weary Jacob glanced up at me and smiled. "So much like you, Orah, to seek respite as I do from the preparations for battle." He slid to one side and brushed the dried leaves from the surface of the rock. "Come sit with me. This place offers tranquility enough to share."

I settled next to him, hands folded in my lap, and we both stayed silent.

After a minute, I stroked his arm with my fingertips until he turned to me.

His smile changed into a grimace.

I reached out to comfort him, but my hand hovered in the space between us, unable to bridge the gap. "I'm sorry you have to use those wonderful hands to fashion tools that might cause others harm. You didn't follow me here for this."

He shrugged. "It's not your fault. It's the way of the world."

"I'm not sure I understand the way of the world anymore. Everything I once believed is changing around me."

"How so?"

"I can't say, but it seems to be everywhere. I feel it in the way the wind blows through the leaves, in the sounds echoing off the rectory walls when people talk, in the reflection of the sunlight off the water, in how time passes—it's all changing. Each change in itself makes sense, but bit by bit, a vaster change is coming, like when the first drops of rainfall build into a stream, and then gush forth in an all-consuming flood."

Jacob grasped my extended hand in both of his. "I feel it too, and perhaps it's preordained. The earth mother spoke of the great circle, not only for each of our lives, but for the whole of humankind. We are creatures who want, she said. Some, like me, can find contentment in simple things, like crafting wood with my hands."

"Thomas too," I said with a half-smile. "All he ever wanted was to make music."

"Others, like you and Nathaniel, are less content and long to change the way things are. When the two of you arrived on our shore, you brimmed with want. Why else would you risk crossing an ocean you once believed did not exist?"

"We wanted a better life for our people."

"A worthwhile goal, but the earth mother taught us not all wanting is good. Wanting too much can lead to evil."

"How can wanting too much be bad?"

"While still in the machine masters' city, she studied history from before the cataclysm, the time your people call the darkness. She found that in every era, some believe one way and others the opposite, all with an equal passion. Over time, those of like mind cluster together, and their passion feeds on each other. Like the people of the earth and the machine masters in their mountain city."

"Or the children of the light and the vicars."

"Yes, exactly, but eventually passion becomes purpose, and purpose drives the need to convince others. We become like men shouting from opposite banks of a broad river during a storm. One cries out, the other reacts. The first shouts back as his compatriots cheer—but no one on the far side listens. The discord grows until each group marches into battle, bearing the banners of their faith, convinced in the righteousness of their cause. They give speeches and play music to demonize their enemy, until their humanity vanishes, and they become willing to kill.

"I've never been one to shout across a river. My wants are simple. If what I craft pleases others, I'm pleased as well. If it's useful, even better. One of my happiest moments was making the spinning wheel and loom for you. Those devices provided benefit to my people, but best of all, they made your lovely smile glow. This time, I fear, will be different."

"How so?" I said, afraid to hear the answer.

"This time the results of my craft may leave blood on my hands, and suck the joy from the world."

Chapter 16

Riverbend

I scrambled up on a waist-high rock at the side of the road to better view our troops, but even from that vantage point, the column had no end. The flow of followers stretched for more than a thousand paces, snaking its way toward Riverbend. Men of varying ages and builds plodded along, burdened with packs of provisions... and a hefty dose of foreboding. Each bore their weapon of choice, some with axes on their shoulders and others wielding hoes, or scythes, or any tool with a pointed end or sharpened edge that might be swung with force.

Thomas had assembled a band of players, more than a dozen who played his marching tune with flute and drum. With so many troops, Caleb had asked them to scatter, so the music would carry up and down the line, keeping spirits high.

Zachariah pranced among them, proudly tooting his flute, too innocent to realize what lay ahead.

For the past two weeks, we'd marched to their beat, until at last the landmarks on my map showed us nearing our destination. In anticipation of our arrival, those with special roles donned their new uniforms. The mass of troops kept the customary black tunics, once ordained by the Temple of Light, but Jacob and his armorers wore blue with yellow armbands bearing the insignia of a crossed axe and stave. This marked them as non-combatants who would stay behind the lines to keep the troops supplied and the blades sharpened.

Devorah headed the healers, dressed in bright red with a white star upon their chests, visible enough to locate in the fog of battle. Though only she and Kara could mend, the others had been trained with a mix of medicines gleaned from the traditions of my people and the wisdom of the earth mother. Behind them trailed the litter carriers, ready to evacuate the casualties from the battlefield.

Most prominent, at the center of the column where they might be best protected, marched the bearers of the cube. Since Kara had exposed the dreamers' magic to our troops, Caleb had elevated their status. These guardians of the dreamers now wore the silken white robes once reserved for temple ritual, and added festival-like wreaths on their heads. They bore the black cube, the mending machines, and other devices on elaborate platforms, decorated each day with fresh flowers.

As word of our arrival reached Riverbend, a smattering of locals lined the road and cheered as we passed by. Caleb halted the troops before entering the town, giving them a chance to rest and refresh near the cemetery where Nathaniel, Thomas, and I had rested years before.

I stared at the somber stones, praying we'd have no need to erect new ones, or worse, to have to clear land to make space for additional plots.

By the time we reached the main square, a crowd awaited us, and at its head, a young woman with a familiar face.

She stepped toward me and made a small curtsy. "Hello, Orah. Your arrival at Riverbend is both timely and welcome."

I recognized the voice at once—Lizbeth, the shoemaker's daughter, who had provided us the final clue to the keep. In our time apart, she'd grown taller than me, and had blossomed into a lovely woman, though a tinge of sadness marred her once innocent features, the result, I assumed, of her receiving a teaching at such a young age.

She held a bouquet of daisies, which she presented to the leaders of our troop, one at a time.

Nathaniel smiled down at her and accepted his with grace, greeting an old friend, but the flower appeared lost in Caleb's calloused hand.

After a proper welcome ceremony, we reconvened with Lizbeth and the town elders around the banquet table at the local inn.

A round of drinks was served, and a gray-haired man offered a toast, thanking the light for our safe arrival and praising us for our bravery and support. Then he turned to Lizbeth. "With pride, we commend to you the last keeper, whose family guarded the secret of the keep across generations. To her, we grant the honor of relating our current situation."

Lizbeth stood at the head of the table and gestured to the north. "The vicars have assembled their force on the field by the bend in the river. More come every day. We've built barricades and trenches to the east of town, and many of our neighbors from surrounding villages have gathered to help defend it. So far, the deacons have left us alone, but if they decided to move, they'd sweep us away. Now, thanks to you, they'll think twice before marching."

Caleb raised a hand. "Can you tell us more about their force—the number of fighters, where they're situated, and how they're organized? Time is not our friend. The more we know, the better we can plan our attack."

She focused on him as he spoke, and then glanced out the window as if assessing the enemy encampment. "The deacons control who may cross the lines, and swear those who do to secrecy, but their stealthy curtain is not without holes. They've conscripted workers to do their labor and still demand their tithe, now not as gold but as food and supplies." She signaled to an elder who waited at the back of the room, by the stairway to the inn's bedchambers. "Please fetch Miss Junia."

After the elder disappeared up the stairs, Lizbeth leaned in, pressed both hands flat on the tabletop, and lowered her voice. "The woman you're about to meet is one of the town's bakers. They let her into their camp to bring fresh bread daily. She's offered to tell us all she's seen, but understand that in doing so, she risks her life."

Caleb tilted his head to one side and glared at Lizbeth across his nose. "How can we be sure she tells the truth?"

Lizbeth let out a long sigh. "Like many here, her husband of forty years was conscripted to remove the thistle and undergrowth, and to build the new road. He was old and in poor health, but they showed no mercy. He passed to the light two weeks ago, and Junia seethes with rage."

Moments later, the elder returned with a woman in tow. Gray locks curled about her ears, and bulging veins laced her hands and neck, but she held her head high.

Lizbeth met her at the foot of the stairs and guided her to her own seat while she stood aside. She rested a reassuring hand on the woman's shoulder. "Please meet Miss Junia, along with her late husband one of the finest bakers of the north river valley. The vicars chose her to gather bread from the others and deliver it to their camp." She turned to the woman. "You are among friends who will keep your counsel secret. Please tell them all you've told me."

Miss Junia's eyes burned with a fierceness as she met the gaze of each of us around the table. Then she stiffened her back, raised her chin, and spoke with words crisp and clear.

"The vicars organize their men in a grid, two encampments wide, with one on either side of the road to allow provisions to move in between. As of yesterday, these groupings stretch twelve long, and each holds twenty men."

"Are you sure?" Caleb said. "A miscalculation may be deadly to us all."

Miss Junia reached into her tunic pocket and withdrew a crumpled piece of paper, which she faced outward and waved at us. On it were words printed using what I once believed to be temple magic. "Every day, they place an order for bread. Yesterday, they demanded a hundred and twenty loaves, five per unit, each to be shared among four men."

I calculated in my head. Twenty-four camps of twenty deacons. Nearly five hundred men. A force less than half the size of ours, but likely better armed and trained.

Time to thank Miss Junia and commend her for her courage, but Caleb wasn't finished. "Their weapons. What arms do they carry?"

She stared at the ceiling and thought a moment before replying. "Each bears an axe with a short handle, no longer than my arm, with a pointed pike at its top, and a long knife, its blade as long as the axe is wide. When I arrive in the morning, I see them training and hear their grunts as their masters berate them."

Enough. I went to the old woman and embraced her. "Thank you so much. You've done a brave service for our cause."

As Lizbeth helped her stand, she stopped and turned to me. "One more thing, Miss Orah. Every day, the order increases."

"By how many?" I said.

She raised a knobby right hand with all the fingers extended.

"Five," she said. "Five more loaves each day."

No time to wait, as our advantage in numbers diminished by the hour.

***

We'd taken the past two days to rest our troops from their long march, and to lay out plans. This afternoon, the council voted.

Time to act.

That night, after dinner, I left Nathaniel, exhausted from his training, and wandered alone through the village, beyond the barrels and staves of the cooper's workshop to the edge of town. There, under the ghostly sheen of a half moon, I found Caleb staring at the road ahead.

"No sleep tonight?" he said.

I shook my head. "And none for you as well?"

"I worry about the men. They mean well, but the people on this side of the ocean have become too gentle and kind. The vicars' tales of the darkness and the threat of their teachings have made them meek. I fear for them."

"Are you not afraid for yourself as well?"

"Me? No. When my wife died, a part of me died as well. You can't fear death when so much of you has already died."

He went silent, staring up at the moon.

I waited a moment, and then gave voice to a question I'd pondered since the dreamers first shared his story. "What was she like?"

"My Rachel? A wonderful woman, my dearest friend. A brilliant scientist with boundless energy. More than any of the others, she longed to push the limits of the unknown, and that daring was her undoing. I remember her smell, her touch—like she stood beside me today—but I struggle to recall her face. When they took her to the disintegration chamber, they wrapped her body in a shroud, but against convention, covered her face as well. They claimed no mind remained, but still she breathed, and no one dared gaze into those glassy eyes as they carried her away.

"Every day, I'm haunted by questions: What if they had given her more time? What if they had left her on life support? Might some future research have restored her mind? I'll never know the right and wrong of it, whether they ended her life rashly or, in an act of mercy, granted her peace."

"Is that why you're so willing to fight and maybe die for someone else's cause?"

He turned, and his eyes bore into me. "Not someone else's. The injustice I found here affects us all. I fight this battle by choice." He pointed to the east, where the Temple's encampment lay. "Tomorrow, that's where I choose to be, with my men and on the side of right. A man can't choose where he's born, but he can choose the place to die."

Chapter 17

Monsters and Men

Two hours before first light, I swung my feet to the floor and sat dazed at the edge of the bed, until the plan I'd agreed to for that day startled me awake. Such madness, to abandon the safety of the inn and rush off—not to some sheltering village, but to a battle where men would die.

The night before, everyone in our would-be army had sharpened their weapons and mustered their courage, and penned notes to their loved ones and made peace with the light. Now, after a quick breakfast, Caleb had assembled the bleary-eyed troops in the dimness of pre-dawn.

Before we marched, I scampered up and down the line one final time to check that all was well.

I caught Zachariah tucked away near the rear, grasping a thick branch in one hand and a rock in the other.

"What are you doing here?" I hissed.

His eyes shone moist in the faint light. Even at ten years old, he sensed the sorrow to come. "I want to go with you, to protect you from the bad men."

I bent so low my eyes were level with his, and grasped him by the arms. "You swore to obey without question. Stay here with Thomas and the other players. Stay and don't follow, no matter how long I'm gone, but if you hear a tumult coming from the east, flee as far and as fast as you can, and never look back."

No need to give instruction to Kara or Devorah. They'd already set up the mending machine on the green to catch every second of the sun's rays. Others among the healers prepared pallets of bandages and medicines alongside the litters, bustling about expressionless and steeling their minds for whatever might come.

The rest of the troop shuffled their feet as if marching in place, and blew into their hands, waiting in the cold before dawn for their orders. In the glow of torches lining the village, I caught glimpses of faces, some frightened but most excited, each gazing to their left and right to acknowledge the whispers of encouragement from their comrades. Some slid the pad of their thumb along the edge of their axe or blade, testing its sharpness.

At last, convinced our preparations were complete, I dashed to the head of the column, where Nathaniel glared at the horizon, his outsized silhouette standing stark against the brightening sky.

I took a second, no more, for a quick embrace. We said not a word, but one thought resounded in my mind: *No matter what happens, our love will survive.*

A questioning glance from Caleb, and I nodded, little more than a tilt of the head. He raised his right arm and motioned us forward.

As we trod through the gloom, the dank morning air grew thick with the smell of wet moss, and the silence deepened, as if the forest was trying to reject this invasion of its territory.

My hearing became acute, catching the smallest of sounds—a bird awakening in the trees, a squirrel scampering through the brush in terror of our might—but there was something more. Though we left the players behind—no sense warning the deacons of our approach—a dull sound pounded in my ears like a distant drum. My heartbeat, most likely, or the echo of battles past. I shook my head to silence the sound, but it refused to go away.

We marched through fields of goldenrod growing high as a child's shoulder, with butterflies flitting above them. None of the would-be soldiers noticed, all eyes focused on the road ahead. Was this how armies had marched into battle during the time of the darkness, in stealthy silence, staring into the distance but seeing only the void?

A hundred paces from the rock face that marked the entrance to the enemy encampment, a temple sentry high up in a tree spotted us. He blew two long notes into a ram's horn.

Caleb gave a signal of his own, the screech of a hawk that rippled up and down the column. In response, his well-trained troops took off at a run.

From the far side, deacons awoke, but too late.

We quickly overpowered the sentries and surged into the camp.

Just as Miss Junia had described, our enemy had organized in parallel rows with a broad road in between. Our leaders shouted orders. The lead squads formed wedges, human arrows aimed at the heart of the first two camps, while the remaining squads surged forward. As we encountered subsequent sections, our troops divided again—the exact plan of attack drawn up the day before.

One by one the encampments fell, surrendering to overwhelming force. The enemy might have been better trained, but my people had right on their side, and passion prevailed.

My heart lightened as I glanced to my left and to my right.

Overwhelmed deacons had laid down their arms or lacked the time to fetch them. A scuffle here, the bloody swing of an axe there, but few injuries. Our victory seemed at hand.

Then, out of the morning mist, a nightmare appeared, one Miss Junia had failed to foretell.

From the rear of the camp, rows of deacons emerged marching shoulder to shoulder, some sort of elite force kept in reserve. These wore gold tunics beneath vests of chain mail, with metal helmets on their heads, appearing like the knights of Nathaniel's legend. Much like the deacons who'd ambushed us, they'd painted their faces green and black, but in place of the usual weapons, they brandished before them staves.

Something was amiss. These were the elite, more disciplined and so well armored that our axes and knives would struggle to harm them. Why did their weapons seem less than those of the rest, nothing but flimsy staves with a blunt end, thick enough to stun but not much more? Had we caught them before they'd properly armed?

I hesitated, trying to understand.

Caleb had no doubt. He aligned the men in waves and signaled for them to charge, but before the two sides clashed, dusk seemed to turn to noon as flames flashed from the end of the staves, followed by a series of loud cracks and a pungent odor like spoiled eggs. Men screamed and several fell. When the smoke cleared, dozens of our comrades lay on the ground.

Faced with the unknown, our troops faltered, looking to their leaders for guidance amid whispers of temple magic.

The row of golden deacons surged forward, pounding their boots into the dirt and grunting with each step, but I focused on their hands as they fiddled with a latch at the back of the staves. In the gloom of pre-dawn, I recalled a similar image from the helper screens in the keep, weapons of war from the darkness.

I shouted to Caleb. "Turn them around and flee."

He hesitated, then grasped my meaning and gave the order. Our men turned to run.

Another volley fired from the sticks, but with our troops in full retreat, most missed their mark.

While they prepared to fire again, our brave litter carriers raced about, gathering up the wounded under the veil of smoke. I helped one to his feet, a boy I hardly knew, and sent him on his way.

Time to flee myself, to regroup in the village behind the safety of the barricades.

But where is Nathaniel?

I closed my eyes and listened for his thoughts, my friend since birth.

Amid the muddle of shouts from the battle, I discerned a moan from my left, a plea weakly spoken. "Orah."

I found Nathaniel crumpled on the ground, one arm raised, groping at the air with fingers moist with blood. A blotch of red seeped across his tunic, staining it two hands below his right breast. I grasped him by the elbow and tried to help him stand, but he stumbled back down.

"No good," he said. "Save yourself."

Suddenly, I was back in Little Pond on that morning so long ago. "Save yourself," he'd said, but I refused to leave his side, and we'd marched in to face the stoning together.

I wouldn't leave him now.

I handed him his stave, which had fallen by his side, and he used it to yank himself to kneeling. Then digging in my heels and arching my back, I tugged on his free arm with all my might.

Light give me strength.

He staggered to his feet, but wavered and slipped back to one knee, dropping his stave as he fell.

I bent low and urged him to try again.

His hand rose as if on its own, and reached out to caress my hair, but he stopped when he saw something over my shoulder. His eyes widened, and in their reflection, I caught a lone deacon approaching.

As our enemy edged toward us, gripping his knife with both hands and raising it above his shoulders preparing to strike, I held my ground, shielding Nathaniel's body with mine. When the deacon continued to advance, I picked up the stave and aimed its point at his heart, though I had neither the training nor strength to cause him much harm. If he'd lunged at that instant, I was prepared to die.

The words slipped from my lips as if on their own. "I love you, Nathaniel."

The deacon and I stared at each other, and after what seemed an eternity but was no more than a few seconds, he dropped the knife and showed his hands palms out.

I handed the stave back to Nathaniel, no longer weapon but crutch, and gaped at the man wide-eyed. "Why?"

"There's one thing worse than death," he said. "To lose who you are, to become more monster than man."

Then he turned and walked away.

I startled to a heavy hand landing on my arm and spun around.

Not enemy but Caleb. He passed me his axe. "Take this and run. I'll carry Nathaniel."

He grasped Nathaniel's wrist with a thick hand, and slid the other beneath his thigh. Then, in one powerful motion, he slung Nathaniel over his shoulders and whisked him away.

Chapter 18

After the Battle

Our troops staggered back to Riverbend in a more somber mood. No one spoke, and our boot steps seemed muffled as if the smoke from the battle had dampened all sound. Far away, a crow cawed. Puffs of clouds drifted across the sky with the same indifference as before. A light breeze blew, rustling the leaves, and more than likely the earth itself kept rotating as the helpers in the keep once claimed. None of these cared about the tragedy that had transpired this day.

All of us—wounded and well—slogged along until we passed through the protection of the barricades. Ever diligent, I took time to station troops at the wall in case the deacons followed.

When I arrived at the village green, litters lay scattered across the lawn. The sun had cleared the treetops, bestowing its full power upon the mending machine, but its glare also highlighted the splotches of red staining the green grass. I started to count the wounded, but stopped. Too painful.

Some moaned in agony; others pressed their lips together and suffered in silence, as if in sympathy with those silenced forever.

I darted about, searching until I located Nathaniel, one of the silent ones staring at the sky. A healer had cut open his tunic and placed a clean bandage over his wound, with orders for him to press down to stanch the bleeding.

I checked the mending machine. Kara had just finished a healing, and her helpers were removing the patient from the slab.

I glanced back at Nathaniel as he tried to hide his pain, the blood still oozing from his chest. "I'll tell Kara to take you next."

He shook his head, wincing with the effort. "No. I can wait. Others need help more."

I recalled him emerging from the dreamers' cocoon, wondering if he'd return to the man I loved. How much harder to bear the suffering of one you love than to endure the pain yourself. How much greater the pain.

Minutes turned into hours as one wounded warrior after another entered the brightly lit tunnel. Most came out healed. Some with more serious injuries did not, and these the helpers covered with sheets and carried away.

Kara worked feverishly. Only when near collapse did she allow Devorah to take over.

The healers had laid out the litters in order of need, with the direst wounds first.

Nathaniel insisted he go last, that he could wait while those with more painful injuries went ahead, but his gritted teeth and pallid skin said otherwise.

As leaders, we should expect no special treatment, yet I hoped for Devorah to tire soon so a revived and more experienced Kara could treat Nathaniel.

At last his turn came. Devorah had been left to deal with the lesser wounds, and with only a few weeks of training, she'd done well, healing a half dozen, but the strain of the mending showed in her wan features.

"Can you do one more?" I said.

We both glanced at Kara, who lay prone on the lawn, still drained from her efforts.

Devorah nodded.

Four healers lifted Nathaniel onto the slab, and his long frame slid head first into the tunnel. The bright light flashed while I prayed.

When the mending finished, Devorah smiled weakly. "I did it. He's healed." Then she collapsed in my arms.

I led her to a bench by the gazebo and sat her down. "You did well for your first healing."

She stared at me, her face drawn and with tears in her eyes. "The mending machine is a miracle with a mind of its own. It lets me see inside the body, gives me choices, and I direct the repair. I found a piece of metal that had pierced Nathaniel's chest. It had cracked a rib and ripped the flesh inside. I used the synthesizer to dissolve the metal, rebuild the bone and mend the flesh within and without. He should be fine in a few days."

Now my own tears flowed, and I embraced her. I held on, letting the sobs that racked her slight frame subside.

When we separated, her expression still bore a look of devastation.

"You must be tired," I said. "The mending takes so much concentration, and here you're newly trained."

A cloud cleared away from the sun, letting a slanting beam fall upon us like a ray of hope. Devorah held up a hand to shield her eyes and gazed at something far off. "Tired, yes, but that's not why I weep. Through the machine, I find rents in the tissue and cracks in the bones, but I also feel the wounded's pain. That burden alone is hard enough, but unlike the fall that broke Zachariah's arm, no accident caused this damage. These injuries were caused by those intending to do harm." Her lower lip trembled, and she shook with rage. "The earth mother preached of sorrow in this world, but she never prepared me for such evil. If we are the stuff of stars, how can we act like beasts of the field?"

Without another word, she rose, staggered to where Kara lay, and helped her mentor to stand. The two embraced, sharing a moment few of us could comprehend.

I followed the litter bearers to the guest room in the rectory, where the healers placed Nathaniel on our bed. He rested there, weak as Zachariah had been, but with the anguish gone from his face.

I stayed by his side until his breathing settled into its normal rhythm and his eyes drifted closed. Time to go outside. The troops needed me to assure them all would be well. As a seeker of truth, I'd raise my chin and pretend to be strong. I'd willingly act the lie.

Before I reached the door, Nathanial called me back. I settled on the bed and leaned in to hear his mumbled words.

"How many... killed?"

"Twelve." My voice cracked, and I paused to collect myself. "Twelve fathers and sons, twelve husbands and dear neighbors."

He turned away and buried his face in the pillow. "How did we come to this?"

I wiped the sweat from his brow and brushed the hair from his eyes. "The earth mother claims we've been like this throughout history. People keep striving until their passions overflow into violence. How can we live with such sadness?"

He placed a hand behind my neck, pulled me close, and kissed me, but his words sent a shiver down my spine. "Though dark clouds gather, we'll face this storm together, and one day, we'll find a way to avenge."

Then his eyelids drooped, and he slipped into sleep.

***

Once the pain had eased from Nathaniel's features, I put on my leader's mask and stepped outside to mingle with the troops. After an hour of urging them on, I'd pretended enough.

In the days before the battle, an excited Jacob had shown me his sketches of the Riverbend grist mill. He'd extolled the benefits of such a simple machine, but also commended the setting as a respite from making the tools of war. I thought now how I needed a respite as well, a place from a more innocent time.

I followed the path he'd described, the rush of the stream through the reeds guiding me on. At the mill, the splashing of water over the slats of the wheel triggered fond memories—strolling down a similar trail in Little Pond, swinging my arms through the waist-high heather and feeling their kiss on my hands, and having Nathaniel, unbowed and unscathed by my side.

I settled on a bench by the stream, pressed my eyes closed, and fought off the urge to cry.

As I sat there, a voice interrupted my thoughts.

"Jubal told me you headed this way," Caleb said. "I'm glad Nathaniel is healed. I know how hard it is to watch the one you love suffer."

The crunch of his boots on dried leaves stopped close enough that I heard his breathing. He waited, but I refused to open my eyes, preferring to wish the world away.

"You can't ignore what happened," he said. "The troops need you to lead, and we have little time."

I opened my eyes and blinked at the sunlight glaring off the water as it splashed across the slats of the wheel. "I don't want to lead anymore. I'm tired of causing pain to those who follow. Let someone else take their turn."

"You should have thought of that before you started what your people call the great change."

I turned to face him. "What would you have me do?"

"The enemy will come for us, but not today. The weapons they used to drive us off were too few, and next time, they won't have surprise on their side. They'll wait until they're better armed, after the gray friars provide them with more powerful weapons. They won't come tomorrow, because we still have numbers on our side, but maybe in the next week or two. No longer than that. When they come, more will be injured and more will die."

I gritted my teeth, denying the truth he spoke, and stared back at the wheel, not to find answers there, but to seek the comfort of forgetfulness.

"Please, Orah, I've seen the depth of your courage before, ever since you confronted me in the earth mother's village. Don't let that strength abandon you now. I can train the troops and give them orders, but with Nathaniel wounded, they look to you, the remaining seeker, for guidance."

I fought off the mood. Nathaniel lay healing and I was alone. My people depended on me.

"What if we undo the harm we've done and retreat?" I said. "Let our troops go back to their homes, to their families and farms, to their spinning wheels and looms, to their blacksmith's anvil or carpentry shop or whatever crafts they ply. Let them blend in with their neighbors. The vicars will be hard pressed to identify those who rebelled and those who did not."

"Perhaps, but they'll know me and my men, and you, Nathaniel and Thomas. They'll know the escaped scholars and Lizbeth and the vicar of Bradford. They'll know our friend, the prior, and Miss Junia. They'll know Kara and Devorah, who will insist on staying to mend the injured, and Jacob and Zachariah, who'll refuse to leave your side. I might escape with my men over the mountains and sail back to the safety of my native land, as my ancestors once fled the Temple of Light a thousand years ago, but the rest have no such choice. They'll hunt them down, and you and Nathaniel foremost, no matter where you go."

I shook my head, rejecting his words, and forced myself to focus on the slats of the wheel as they rose from the shadows and emerged into the sunlight.

Caleb grasped me by the shoulders and turned me until our eyes met. "We can't fight them without better weapons. Your people have only one hope, and you know where that hope lies."

I squinted at the stars dancing off the water and, as I stared, the setting transformed into a black cube with bits of lightning flashing inside.

Chapter 19

A Vote for War

I insisted the meeting be kept small, mostly those who had dwelled in the dream: me, Caleb, and Kara, with Nathaniel too weak to attend. No need to involve others in matters they did not understand. Though the vicar of Bradford knew little of dreamers, I invited him as well. He'd accompanied us on our trek so he could minister to the troops, and now I coveted his counsel for such a difficult decision. This meeting dealt more with the spirit than science.

Before describing the purpose of the gathering, I swore everyone to secrecy.

Kara leaned in with her elbows on the table, made a bridge with her hands and rested her chin upon it. As I described my plan, she hardly blinked.

When I finished, I fixed on her. Of those in the room, only she had the ability to carry out what I proposed.

She straightened, took in a stream of air and let it out. "I've brooded on this option for a long time, ever since we shared our memories. I could guess what your vicars would do. Can we match them? Of course. Your craftsmen have most of the skills I need and with mentoring, I could teach them what they lack. But what good to match our enemy? Let me ask the dreamers for more."

A panic fluttered within me, as I envisioned the horrors Thomas had described from his teaching. "Like the false sun that burned people to ash, or the liquid that melts flesh from bone?"

She shook her head. "No need to go that far."

As we debated, the vicar of Bradford stood and paced to the cabinet with the image of the sun carved into its front. With his back to us, he seemed to be studying the icon that had once been the cornerstone of his faith.

When Kara finished, his shoulders heaved up and down, and he turned around to face us. "I understand little of such matters, but you speak of the forbidden, actions I'd never before condone. Yet in these past weeks, I've witnessed cruelty beyond imagining, atrocities I struggle to accept even now."

I slipped between him and the sun icon, and let my fingertips trace the symbol of what I'd once called the giver of life. "I invited you to this meeting, not for your knowledge, but for your wisdom about right and wrong. Will asking the dreamers for weapons cause more harm than good? Will this single step send our world sliding back to the darkness?"

He sucked the air between his teeth and shook his head. "I have less wisdom than you presume. We know from both the book of light and the history found in the keep that our ancestors nearly ended our existence. What we've witnessed is but a trace of the horrors they committed. Like you, I was taught to beware the stray thought, because once we allow a hint of the darkness to seep into our minds, something wicked in our natures rears up and drives us headlong down that slope. Good folks find ways to justify cruelties they'd never dream of tolerating before... just as we're doing now."

Caleb joined us, his broad frame blocking the sun icon from view. "Noble thoughts, but my people suffered the same cataclysm. After we crossed the ocean, fleeing from your temple, we struggled for generations to rebuild our lives, but unlike you, we never abandoned the pursuit of knowledge. Now only that knowledge stands between you and your destruction at the hands of so-called magic stolen from the keep. Tell me, wise elder, if we dismiss Orah's proposal and choose the way of peace, what do you predict will happen? Will your former colleagues rediscover the light and forgive us all, or will they punish us in ways so harsh they give new meaning to the darkness?"

Though the smaller man, the vicar of Bradford stepped toe to toe with Caleb, so close I imagined the heat passing between their eyes. "My temple offers a broad canopy, which encompasses many things. Not all have been good, but over the centuries we've maintained the peace and preached kindness to everyone. To my distress, a disease now rots the Temple from within. I reject the usurper as my leader and condemn the harm he's done, but we mustn't ignore the sins of the past. The evil can grow worse, horrors without end that threaten once again to consume us all. We should take care before making this leap." He turned to Kara. "Your dreamers.... Can they conjure up weapons that will defeat the deacons, yet do minimal harm?"

"To answer your question," she said, "I'll need to meet with them first."

***

I went to my room to fetch my bonnet and check on Nathaniel. Kara had insisted he'd sleep until morning as his body recouped from the mending. I bent low and brushed my lips to his forehead to measure his health. His skin felt cool but not clammy.

I tiptoed to the bureau and slid open the drawer an inch at a time, trying to make little noise, and withdrew the white bonnet. Before returning to the others, I hovered over Nathaniel, knowing how much he needed the sleep, but wishing him awake for a minute or two, long enough to share my burden and seek his counsel. Not a twitch as he slept more soundly than before.

Kara, Caleb, and I regrouped in the anteroom to the dreamers' chamber. We ordered the bearers who guarded them to wait outside, making sure no one entered.

Though they'd carried the black cube for many a week, they'd rarely witnessed us communing with the disembodied minds. Now Jubal and three other stout men stood on either side of the door, shuffling their feet and wringing their hands, with the look of those expecting the dead to arise.

When Kara spotted my bonnet, she held up a hand and shook her head. "Better I do this alone."

"Can't we commune together as we did in the dream?"

"The cube is different, not a sharing of minds, but one of the living conversing with the dreamers, asking questions and hearing their answers through the sensors. We've never tried two at the same time. Unencumbered by their physical bodies, they think so much faster than we do. We may become confused and struggle to grasp their responses.

Moreover, I'll be asking for complex plans using technology I understand far better than you. You'd only slow me down."

I opened my mouth to object, but Caleb stopped me. "Time is not our friend, and lives are at stake."

I imagined the gray friars hard at work, querying the helpers to find more efficient ways to kill. My thoughts flew off to dark places, to a world of unchecked evil. I pictured Nathaniel's anguish as blood seeped from his wound, and the battered faces of Thomas, the arch vicar and the prior. Their faces transformed into my mother and Miss Junia, who would surely be punished, and to Lizbeth and Zachariah.

I bit down on my lower lip and agreed. "Let me at least accompany you, so I can support you in spirit."

She nodded but glared at the bonnet clutched in my hand. "Leave that here. If you yield to temptation and intrude, you'll disrupt my connection, and I'll need to start over."

I handed my bonnet to Caleb and entered the chamber, latching the door behind me. The black cube lay on its carrier in the center, surrounded by clusters of flowers—more than ever before, a growing tribute from people who viewed it with awe. The blues and reds and the brightest of yellows pleased the eye, and their scent filled the air, a foolish embellishment, since the dreamers sensed nothing of the physical world. Only Kara and I provided their eyes and ears through our bonnets.

Kara aligned the sensors to the pressure points on her scalp and focused her mind. So young, no older than I was when I first set out to the keep.

"Are you ready?" I said.

She nodded and placed both hands on the cube palms down, an unnecessary ritual adopted more for our own comfort than for the benefit of the minds within. As I imagined the familiar tingling in her fingertips, the bits of lightning stirred, not from the touch of her hands but from her thoughts transmitted through the bonnet. She closed her eyes.

As I waited, the pounding of my heart seemed to echo off the walls. I caught other sounds as well—a thud like a tree limb falling outside, the groan of a floorboard under weight, or the creak of a door swinging wide—but I never took my eyes off Kara.

After what seemed like forever but was less than an hour, she stepped away and opened her eyes. Her head tilted to one side, as she wiggled the bonnet free and fluffed up her hair where the sensors had matted it down. I tried to catch her eye, but she glanced away, gazing instead off into the distance like a sailor seeking the horizon.

I unlatched the door and let Caleb in.

He eyed the cube as he always did, with a mix of wonder and rage. More than any of us, he appreciated its power, but loathed the science that had destroyed his Rachel's mind.

The bearers guarding the entrance peeked in, but feared to come near.

I closed the door behind Caleb.

"Can they help," he said.

Kara nodded, though the gesture lacked energy. Perhaps she was still tired from the mending. "All I need is a blacksmith, a carpenter, and four wooden carts. The rest I can cull from my box of parts. While I construct the devices, pick eight stout men I can train, those who can be trusted to obey without question and not flinch under pressure." She faced me for an instant, but before I could read her mood, her lids drifted lower, and her gaze shifted to the floor. "Of course, I'll await your word to proceed."

Something made the hairs on the back of my neck stand on end. Kara had supported me in the mountain fortress when I feared losing Nathaniel. Together, we'd mourned the death of her grandfather and shared our deepest memories in the dream. She'd accompanied me across the ocean to help in my cause, and through it all, she'd become like a sister to me.

Why then, in this moment of peril, does she refuse to meet my eyes?

Perhaps my imagination, or the way one feels when the unthinkable becomes possible.

Kara waited for my response. All that remained was to give the order.

I tapped my teeth with the tip of my thumb, and glanced from her to the lightning in the cube. "I'll need until tomorrow. A choice this dreadful deserves a night's sleep. In the morning, I'll decide."

I turned to walk away, but Caleb grabbed me by the elbow and spun me around. "Why wait? Nothing will change by morning, and Kara should start right away." His harsh features softened. "Please, Orah, be a leader now."

I yanked my arm away and glared at the two of them, so deafened by the blood rushing through my temples that I spoke too loud. "Do it, and may the light forgive us all."

Chapter 20

The Cause of Strife

That night, I dreamed of my unborn child. I heard her crying in the crib and rose to comfort her, floating along in that way people do when they dream, my feet barely brushing the floor.

I picked her up and pressed her to my breast, but she failed to calm. I offered food and drink to no avail. As a last resort, I rocked her in my arms, swaying from side to side and singing the song my mother had sung to me after my father died, the same one I sang to Nathaniel through the peephole during our imprisonment.

> *Hush my child, don't you cry*
> *I'll be here with you*
> *Though light may fade and darkness fall*
> *My love will still be true*
>
> ~~~
>
> *So close your eyes and trust in sleep*
> *And dream of a better day*
> *Though night may fall, the morn will come*
> *The light will show the way....*

She stopped crying and stared up at me, mouth agape, but before I finished, she interrupted.

"How can there be a better day," she said with a voice too wise for her years, "when you're about to lead us back to the darkness?"

"I'm not leading us back to the darkness," I said, unperturbed by this infant speaking in such an adult way. "I'm fighting for the light."

119

"I don't understand the difference."

I began to answer in my schoolgirl, I-know-the-answer tone, but whenever I tried to say the word 'light,' 'darkness' came out instead. As I stuttered, trying to explain the universe, the room dimmed. Through the window, I spotted storm clouds racing across the sky, consuming first the moon and then the stars. A sudden gust blew out the only candle in the room, and we were cast into darkness as deep as a teaching cell.

As I gazed into the gloom, the air above me shimmered and a vicar appeared, the one who had dragged me and Thomas off to our teachings so long ago, the man my people now called the usurper.

He bared his pointy teeth and leered at me with black button eyes. "So, Orah, whose name means light, you stepped into my trap. Perhaps we should change your name to something more appropriate. What word in the forbidden language means darkness?"

He twirled his fingers above his head, and the gust grew into a gale.

I clutched my child more tightly, but the strength abandoned my arms. A wicked wind snatched her from me and swept her through the open window, high up into the clouds and lost into the night.

***

When I awoke, I lay in a cold sweat, eyes pressed closed, afraid to confront the day. What kind of world would I bring my child into? Or would Nathaniel and I, like the last of the keepmasters before us, deem it unwise to bring offspring into such a troubled world?

I opened my eyes to a stirring at my side and found Nathaniel sitting on the edge of the bed, chin propped up in his hands and staring out the window.

"Are you all right?" I said.

"Just tired. What did I miss?"

I described the plan I'd approved the day before.

He brushed a lock of hair from my eyes. "You did the right thing. I would have done the same."

Now that I'd shared my burden, my lower lip began to tremble. "I'm not so sure. I'm afraid where this will end. Will we stumble like our ancestors, step by foolish step, back to the darkness?"

He lay back down, and I rested my head on his chest, letting his heartbeat calm me.

He wrapped a comforting arm around me. "You saw what happened. We have no choice."

I turned to face him. "No choice? We sought a better world. Is this the world we wanted?"

My head rose and fell as he sighed. "What we want no longer matters. Look at the harm they've done, worse than we ever believed possible. They threaten all those we love and everything we hold dear. A time comes when the blood rushes and the heart should dominate the mind. If someone attacked you, I'd fight back and kill them if necessary, without thought, as I hope you'd do for me. I might have died if not for the mending machine. Isn't that worth fighting for?"

"But when does this cycle end? They harm us, we harm them. Will we all be destroyed? There must be another way."

He rose on wobbly legs and took a halting step—only one, but it felt like the breadth of the ocean.

He spoke with his back to me. "You think too much. Now's not the time for thought. Once, in the keep, you dismissed my notions as childish illusions. Now you're the one with illusions. Open your eyes. What does it matter whether we call it darkness or war? There can be no peace until we win—by any means."

I crept up behind him and rested a hand on his bare shoulder. I knew I should say something, should argue or disagree, but my words died in the hollow of time, sinking soundlessly as if tossed into the bottom of a darkened lake.

He staggered away to the bureau and pulled out his tunic. While he dressed in silence, he glared at me with a look like fog on the sea, a cold mist that wends its way into your heart and remains there for a long time... until it becomes a part of you.

***

Though still weak, Nathaniel went off to join the men training, claiming that watching them and listening to their grunts inspired him.

With the troops drilling and an audience of townsfolk cheering them on, and with Kara and her cohorts hidden away and preparing for the battle to come, the center of Riverbend lay quiet. I wandered off, my mind in a haze. At the outskirts of the village, music came wafting on the breeze—not a tune, but a toot here and there. I followed the sound down a side trail off the road.

On a bench at the base of a broad elm, Thomas was crafting a new flute with knife and sandpaper.

When he looked up, I raised a questioning brow.

"For my pupil, Zachariah," he said.

I forced a smile. "I'm happy you've taken him under your wing."

He flashed his usual grin. "You're just glad he's following *me* around instead of *you*." As he took me in, the grin vanished. "You look awful, like you just came out of a teaching."

"My face shows how I feel."

The corners of his eyes drooped, and he crumpled his brow. "It's not Nathaniel, is it? Is he all right?"

"Nathaniel's fine, or at least his wound has healed, and he's itching to rejoin the fight. I don't...." I glanced up to the treetops and bit down hard on my lower lip, afraid to say more.

He brushed the surface of the bench beside him. "Come sit and stay awhile. Share your woes with me."

I settled next to him, massaged my cheeks with my fingertips, and breathed a sigh. "Where to begin? Maybe I should have accepted the vicars' teaching, gone home a loyal child of the light and never left Little Pond again."

"You can't think that way. If you accepted the teaching, we'd never have found the keep."

"What did *that* accomplish? Now I'm a seeker of truth. Hundreds follow me and place their lives in my hands, but truth's an elusive thing. Are we better off today than before?"

"I am." He waved the flute in the air. "You gave me the freedom to make music as I please."

"Music, yes, but what about all the suffering we've caused?" I folded my hands in my lap and stared at them. "What about the sorrow yet to come? I once thought I had all the answers, or at least I pretended I did, but now I have none."

Thomas lifted my chin with one finger and turned my head until I faced him. "They claim I'm a seeker of truth as well, though a minor one compared to you and Nathaniel. Maybe for once I can answer some of *your* questions."

I studied him as he waited for my response, my childhood friend. His boyish features still appeared young despite the trials he'd been through.

I smiled. "My first question? What is the cause of strife?"

He scratched his head and narrowed his eyes. "You couldn't start with an easier one? Something like what's for dinner?"

"You offered."

"Very well, but be warned my answer may be nonsense, the babble of a musician."

I leaned in and focused on his eyes. He and I had been apart much of the past three years. I now perceived a depth in those eyes I'd never seen when playing adventure games in the NOT tree or on our search for the keep.

How much he's changed. "I'm listening," I said.

"You always told me we need to strive, to try to be more than we are, but that goal never appealed to me. I'm one of the contented with limited needs. For those like you and Nathaniel, whom the vicars call dreamers of dreams, striving is needed to live, like food or water or air. That's why you couldn't stay in the keep and had to go off and start your revolution." He leaned closer to me. "That's why you had to cross the sea. I always wondered—what happens when goals collide, when the passion and strong will of those like you clash with the goals of others? Neither side could back down, because to do so would be to give up who you are, leaving no choice but to fight."

"Does that mean people like Nathaniel and I are by our own nature doomed?"

He shrugged. "How would I know? I find my solace in the grain of this wood, and in the sound of the music it makes."

I slumped on the bench and buried my face in my hands. Thomas rubbed my shoulders until I glanced up at him and smiled.

He offered me the flute. "Would you like to learn to play?"

I shook my head and laughed. "You know I have no talent."

"If I can teach Zachariah, I can teach you. Of course, you'll never be as good as me, but you can still take pleasure in it."

He thrust the instrument at me. "Cover the first, third, and fifth holes with your fingers."

I did as he asked.

"No, not like that. It's not a weapon. Hold it more like a caress. The music won't come if you don't show it love."

"I can't do this, Thomas."

I offered him back the flute, but he refused. "Four notes, no more."

I covered the three holes again and blew. To my surprise, it made a pleasing sound.

He shifted my fingers to different holes and told me to try again.

I blew into the mouthpiece, and the note changed.

"Now two more, and we'll put them together into a tune."

I did what he asked. As I played, the tension drained from my shoulders, my burden not relieved but for a time forgotten.

"One last thing. Play the first three notes as before, then take in a breath, blow the fourth, and hold it."

"For how long?"

"For as long as your heart tells you to."

I set the flute down on my lap, licked my lips, and repositioned my fingers on the holes. I played the first note, the second and the third, and then took a deeper breath and blew.

Thomas was right. The sound wafted into the air and lingered, and for those few seconds, the whole world was healed.

***

For the next two days, Kara worked with little sleep. She spent no more time with the black cube, but rather with the other cargo she'd salvaged from the machine masters' city—what she called her box of parts.

To maintain secrecy, she did most of her work indoors, surrounded by a tripling of Caleb's trusted guards.

During that time, Nathaniel and I shared our meals but little else. Words trickled between us in dribs and drabs, as if the thoughts that had flowed since childhood had dried up.

At the end of the second day, as we sat in the common room of the inn silently eating our evening meal, Kara emerged from her labors, her face worn down by something more than exhaustion.

I held my breath as she approached, stopping an arm's length away.

She seemed to have strength left for only two words: "I'm ready."

Chapter 21

A Greater God

Another night, another dream, this time of Nathaniel still as death in the dreamers' cocoon, his mind downloaded to a machine. I needed to wake him or he'd die, but each time I reached for the abort button, it slipped from my finger and floated off into the icy blue mist leaking from inside. I circled the cocoon, chasing the elusive control until first light filtered through our bedchamber curtain and woke me.

***

The next day dawned in silence. Everyone rose and went about their tasks, drilling until Caleb's latest tactic became second nature.

This time, the attack would wait until dusk and use a different formation. The bulk of our troops would spread out wide in a crescent to provide less of a target for the deacons' darkness weapons. Behind them, four clusters of handpicked men—comprised of those whose stubborn bravery would let them hold their position despite casualties—would huddle around carts covered with canvas. Each cluster would be hidden behind a banner, depicting the opposite of the tapestry that hung in the vicars' teaching chamber. In place of the battle of darkness and light, this image showed lightning flashing from storm clouds and striking the vicars down.

The Temple had taught me the power of ritual, theater to control men's minds. Now we'd use the same approach but to conceal our true intent—the dreamers' surprise.

125

At last the hour arrived. More than a thousand souls lined up, their determination so strong the air crackled around them, but each of them understood the risk. They'd lived the day of battle before.

I reviewed the troops one last time and gave Caleb the signal to advance.

As we trudged along the road, fingers twitched around the grips of weapons, and eyes flitted from side to side. Trees lurked like enemies lying in ambush, their gaze zeroing in on the intruders like beasts stalking their prey. The forest bristled with a dark and magical power, making me tremble like a lost little girl. At that moment, an ancient fear welled up within me, and I believed the trees might attack... or swallow me whole.

At one point, I conjured up an old woman at the side of the road, glaring at me from behind knobby eyes. Her gnarled arms stretched out as if to grab me in their clutches and carry me away. I squinted to view her more clearly.

Not a woman. Not a person at all. Just some crone-like tree with knotted trunk and branches twisted by endless gales.

Ten minutes later, we reached the bend in the north river. The ram's horn sounded as expected, and the advance guard fell back as we charged. Ahead, the elite deacons in gold tunics emerged, but twice as many as before.

This time, instead of pressing forward shoulder to shoulder and firing their sticks, they separated, creating spaces between them. From these gaps, others ran out, bearing not weapons but rocks the size of an apple.

Had the Temple reverted to their heritage, a stoning for apostasy, but this time on a massive scale? If so, they'd find a surprise.

Our troops scattered, dodging the rocks, with only a few of those finding their marks, causing little more than bruises, no harm at all, until....

...Until the rocks landed.

The earth shook with ear busting booms. Dust flew everywhere and men screamed. Dozens of our troops fell to the ground, some with arms and legs missing, others with flesh rent beyond repair. No mending for these.

From the memory of my teaching, the arch vicar's voice resounded. "And now, Orah, whose name means light, you will understand the darkness... to the depths of your being."

Amidst the smoke and dust, and the screams of dying men, a different voice arose.

"Now!" Caleb yelled.

The guardians of the carts dropped their banners and removed the canvas, revealing what had once been the topmost turrets of Kara's repair machines, the ones used for cutting and welding. Their tips glowed red and beams spewed forth, as the bearers swiveled them to the left and right.

Golden tunics blackened, and the ranks of the elite collapsed. Bodies dissolved amidst the stench of burning flesh.

Seeing their best so easily vanquished, the remaining deacons fled, leaving weapons and provisions behind. They dashed up the paved road, built with the forced labor of my people, until they vanished around the bend.

A cheer went up among our troops, but not for long, as the fate of their injured comrades sunk in. Litter bearers raced about, gathering those wounded who might still be healed.

Nathaniel, Caleb, and I waited to make certain the healers had evacuated all who could be saved, and then ordered the retrieval of the remains of those less fortunate, to be brought to the Riverbend cemetery and buried with dignity.

I staggered back to the village in a daze, my eyes focused on the road ahead. No, not the road, not even the horizon... but to a darker place I feared to go. I took several breaths to test the air, but all I smelled was the normal fragrance of trees. I cast about, studying the surrounding plants and flowers—nothing unusual. Despite how it seemed, the world remained the same. The forest had changed neither shape nor color nor scent.

Only the people had changed.

I lingered at the spot where I'd imagined the old woman. Now, in the light of an ascendant moon, I realized my mistake. The gnarled tree stared back at me with knots where a mouth, a nose and eyes would be, a face I might draw on paper if I wished to depict the horror of the day—the essence of the darkness.

Nathaniel called me back from the void. "Don't dawdle. The deacons may be defeated, but no sense risking a stray looking to avenge his friends."

I reached out and grasped his hand, needing his strength to flow through me. We quickened our pace and caught up with the stragglers.

Ahead, the north river wound through a flat stretch of land, looking cool and inviting, like it might wash the blood away. At one point we passed a dog standing by the side of the road, staring at the parade of the disillusioned.

At the center of town, I found a repeat of the scene from the prior battle: the grass littered with wounded, Kara and Devorah frantically mending, and their helpers tending to those who waited their turn. But this time, twice as many lay still and pale.

How many more will meet their fate in battles to come?

As I wandered among the survivors, encouraging them and comforting the wounded, darkening clouds cloaked the moon, and a light drizzle began to fall. Raindrops splattered on the torches that lit the field, making them sizzle and smoke. I squinted, and moisture formed on my eyelashes, blurring the torchlight and softening the sickening scene. How easy to pretend the battle had never happened, and that the bodies before me slept.

I gazed past the carnage, struggling to understand how the search for truth had brought us to this, when a new sight caught my eye. Beyond the field filled with litters, the troops had gathered in a half-circle, hundreds of them crowded together and facing forward, with those in the front kneeling.

I drew closer, rose up on tiptoes, and peered over the shoulders of those who stood at the back.

In the center of the circle stood the black cube, surrounded by its usual display of flowers—daisies and daffodils, white lilies and a bouquet of blood red roses—but something new had been added.

I squeezed through two burly men to get a better look, and gasped at what I saw. On the ground before the cube, someone had placed trophies from the battle, a pile of deacons' axes with spikes at the top, a pair of fire sticks, and seven golden tunics charred and drenched with blood.

As I stood there, mouth agape, one of them recognized me, and a murmur spread through the crowd. "Orah, seeker of truth."

The words rippled across the men like a wave and then silenced, but not for long.

All eyes turned to me, and one man with a deep baritone called out. "Hail to the seekers of truth."

The others picked up his rallying cry and repeated it, until someone added a second chant.

Only when the chants converged did I make out the newest words.

"Hail to the light in the cube."

Chapter 22

Children Unborn

Nathaniel and I stood hand-in-hand at the rear of the cemetery, heads bowed and avoiding the attention of the crowd. At the front, too many litters lay covered with white sheets and decorated with day lilies. Behind them, too many holes gaped in the ground, and the air reeked with the odor of freshly turned sod.

The vicar of Bradford spoke for the dead, his every word ringing out despite his subdued tone. As he recited the name, age, and home village of each of the deceased, none of the assembled made a sound. No one so much as shifted from one foot to the other, as if fearing to disturb the sacred soil. Even the breeze paused out of respect.

After the ceremony, Zachariah approached me, dragging the vicar by the hand.

"Come with us," he said. "The vicar wants to show you what we found."

They led Nathaniel and me to a gate in the stone wall at the back of the cemetery, unmarked and plainer than the elaborate wrought iron arch at the front—one we hadn't noticed before. Beyond it, a mossy path snaked deeper into the woods.

A hundred paces in, we came to a second cemetery, with headstones smaller than the first and clustered closer together. A single granite monument loomed above them in the center, with these words engraved upon it.

Riverbend Children's Park

A resting place for the angels
Who dwelled too briefly among us

We strolled past the stones, stooping to read the names and dates on each one. The first, a child of only three, and the next less than a year....

"I checked them all," Zachariah said. "None as old as I was when my parents left for the dream."

The vicar of Bradford waved his hand to encompass them all. "Why must such innocents die so young? Why must so much potential be lost? Each of these may have become a seeker and discovered miracles of their own, if the Temple had not stifled our growth. You've shown me the possibilities in the knowledge you found in the keep, and now in the healing science brought from the distant shore." He sighed and glanced to the heavens before fixing on me. "You asked for my wisdom about right and wrong, whether seeking weapons from the dreamers would cause more harm than good. We've witnessed much suffering this day, and I grieve for those who've been lost, but despite the tragedy, we must continue our struggle. We must never return to stagnation. We must fight for the children unborn."

As he spoke, Zachariah paced from one end of the row to the other. Then he returned to the first and started to sing in that lovely voice I'd discovered in the hall of winds. I recognized the verse he'd composed for his mother, but now he'd changed the words.

Sweet child with eyes that shine
To heaven, take my rhyme
Keep this poem so you will know
All of us love you so

He shuffled from stone to stone as he sang, brushing each with his fingertips while tears streamed down his cheeks.

When he finished, the vicar of Bradford reached out and grasped his hand. "Come, Zachariah, leave the children to rest. We have work to do, to make a better world. We owe it to them and to all the friends we've lost these past days."

The four of us trudged back to town in silence, each absorbed in his thoughts.

At the rectory, before parting ways, the vicar paused and confronted us. "When you first came to Bradford, and I sent you off to find the keep, I envied your adventure. I don't envy you anymore. The light has chosen you to be the leaders of a great but perilous cause. May you lead wisely."

Once in our bedchamber, I closed the door and leaned with my back against it, relieved for the moment of the need to pretend. My chin sagged to my chest as my shoulders slumped under the weight of this hideous burden. I wanted to flee back to Little Pond, to mount the podium once more and relive my coming of age, to make different choices and return to a more innocent time.

Nathaniel and I stared at each other like scared children. He stood with hands at his side, balling them into fists and stretching the fingers out again and again, as if trying to decide whether to fight or yield.

I steered him into the full glow of the candlelight to better read his eyes. They reflected back at me, pained and glistening.

He licked his lips to moisten them, and when he spoke, his voice came from far away, not so much distant in space but in time, the voice of the boy of my youth. "I was wrong, Orah. I'd learned nothing from those foolish days when tales of knights filled my mind. I'm the one who's been dazzled by illusions, not you. I was so poisoned with hate for the vicars, for the harm they'd done, I turned a blind eye to what we've spawned, a horror grown out of control."

I rested a hand on his cheek and watched his mind churn. *My Nathaniel.* "Out of control? Yes, but they still expect us to lead. What should we do now?"

He stepped back and gazed up at the wooden beams of the ceiling, as if hoping to find answers there. His jaw twitched and the vein in his temple throbbed. "The gray friars follow their master's command, to delve deeper into the knowledge of the darkness. You and I have watched the images on the screens, recordings of past atrocities. More than most, we understand how devastating war can be." He closed his eyes and took three measured breaths before reopening them. "They'll attack again, this time with more terrifying force than before. We have no other choice. Our sole salvation lies with you and Kara, and the white bonnets you wear."

***

I joined Kara in her bedchamber at the inn, the one where years before I lay awake deciphering the keepers' rhyme. I checked the hallway to make sure we were alone, and then closed and locked the door.

I lowered my voice so no one outside could hear. "I dread where this request might lead, but we have to ask."

Kara pressed her lips into a thin and bloodless line, and shook her head. "Unlike your friends in the keep, the dreamers are living minds. Who knows how much more they'll help? Without their assistance, my skills have limits."

"The gray friars work day and night to make more powerful weapons. We need to do the same."

"What if the dreamers won't—?" She turned her back on me and stared at the wall, unwilling to meet my eyes.

I grasped her by both arms and spun her around. "Then our enemy will win, and all those we lead will be imprisoned or die."

She twisted the white bonnet in her hands as if wringing out moisture from a dishrag. "I'll speak with them, but I make no promises."

I showed my own bonnet. "This time, I go with you."

"No!" Her voice rose, forcing me to step to the closed door and listen for footsteps outside.

Not a sound.

I turned back to Kara, and my eyes narrowed. A tremor in her fingertips made me view her in a new light. She'd always been honest with me before.

Is she being honest now?

My back stiffened, and the air around me went thin, so my words emerged muffled. "If I can't go with you, I'll speak to them alone. With so much at stake, I need to assess their response for myself."

The blood drained from her face, but she still averted my gaze.

When she had no more to say, I swept past her and out the door. I marched to the chamber that housed the black cube when not in the sun gathering strength from its rays, and ordered the guards to let no one in, not even Nathaniel or Kara.

Once alone with the dreamers, I adjusted the white bonnet until the sensors rested firmly against my scalp. Then I stepped to the cube and placed my palms on its surface. At once, my fingertips tingled, and the buzz of a hundred thoughts surged in my mind, but this time, I kept my eyes open, needing to maintain a part of me with the living.

"Orah," the speaker said. "We've met with Kara five times since we spoke with you last. Are you well?"

"I'm well, but the latest battle with the deacons went badly. The gray friars supplied them with new and unexpected weapons, and a number of our companions died. We would have all been destroyed without the weapons you provided Kara."

132

Their thoughts surged, and I waited as always for them to subside. Seconds passed but this time rather than diminishing, the buzzing increased, rising to an unprecedented level so I was tempted to cover my ears, though none of it made a sound in the physical world. My mind cried "stop," the dreamers' equivalent of a shout.

The buzzing quieted, and I cast out a new question. "Why the uproar?"

The answer rang out from the speaker, distinct and surrounded by silence. "We provided no such weapons."

I recalled Kara's face when I left her, lips parted, eyes wide, and one trembling hand reaching out to stop me. "But she told me you...."

"Ah. A lie. A story made up to deny a fact. She must have used her own knowledge, because we refused to help."

No further explanation came my way, and I was afraid to ask. I thought of the founder of the keep years before denying my request:

We decided the abuse of knowledge brought the world to its current state. It seemed foolhardy to encourage you down a similar path. We determined to eliminate weapons from the keep. Of course, the foundation is here for you to re-invent them if you insist, but we refuse to help.

I held my breath — that precious commodity the dreamers lacked — and waited until I wondered if the bonnet had ceased to function. Then I cast my question through the sensors, almost hoping for no response. "Why did you refuse?"

The answers flowed in a stream.

"Our ancestors had enough knowledge...."

"To nearly destroy our world...."

"Now our science is much more advanced...."

"We could invent more powerful weapons if we chose...."

"An interesting engineering problem...."

"But why would we?"

A question I'd asked myself, until I pictured the field of litters covered with sheets. "You may not have hearts, but you are creatures of logic. Compute this. Without your help, Kara and I and all the others will die."

The speaker's thoughts remained measured, as if explaining a complex lesson to a child. "Though we have no hearts, we understand mathematical models. As each side does more harm to the other, the violence grows. Those close to the victims seek revenge, and the number of casualties increases. Even allowing for a generous percentage of reasonable people—those willing to forego revenge—the violence climbs asymptotically over time, approaching a singularity—a rate of acceleration that approximates infinity and becomes irreversible."

My head ached as if the bonnet had taken on too much weight. "I don't understand."

Other voices chimed in.

"Use her background and education...."

"Explain it in her terms...."

I waited.

At last, the speaker's words burst through the sensors to my brain.

"What you ask may lead to a cataclysm more destructive than what you call the darkness—the end of all things."

***

I removed the bonnet, and the buzzing in my mind ceased. Nothing new to learn. My feet stayed rooted to the floor as I gazed transfixed at the lightning flashing in the cube. I rocked back and forth and hugged myself as if the cataclysm had already occurred, and I were the last person alive.

I slowed my breathing and closed my eyes, trying to return to my center, the part of me that housed my deepest beliefs, but all was covered in fog. I peered through the haze, hoping to peel back its layers and discover a glimmer in the dark.

I found only despair.

The gray friars would extract the information they needed from the indifferent helpers and build new weapons to meet their master's demands.

Without the dreamers, Kara offered nothing more than tricks and a smattering of machine parts.

The deacons would come. We'd all be destroyed.

From the depths of that despair, a wellspring of courage arose within me, a trait suppressed since arriving back on my home shore. My mother and father had given me a name that means light, and my whole life, I'd rejected the darkness in all its forms. Now, in a flash of insight, the glimmer I sought appeared, like looking out the window of our bedchamber after a storm to discover the rain-soaked branches of the willow gleaming like a thousand blades in the moonlight.

Time to confront Kara.

I knocked on the door so as not to surprise her, and waited until a melancholy voice bid me enter.

She sat on the bed, staring at her hands folded in her lap. She looked up at me, eyes pleading. "The mending... it's like seeing into the hearts of tormented souls. So much pain. I had to find a way to help." Her reddened eyes drooped at the corners. "I'm sorry I lied to you."

I settled next to her, and we embraced. "I understand what you did. You saved many lives."

"But what do we do now?"

I grasped her by the arms and forced her to face me. "By now, the usurper has learned of our latest weapon. We know the limits of the keep, but he can only imagine the power of the dreamers—other than that they're a thousand years more advanced than the keepmasters. Despite the efforts of his gray friars, he must dread what we'll do next."

She pulled away, her shoulders slumping and the pall of defeat clouding her features. "You don't understand. The dreamers won't help, and without them, I'm little more than a child playing tricks, using nothing but what I learned in my lessons and a box of miscellaneous parts."

I drew in a long breath and let it out slowly. "Only you and I know the dreamers' response, and no one else has access to them. We can use that to our advantage."

One brow raised, and she wrinkled her nose, causing a crease to form between her eyes. "I don't know what you mean."

"I mean... you already told one lie. Now... together... we'll tell another."

Chapter 23

To Dream No More

I asked Nathaniel to join me on a stroll to the grist mill, needing private time to explain my plan. We meandered along the winding path, holding hands and swishing our feet through the dried leaves, as we used to on our way to the NOT tree. Once there, we settled on the stone bench by the stream. The sunlight off the water captured my eye, and for a moment I felt no longer in Riverbend but back home in Little Pond, as if finding the keep had been imagined, just another of our adventure games.

Memories of childhood flooded my mind. "Do you remember the first time we visited the mill? I thought the wheel a wondrous device, but saw only the sparkles. As I grew older, I discovered the shadowy place where no sun reached, and imagined demons lurking there. Now I find those fears may be true... in a way."

"How so?"

"This mill wheel is like the earth mother's wheel of life, always cycling between light and dark. What if all we've accomplished has been to climb to the sunlit crest, and now we're about to descend back into the darkness?"

He crumpled his brow and eyed me across his nose. "What are you trying to say?"

I turned to him. "The dreamers refuse to help. No one but Kara and I know, and now you as well."

He drifted to the wheel like someone newly awoken from a deep sleep, and stretched out an open palm, letting the icy water splash off his hand. When he spoke, his words chilled like the water. "So much for changing the world. Maybe the founders of the Temple were right. What if we were meant to live simple lives, to take nature in stride and spend our existence content like sheep in the fields? If we'd accepted that life, those who died for our cause would be alive today, those who followed us would be safe in their homes, and our journey wouldn't be hurtling toward a horrible end."

My heart ached to hear such words from Nathaniel, and I rushed to embrace him, holding on as if to keep the hope from leaking away.

After we separated, I kept my gaze fixed on his, nodding ever so slightly to draw him back from the brink. "What about those who died because the Temple stifled our progress? What about my father and your mother? What about the children in the cemetery? If they lived on the far side of the sea, some might have been saved."

In my rush of words, I'd taken in no air, and now I paused to breathe.

Nathaniel waited, knowing I had more to say, my friend since birth. "You're planning something, Orah. I can tell."

"As you once told me, the ending hasn't been written yet. Everyone else, including our enemy, expects us to return to battle with new and more powerful weapons."

His shoulders heaved up and down, and he shook his head. "But there'll be no such weapons."

"Yes, but truth is sometimes elusive. Temple magic had nothing to do with the voice in the sun icon, yet still we believed."

"You mean...."

"We bluff. The vicars witnessed a hint of the power we brought from across the sea. We use their fear of the dreamers to threaten them with extinction. We force them to sue for peace."

***

The next morning, I summoned the prior, the man who had escaped the torment of the deacons to seek refuge with us, and who had been healed by the mending machine.

We waited at a round table, Nathaniel, Caleb, Kara, and me, with guards blocking the door to ensure secrecy.

When he arrived, I offered him a seat and a mug of hot tea, and gave him time to settle before beginning. "What I'm about to request of you is more than I have a right to ask, and if you decline, I'll understand."

He wrapped his hands around the mug and stared at the steam rising from his drink. After a moment, he took a sip and fixed on me. "I'm in your debt, and will do anything in my meager power to help."

"Are you willing to return to your former masters, those who abused you so?"

He grasped the edge of the table and pressed down until his body unfolded to upright. A tremor racked his frame, but he steadied, lifting his chin like an elder about to address a Little Pond meeting. "Each night, I dream of my time with my captors, and each morning I awake in a cold sweat. Now, as my days dwindle, I live in terror of returning to their grasp. Yet you not only healed my body. In the depths of my despair, you gave me hope for a better world. I'll do anything you ask if it serves your purpose, though it costs me my life."

"I need you to deliver a message from the seekers of truth."

Caleb stood and wrapped an arm around the prior's shoulders. "Why him? Despite the mending machine, he still bears his captors' scars. What might they do to him if he returns? Better I send one of their own instead, a deacon we've taken prisoner."

I wavered, for an instant wondering what kind of monster I'd become, cursed by the burden of leadership. Then that same burden made my back stiffen. "No. We need him, a learned man. He knows the secrets of the keep, and now he's experienced the miracles of the dreamers. He's walking proof of their power, the perfect man for this task, the one they're most likely to believe."

From my tunic pocket, I pulled out the text Nathaniel and I had composed the night before, and smoothed the paper on the table.

The room lay still while I recited the words, with not so much as a creaking of the floorboards or a body fidgeting in a chair.

To the leaders of the Temple of Light
From the Seekers of Truth

We find ourselves at a crossroads. You chose to fight the people using knowledge from a place you once condemned as of the darkness. From this leader of the gray friars, we know that they work day and night to recreate forbidden weapons that once nearly destroyed our world.

Now we, the seekers of truth, have traveled across the ocean and brought back science beyond your conception, a thousand years advanced from the keep. What you witnessed at our most recent victory is but a hint of what's to come.

We grew up with your sermons and have no desire to send our people tumbling headlong down the slope to the darkness. Yet if you escalate this war, we will have no choice but to ask those far wiser than the keepmasters for more powerful weapons that will destroy you all.

At this crossroads, we ask you to pause and consider your fate. We're willing to meet at a site of your choosing, to talk peace and give you one last chance to choose the light.

The prior nudged the much larger Caleb's arm aside and nodded to me. "I'll do as you wish."

I sealed the missive and handed it to him.

And then we waited.

***

That summer when we first found the keep, the days flew by as I raced from one helper to the next, searching for solutions while our dreaded decision loomed.

Now, while awaiting the usurper's response, the hours and minutes crawled. Morning came early as I struggled to sleep, and a sluggish sun plodded its way across the sky.

Late on the second day, as most of the troops retreated to their lodgings to prepare for the evening meal, a murmur spread through the camp, which soon turned into sharp outcries and the thud of running feet. The prior had returned, and with him an envoy from the Temple.

The envoy recognized me and made a small bow, no more than a dip of the head. "I come in response to your message, bearing an answer from the Grand Vicar, the human embodiment of the light in this world. His holiness has agreed to a meeting."

Caleb and Nathaniel came running up behind me, and together we took in the man. From the red stripes on his not-quite-square hat, I deemed him an arch vicar, though his dress was embellished beyond the traditions of the clergy. He now wore a sash across his chest, bedecked with gold medallions, and a cape of white silk clung to his back.

Nathaniel squared his shoulders to the man and rose to his full height. "The purpose of the meeting?"

The envoy took a deep breath and steadied himself, rising in stature as if trying to match Nathaniel. "To discuss a path to peace."

"And the place?" Caleb said.

"The clearing by the river where the road begins to climb, at the northern edge of what had been our encampment."

Caleb scowled at him. "Too close to your forces, too far from ours."

"The place has been sanctified by the blood of those who died. His holiness believes it a fitting location, a place that will remind us how devastating a return to the darkness would be. I give you the grand vicar's oath, sworn on the light, that he'll guarantee your safety."

Caleb twisted his mouth into a sneer, but before he could argue, I waved him to silence. I'd grown up believing in the sanctity of oaths on the light, and preferred any chance for peace.

"One final term," the envoy said. "Each side may bring only three, and all should come empty-handed. We can meet tomorrow at noon, if you accept these terms."

I agreed at once.

He lingered not a moment longer, spinning around so fast his cape unfurled in the breeze as he swept out of town.

***

We began the trek to the meeting before the sun reached its peak in the sky. I chose Caleb to accompany Nathaniel and me. Beyond his role as leader of the troops, his imposing figure and exotic accent would emphasize to the vicars that they dealt with people other than the children of the light.

After three years of frequent use, the Temple had cleared the scrub behind the rock face and added a paved roadway wide enough for their fast wagons. What had once required two hours of battling through thick brush now became easy to navigate. In no more than twenty minutes, we reached the spot by the river, where we'd once sent the arch vicar's tracking device floating downstream.

Thank the light, we'd arrived first. I took the time to quench my thirst and organize my thoughts, but soon the roar of a fast wagon overwhelmed the rush of the water.

The vehicle skidded to a stop, and the envoy emerged with a burly deacon in tow, both empty-handed as promised.

Despite the small audience, he used a booming voice to announce his superior. "His holiness, the grand vicar of the Temple of Light." His words began as an echo off the mountain ridge but quickly dissipated into a murmur, as if nature cared nothing for the usurper's title.

From the back seat of the wagon, the upstart emerged. He appeared older now, with a hint of gray streaking his long beard, but the black button eyes burned the same, eyes that had terrified me when he called my name for a teaching, in a time and place so long ago.

"So, Orah, whose name means light, we meet again."

Like his envoy, he was no longer content with traditional dress and more red stripes on his hat. Instead, he bore an even more outlandish cape, with threads of silver woven throughout, making the cloth shimmer in the sunlight, and in place of the not-quite-square hat, he wore a crown of gold.

The deacon unloaded two armchairs from a compartment in the rear and set them facing the water. With no furniture to support us, we settled on rocks by the river bank. As I craned my neck to see the usurper, I recalled the high bench of the vicars in the teaching chamber — another way to look down on us.

I opened my mouth to speak, but the envoy waved me to silence.

Children mustn't speak before their elders.

He cleared his throat and used the temple voice taught in the seminary. "His holiness, the grand vicar, the human embodiment of the light in this world, has invited you here to listen to his proposal. Holiness, please explain."

Invited us here.

I placed a restraining hand on Caleb's arm to keep him seated.

The usurper focused his black button eyes on me. "As forewarned in the book of light, you have been seduced by inventions from the darkness, and look where they've brought us. You stumble along on a slippery path, but you may still repent before it's too late. Will you renounce your sins and swear fealty to the Temple?"

I could no longer contain Caleb, nor did I care to.

He stood from the lowly position, seeming to rise forever until he towered over the usurper. "Do you know me? I think not, for I'm not one of your children, nor do I adhere to your superstitions. My ancestors fled your foolishness a thousand years ago, and while you stagnated, we progressed. Thanks to the seekers of truth, we now return, bearing power beyond your imaginings. *We* demanded this meeting, not *you*, as a last, merciful chance before we destroy you."

The usurper's eyes flitted to the burly deacon who cringed behind him, and he licked his dry lips before responding. "You can't deny we brought peace to our side of the world. That is, until you arrived. Yes, perhaps we overstepped, but our intent remained pure. What crime in being too zealous in preventing a return to the cataclysm that nearly destroyed our world? I come here with honorable intent, prepared to discuss reforms that may allow us to pull back from the precipice and create a better life for all."

The crackle that charged the air between us eased, and I signaled for Caleb to sit.

I answered in his stead. "If the reforms are sufficient, and if you're ready to meet the people as equals, we may find common ground and avoid your destruction. What are your terms?"

His eyes narrowed and widened as I spoke. When I finished, I caught a glance to his right and the hint of a sigh. He motioned for his envoy to respond.

The envoy rose but kept four paces from Caleb. "First, you acknowledge the authority of the Temple to mediate in matters of the soul. You recognize the grand vicar as the human embodiment of the light on this earth, and you continue to tithe, a way to support the good works of the clergy. Anything less than this, and you give us no reason to concede. We will fight you with all available means."

He paused as we glared, waiting for more. When no more came, Nathaniel spoke. "You offer only terms that benefit you, yet we possess the power. What do you offer us in return?"

The envoy checked with his superior who nodded approval. "His holiness is prepared to accept the following: no more teachings or other harsh methods. The Temple will assume your good will. All disagreements will be settled by a new leadership council, comprised of seven members, four representatives from the Temple and three from the children of light."

Caleb slid to the edge of his rock, but remained seated. "You misunderstand our relative positions. From the part of the world where I come from, you are primitives. Even your keepmasters are backward compared to us. We can destroy you at will and have no need to negotiate terms. Don't waste our time. We offer you this one final chance as an act of mercy."

The grand vicar looked to his envoy, a hint of fear flickering in his black button eyes. The envoy glanced back with a shrug.

They are entering new ground, concessions they hadn't rehearsed. No more theater for believers.

"Despite your threats, we shall choose the light over your darkness.

In the name of peace, his holiness will grant you an even number of representatives, provided you agree to the other terms."

I'd stayed seated, waiting. Now I rose, so much shorter than Nathaniel or Caleb, but I loomed over the usurper. *I've come a long way from my teaching.*

"No. The seekers of truth demand more. Five representative to your four, or when next we return, we'll teach you the meaning of the darkness...." I rocked forward on the balls of my feet, coming close enough so that he could feel the heat of my breath. "We'll teach you to the depths of your being."

I caught a shudder, hidden beneath the folds of the usurper's cape.

He signaled to his envoy, a barely perceptible dip of his head.

"Very well," the envoy said. "His holiness agrees, as long as you accept our final term, without which we'll fight if need be until the end. We shall preserve the essentials: medicines, communication devices and means of travel, anything to benefit the people. We shall no longer limit what may be read or taught. We'll make the printing of books available to all, so your precious freedom of thought can flow. Over time, the people will rediscover the past, but at a more reasonable pace, giving time for their souls to mature. Perhaps, in a few centuries, you'll be wise enough to use this knowledge for good."

My mouth opened and closed. I began to speak and stopped.

What is he saying?

"But we already possess such knowledge," I said.

"Not if you agree to this last demand."

"I don't understand."

"To end the violence and return to peace, these apostates from across the forbidden sea must go back to the distant shore—" He glared at Caleb, as if daring him to interrupt. "—and the keep along with your so-called dreamers must be destroyed."

***

The usurper and his henchman entered their fast wagon, and in a hollow display of power, roared their machine and raced off. He'd given us two days to consider his offer, as once his former master had given Nathaniel time to choose between my teaching or committing his life to the Temple.

We waited until the dust had settled and the stench cleared, and plodded our way back to Riverbend, staying somber and silent until we passed out of sight of the clearing.

By the rock face, Caleb turned to me with a gleam in his eye. "What a fool. He offers a bargain you should rush to accept. They don't understand the dreamers. They don't realize they still dream on our side of the sea. They'll destroy the source of their power, while we lose nothing. The war will end, and all the knowledge of mankind, far more than what lays in the keep, will stay safe and secure in the mountain fortress. You gain peace and freedom for your people at little cost, and none besides the three of us and Kara will know the truth. As for me, I'll be glad to be done with your world and go home."

I gazed at the rock face full of wisdom for the ages, and it glared back at me unblinking, with accusing eyes. Unable to bear its stare, I glanced away, past it to the bend in the North River that gave the town its name, and beyond to where the troops awaited, dependent on my good judgment. I owed them peace. We'd won the battle and made life better for all.

Caleb was right; few would know the truth.

But I will know, and the truth I know is that I gave away our future and agreed to a lie.

Chapter 24

The Essence of the Darkness

I went first to tell Kara about the meeting, since she and her dreamers would be the most affected. I found her in her bedchamber at the inn, as usual tinkering with her box of parts.

She eyed me, trying to read my mood. When I stayed silent, she licked her lips and let out a nervous laugh. "Well, what's the verdict? Do we pack up and run for our lives, or fight and die?"

"No need to do either," I said.

"Then the meeting went well?"

"Well enough. As I hoped, the usurper fears our power and made concessions for peace. Under duress, he agreed to shift control from the vicars to the people, as long as he maintains his position and the special status of the Temple... with a few additional conditions." I fixed on Kara. "Some will affect you."

"Such as?"

"If we agree to the new order, they'll destroy the keep... and they expect us to destroy the dreamers." When the corners of her eyes drooped, I added, "only on this side of the ocean. They know nothing, of course, about the mountain fortress or the minds that still reside there. And one final demand, that you and all those who sailed here with us be banished from our land."

She removed the white bonnet, ruffled her hair where the sensors had matted it down, and settled on the bed, staring at her slender fingers intertwined on her lap, like viewing some curiously crafted object.

I gave her time to let the news settle in. "Are you all right?"

She glanced up. "For a moment, I imagined losing my parents for a second time, but they taught me to think logically. The dreamers—including my parents—are nothing more than bits of lightning in a cube, one which itself is a replica of those minds still dwelling in the mountain. If we destroy it, the only memories lost would be those gained from our interactions since we built it. Once I return to the machine masters' world and reenter the dream, they'll reclaim most of those.

"The tradeoff you propose makes sense. Your people achieve the freedom you sought and a much needed peace. They'll take a step back, but over time, the restrictions will ease. We'll build more boats, trade with you and share our knowledge." Her lips curled upward into a weak smile, but her eyes glistened. "The worst part is that, at least for now, the barriers that had separated our worlds will return. You'll stay with your people, and I with mine. We'll remain apart until the Temple changes, perhaps... for the rest of our lives."

I settled beside her, and we clutched in a long embrace.

***

Caleb, Nathaniel, and I briefed the leaders, and they spread the news among our troops: peace was at hand, if only we'd agree.

I spent the remainder of the day answering a thousand questions.

Yes, we'd control our own fate.

No, we'd still need to tithe.

Yes, the usurper would maintain his position, but in a more benign role.

No, teachings or other harsh punishments would be banned.

Yes, the Temple would allow us to print our own books, and read and think what we choose.

And most disturbing, in exchange for peace, our friends from across the sea would have to go home, and we'd sacrifice the keep and the dreamers.

That night, a wild wind whistled through the streets of Riverbend. I lay in bed, listening to it howl, straining to catch a hint of what it might portend. I imagined the four horsemen from the hall of winds—desolation, despair, destruction, and death—fleeing from the town, driven out by the power of reason.

146

How could such reason agree to exile our new friends and destroy the genius of the past?

At last, exhaustion overcame my concerns, and I drifted off into a dream so vivid I struggled to distinguish fantasy from reality.

***

I again climbed the mountain alone at night to the fortress of the dreamers. This time, the lava had not yet cooled, but instead glowed bright red, lighting up the field of flowers and bringing a flush to my cheeks. A heavy stillness lay over the glade, and as I watched, the flowers caught fire and burned to ash.

As I trudged up the final approach, I spotted another change.

The gateway to the dreamers loomed no longer black, but gold like the doors of the keep, and the stairs up to them now counted fourteen and three, with a landing in between. Five cloaked figures waited there in a half-circle surrounding the plaque embedded in the granite.

I drew in a lungful of air and began to climb. As I neared the top, the inscription flew up from the stone and blazed in the air as if ignited by the embers of the lava, making them easy to read.

The five figures whispered these words together, like the breath of the dead: "The greatest truth must be... that in every child is the potential for greatness."

The first of the figures emerged to the edge of the landing, a young woman whose face seemed familiar, but one I struggled to recall.

"Don't wrinkle your brow so," she said. "We've never met. I'm Nathaniel's mother."

"Why are you here?"

"Because if you make the wrong choice, we both will pay, you with your husband and me with my son."

"But which is the right choice?"

Rather than answer, she stepped aside and a second figure replaced her: Nathaniel. The wound he'd suffered in the first battle gaped wide, oozing blood with each beat of his heart.

"What should we do?" he said. "A question for heroes. For what we believe in, and for the love we share, make the right choice."

"What's that choice?" I said, desperate for the answer.

"It's not for me to say, but here's a pair who might help." He cleared the way for the others.

The next two approached, cowled figures hidden in fog.

I squinted, trying to make out their faces as they stretched out aged hands, beckoning for me to come near.

When I reached the landing, the first lowered his cowl. Before me stood the mentor.

"Study your lessons," he said. "The answer lies in the pursuit of knowledge."

The second shuffled forward and joined hands with the first. Her smile shone through the fog — the earth mother. "Choose wisely, my child. Choose the light and the earth."

The final figure floated toward me on a cloud, and emerged as the spirit of my father. He gazed down at me and repeated his deathbed wish: "Think your own thoughts, big thoughts based on grand ideas...."

"But at what cost," I cried.

***

The fog swirled and....

Now I walked through the field after a battle. Around me, the wounded moaned, and my nostrils burned with the stench of bodies beginning to decay, but my heart soared. Despite the suffering, our cause had been just, and victory was at hand.

At the edge of the battlefield, a hunched figure lurked in the bushes, watching me.

I crept closer, expecting it to vanish or run away. So familiar, like the old woman I'd conjured up, stalking me on the way to the battle, the one I'd called the essence of the darkness.

An explosion from one of the deacons' rocks flashed a hundred paces away, highlighting the figure's features — a woman, for sure, with high cheekbones and flaming auburn hair. Worry lines etched across her forehead and spiraled out from the corners of her eyes, making her appear tired and older than the world.

The earth mother? Too vague to tell.

"Who are you?" My words emerged more breath than sound.

Without answering, the figure came closer and locked eyes with mine, and at once, I recognized her.

The woman was my future; the essence of the darkness was me.

***

I awoke to a pillow damp with tears, but tears for what? For those dead warriors yet to come, or for the death of truth and dreams? For surely, one or the other must die.

I tempered my breathing and switched off my mind, allowing thoughts to flow as the mentor had taught me. The borders of my consciousness fluttered around like butterflies, but beyond these borders lay a dark abyss.

What if at the boundary of our understanding, the light of reason reaches no more, and so we cast a light of our own making onto the darkness and pretend it's reason? What if that which we see is nothing more than the glimmer of our own hopes, and the shadow of our deepest fears?

I slipped out of bed, padded to the window, and gazed up at the night sky. I thought of time that can never be regained, of rivers and tides, of mountain peaks and lush forests, of rain and lightning and rocks and shadows.

All of these are within me.

No matter what, the war must end, though I betrayed both keepmasters and dreamers, and even if I foreswore the future.

A tumult outside interrupted my reverie. The depth of night still reigned, but voices cried out below, and torches lit in the village square made patches of gold flicker on the wall behind me.

I peered through the curtain to find the source, my mind struggling to comprehend what I saw, but the shadows thrown by the burning torches only increased my confusion.

There, before the inn, a gang had gathered of those who had once been friends and neighbors, and farmers and craftsmen from distant towns. These men turned warriors had dragged the black cube out onto the lawn, embellished it with flowers and totems of war, and were dancing around it.

A chant burned in my ears, and at once I knew.

The darkness in our souls will never let us emerge into the light.

Their shouts rang throughout Riverbend. "Defend the dreamers. Save the keep."

Then their incantations converged into a single, blood-curdling word, proclaimed again and again until it overwhelmed all others.

Revenge! Revenge! Revenge!

PART THREE

VICTORY AND DEFEAT

"So now is the time for your loving, dear
And the time for your company
Now when the light of reason fails
And fires burn on the sea
Now in this age of confusion
I have need for your company"

- Richard Farina

Chapter 25

Revelation

The usurper had granted us two days to consider his offer. If we agreed, the vicars would destroy the keep and we the dreamers. Those who'd accompanied us across the sea would go home, and the children of light would return to a peaceful life under a more benign temple.

If only it were that simple.

After the carnage, I was eager for peace at almost any price. I'd wearied of seeking the truth, doubting if such a thing existed, and had become content to leave the world a little better than I found it.

Much of what we once aspired to would be lost, but some would be gained. Once again, we would grow as a people, although without the wisdom of the past, that growth would take generations. I envisioned how the future would unfold. After a proper respite to let our people adjust—and after this generation of vicars had passed to the light—Kara's descendants would reach out once more and reveal our secret. Over time, using the knowledge saved in the dreamers' mountain fortress, they'd ease our way.

But my people had tasted the blood of their enemy and had come to view the dreamers not merely as allies, but as all-powerful, avenging gods. Nothing short of total victory would satisfy them.

Nathaniel and I stayed awake far into the night, grasping at fragments of hope, groping in the dark as we searched for ways to convince these new zealots to accept an improbable peace—to no avail.

The next morning, after breakfast, I roamed the village, accosting anyone who passed by and preaching the benefits of the proposed truce.

Most listened politely and nodded before extolling the might of the black cube. Why concede so much as a finger's breadth when we commanded such power?

As I trudged about, searching for answers, I noted the curtain to Kara's bedchamber closed.

Still sleeping at mid-morning? Unlikely. Fearing some mischief, I went to check on her.

Caleb had posted guards around the inn, to provide privacy to the leaders, but also to protect us from temple assassins or spies.

Now, as I headed there, a guard at the entrance snapped to attention and blocked my way. "Kara ordered me to allow no one upstairs."

"You know who I am?" I said.

He nodded. "A seeker of truth."

"Then you know she keeps no secrets from me."

While the hapless guard wavered, I brushed past him and went upstairs, recalling her previous lie.

What is she up to?

As I slipped down the hallway to her room, a muffled roar came from inside, loud enough to make the walls shake.

I took a deep breath and knocked. "Are you all right?"

The noise stopped at once, and an instant later, Kara opened the door. Her white bonnet highlighted a scarlet flush on her face, and pieces of parts lay scattered about the floor.

She looked at me sheepishly and waved at the machines. "I was experimenting in case the truce fell apart."

"But you said you couldn't make new weapons without help from the dreamers."

"I can't make weapons, but I can still perform tricks. If your bluff failed, I figured I'd conjure up a bluff of my own."

She squeezed her eyes shut and concentrated. Seconds later the air before me shimmered and a creature appeared, all green with sharp, webbed talons. Overlapping scales armored its chest, and its leathery wings whipped up a storm, though strangely I felt no breeze. Its jaws opened, exposing knife-like fangs, and it let out a roar.

I tried to hold my ground, hardly believing my eyes, but I fell back a step nevertheless.

"Now watch closely," Kara said.

The creature circled my head three times, then hovered in front and breathed out a fireball of flame. I threw up my hands to protect my face. A single thought flashed through my mind—*Goodbye Nathaniel, I'm burned to ash*—though I sensed neither heat nor pain. When the roaring ceased, I checked my arms—no blackening of the skin, not so much as a charring of my tunic.

Kara opened her eyes, and the creature winked out like the lights protecting the machine masters' city.

"Did my creature frighten you?" she said.

I collected myself and gazed at the machines on the floor, recalling my lessons with the mentor, and how we'd practiced with images floating in the air.

"Holos," I mumbled, the only word I could get out.

"Yes, but the deacons won't know that. Of course, I need to figure out a few details—how to simulate a wind to make the flapping of wings more real, and how to create a draft hot enough to convince our enemies to flee from the fireball. Do you think my bluff could work?"

I placed a hand over my chest and slowed my heartbeat. "I pray we won't need to find out. Where did you get the idea for such a hideous creature?"

"When I was little, my parents told me fantastic tales of mythical creatures, just as Nathaniel's father told him about knights. They called this one a dragon."

"You might have warned me first. Your holo could have stopped my heart. Light knows it's had enough strain these past days."

Kara laughed. "I'm sorry. I wanted to test if my ruse would work."

"How did you take a holo from your imagination and make it seem so real?"

She waved a hand at the machines in the corners of the room. "I grabbed these from the synthesizers, not the parts that make food—those were too delicate to survive the voyage across the sea—but the ones that project holos. I've been learning from the dreamers how to make them work.

"The projectors are driven by a complex set of numbers. All they need is the algorithms stored in the archive. Once I have the mathematics to describe an image, with its accompanying sounds and smells, the holo machines can recreate it. Since I joined with the dreamers in their fortress, they have access to all my memories, as well as those of my parents. I started simple—a picture of a little Kara spinning around while my father beamed, and then I moved on to more complex images. The dreamers gave me all the information I needed. From there, programming the dragon into the projector was simple."

I circled the room, gaping at machines as magical to me as the sun icon had once been.

Nothing they do is simple. As I brushed the various devices with my fingertips, a new thought came to me: *How might I use this trick?*

"What else can you project?"

She half shrugged. "Anything they hold in their archives."

"Even from *my* past?"

She nodded. "When you entered the dream, you gave them permission to share your deepest memories. Anything you've ever experienced, anyone you've ever known, has been stored and can be turned into a holo."

Anyone I've ever known.

I recalled the figures I'd dreamed of on the steps of the fortress. Perhaps they could help me now. A special one flashed through my mind, blurred and indistinct, a face I struggled to recall at will.

My heart raced, and I swallowed to moisten my throat. "Can you make a holo for me?"

"Of course, but for what purpose?"

"Sometimes our desires have no purpose and make no sense at all, but in this time of trial, there's someone from my past I'd dearly love to meet once more."

Kara drew in a fleeting breath and shook her head. "The dreamers can give me the algorithms to display anyone, to make them appear and move about in their normal manner—at least as you remember them. I can even replay their voice as it once sounded to you, but the holo you'll see won't be intelligent like the dreamers, not even responsive like the helpers in the keep. It will be nothing more than a three-dimensional moving picture from the archive."

Events swirled before me, all that had transpired since returning from the distant shore. I'd tried to use my brain to solve the unsolvable. What harm in turning to my heart?

I approached Kara and grasped her by the arms. "Can you conjure up for me... an image of my father?"

***

Kara spent a half hour with the dreamers, accumulating the mathematics to make my father appear.

To ease her task, she'd requested a specific memory. "Pick an encounter and describe it in a few words, so they can use those terms in their search."

My recollections of my father were few and vague, foggy images of a seven-year-old or younger. The strongest centered around his death, memories I had no wish to revive.

All but one.

Now I stood with Kara in her bedchamber, surrounded by machines I'd never understand. My breath came in short bursts, and my palms became clammy with sweat.

"Won't I need my bonnet?" I said.

"You won't be joining with the dreamers. You won't be interacting with the holo at all. You'll only be watching and listening."

I circled the outer wall of the room, pausing at each corner to stare at the projectors.

Kara came near and brushed my arm with her fingertips. "Would you prefer I leave you alone?"

"Can you do that?"

"I've programmed the devices and set a timer for when the images will start to play. All that's left is to issue the command. Are you ready?"

I nodded.

She closed her eyes and concentrated. The room filled with light as she turned to leave. "I'll wait outside. Call me when you're finished."

As the door latch settled into place, the shimmering glow took shape, and there, floating in the middle of the room, a holo of my father appeared.

He sat at the edge of what would become his deathbed, barely able to hold his head up, but with arms outstretched, embracing nothing but air. He had a face more handsome than I recalled, but I recognized at once the turn of his cheek and the sadness in his eyes, forever marked by his teaching.

After a moment, he patted the space where the seven-year-old Orah's head would have been, and repeated the words I remembered so well.

"Now, little Orah, don't cry. You have a wonderful life ahead of you. Study hard in school and don't let the vicars set your mind. Think your own thoughts, big thoughts based on grand ideas, and find someone to love."

My lower lip trembled, and I reached out a hand, but my feet stayed welded to the floor. How I wished to step closer, to slip into that spot and be embraced by those arms, though I knew they lacked the warmth of his touch. How I longed to ask him what I should do.

"No," I cried aloud.

This apparition was neither helper in the keep nor dreamer in the cube. Before me shimmered nothing more than my own recollection projected by machines from an algorithm, a specter from my childhood. I was no longer that little girl. I was a leader, and my people depended on me.

I recalled the moment I stood alone with the helper in the keep, absentmindedly requesting pictures of boats and wondering: What if they could print my words? Could they also record my voice? These questions grew into the seeds of the revolution.

Now, seeing my father, my mind churned once again, an inspiration from what the mentor would call the subconscious, but what I still considered a gift from the light.

I whispered goodbye to my father and turned to fetch Kara.

Just a holo, yet it had moved me as once I'd been moved by made-up stories playing out on screens in the keep. Might I now move others instead?

Just a holo. Not like the helpers in the keep or the dreamers in the cube.

Yet in the voice and image of my father, I'd discovered a way forward.

Chapter 26

Plots and Plans

To hatch my scheme, I needed help, so I started with my most trusted companions—my fellow seekers. Nathaniel once spoke of temple ritual as theater to control minds. Thomas loved to perform music for others, a way to touch their hearts.

The two listened as I described my plan, as they once listened while I laid out the path to revolution.

When I finished, Nathaniel grimaced even as he nodded his approval. "I hate this plan, but I'm so tired of conflict I'll try anything for peace."

"And you, Thomas?" I expected his pained expression from the steps of the Temple of Truth.

Back then, he'd argued against me, but finally agreed despite his better judgement because he believed in his friends.

This time, he appeared bemused. He flashed his grin and released a laugh from his belly.

"What's funny," I said.

"You. Even as an adult, everything you do is an adventure game."

I smiled, but my smile faded into a frown. "An adventure, yes. Perhaps even a game, but if we lose this time, people will die."

"What if we refuse to play?"

His question hung in the air.

After four heartbeats, Nathaniel answered for me. "If we refuse to play, people will die anyway. Winning this game is our only hope."

159

Thomas pulled out his flute and tooted a note or two. "All right. Last time, I contributed little. You humored me, tossing me a few morsels — letting me unscrew the plates at the base of the temple trees and post some messages." He stared out a moment, recalling a distant time. "Of course, I *did* rescue you, but only after I had no other choice. This time, I'll do more. To provide the proper effect, your ceremony needs music. I'll compose a tune for you, one worthy of such an event."

"If we all agree," I said, "let's make a pact of the Ponds."

I thrust my hand into the center of the circle as I did that day on the steps of the Temple of Truth.

Thomas grasped my wrist at once, but Nathaniel hesitated before joining. "To complete this pact, we need more than three. We can't do this without Kara. What if she doesn't agree?"

I withdrew my hand, fearing bad luck. "I'll go talk to her now."

***

I peppered Kara with questions. "You created the dragon's image from nothing but numbers derived from memories in the archive, yet you added the roar, a sound you never heard. What about people? If I compose new words, can you make the image speak them in the voice of someone I once knew? You made the fireball glow, but wanted to add wind and heat. What other effects can you contrive?"

Kara scrunched her nose and eyed me sideways. "What are you scheming, Orah?"

"Can we hide these devices in bushes and beam larger images overhead?"

"Yes, but these projectors aren't as powerful as the ones that displayed the city walls. The holos won't show well in the sunlight."

"What if we tried after dark?"

She gaped at me, head tilted to one side. "That might work, but—"

"How far can they project?"

"I'm... not sure. We'll need to experiment."

I patted her on the arm to ease the worry from her brow. "Get some rest. I'll wake you after midnight, and we'll try when no one is around."

***

Kara, Nathanial, and I stood alone in the training field. The air had chilled, but the breeze blew softly, and a moon just short of full provided light for our task.

We'd carried the parts from Kara's bedchamber and positioned them in the surrounding brush, covered with branches to be unseen, all but for a space from where the beams would project.

At Nathaniel's suggestion, we devised a simple test, mixing words and images we'd already tried. No need to involve the dreamers. Not yet.

When all was set, Kara circled the setup one last time, checking the devices she'd checked twice before. Then with her silhouette outlined by the bone-white light of the moon, she donned the bonnet and rested her slender fingers on her forehead, as if trying to draw out some forgotten thought.

I couldn't tell how long she stared at me—not at me, but at the spot where I stood. Time didn't apply here, with the seconds and minutes folding into one. I waited and listened—nothing but the rustle of wind and birds cooing in the night.

At last, she closed her eyes and concentrated. The air at the front of the field shimmered and an oversized image of her dragon appeared, but this time, the creature hovered calm overhead, even dignified. Its mouth opened, but instead of flames, words came out... in my father's voice.

"Now little Orah, don't cry...."

Nathaniel gasped, and I clapped my hands. A moment later, the creature winked out.

Kara removed the bonnet. "A successful test. I knew I could display any image. Now I'm sure I can make it mouth whatever words you compose in any voice you wish, as long as the memories reside in the archive. What's next?"

As I explained my plan, a hint of a smile gathered at the corners of her lips, but the shadows cast by the moonlight kept me from making out the rest of her expression.

"It might work," she said, "but I have a lot to do in a short time. How soon can you give me the details?"

"The usurper expects our answer the day after tomorrow. The ceremony will have to be tomorrow night."

I outlined for her the required images, and promised to provide the script by noon the next day.

As she turned to leave, Nathaniel caught her by the arm. "Can you do it?"

"I won't get much sleep, but I think so... if the dreamers cooperate.

They have minds of their own. Any odd question triggers their curiosity, and they want to know why. They may once again refuse."

How I longed to return to the inn and curl up in bed with Nathaniel. I glanced at him and sighed. "Very well. I'll speak with them now."

***

Still three hours before first light, I approached four sleepy bearers of the cube and ordered them outside, my appearance at such an odd hour only increasing their awe.

Now, I stood alone with the repository of the dreamers' minds, my hands resting on its surface and the white bonnet nestled on my head. I struggled to focus my thoughts. If my plan failed, the conflict would continue and many would die.

"Welcome, Orah," the speaker said. "Does all go well?"

"Not well. We negotiated a peace with the vicars, one that's not ideal but better than war, but our people refuse to accept it. Nathaniel and I devised a scheme to convince them, but we need your help."

"The logic remains the same. It makes no sense to provide you with weapons."

"Not weapons. We need your help to promote an illusion. Our people are not logical like you. Their passions overwhelm their thinking. We plan to use their faith to channel those passions toward peace."

I proceeded to enumerate the images and voices Kara would need, memories from the time when I dwelled in the dream on the far side of the sea. Then I waited while the usual buzzing rose and settled.

"A simple problem," the speaker said. "We'll have the algorithms ready when Kara comes next."

In the twilight state I experienced whenever I communed with the dreamers, my heartbeat slowed and my hope surged, yet my doubts surged as well.

I cast the thought into the void. "The ruse I propose.... Am I doing the right thing?"

Many thoughts swirled, too rapid for me to follow.

When they silenced, the speaker summed up their response. "We've calculated the probabilities with alternative paths. If we turn down your plan, many may die, but if we provide you powerful

162

weapons even more will die. Your idea provides the best chance for peace, although we worry about unintended consequences."

"Like what?"

The buzzing rose and fell before settling into an orderly stream, with each dreamer saying their piece.

"The living...."

"So prone to illogic...."

"To grasping at totems...."

"If you follow this path...."

I jumped in. "How will they respond?"

Then all converged into a single chilling thought: "The future becomes unpredictable, the outcome unknown."

Chapter 27

Priests and Priestesses

Nathaniel and I worked on the script until our eyelids drooped and the words crawled across the page, but neither of us cared for the text we'd composed. As daybreak seeped around the edges of our window shade, we resolved to take time apart, to pause and ponder what we wanted to say.

When we'd sailed to the distant shore, we found people on the brink of war. Though many were far wiser than us, we managed to bring them together. Why? Because as outsiders, we viewed their problems with fresh eyes.

Now, with my own people at war, I sought out those whose beliefs differed from our own, hoping to gain from their perspective.

I wandered the village, praying for inspiration from the light—despite my lagging faith—and found Jacob in his shed, carving away.

"What are you working on now?"

He set down his hammer and stared off as if contemplating the coming battle. "Another of the war carts. I hate them. I hate all they mean, but Caleb insists we might need them." He shrugged his shoulders and sighed. "Best to be prepared, and building them gives my hands something to do."

I brushed the sawdust from the wooden bench at the back of the shed, settled on it, and beckoned for him to join me. "Take a rest from your work and share your wisdom with me."

His brows rose. "Wisdom? I'm no earth mother, but a simple craftsman."

"Sometimes simplicity is the best wisdom. My mind has become so cluttered that simplicity may be what I need."

Jacob's custom was to speak little and only when he had something to say. Now, as he sat beside me on the bench, he folded his hands in his lap and crafted his words with the same care that he crafted wood. "A strange world you've brought us to — so many good folks who can teach me so much, so many useful skills I can learn." He shook his head without facing me. "Yet so much heartache."

I rested a hand on his arm. "We can end this heartache if we accept the usurper's terms, if we abandon the knowledge of the past as your people did not so long ago. Still many among us want to keep fighting and call for revenge. Why would anyone spurn the chance to stop this horrible war?"

Jacob rubbed the salt-and-pepper stubble on his chin. "I work with my hands and leave others to think and live as they choose, but I can tell you what I've observed of my fellow creatures. Most feel a need to define the other as evil, as if they themselves can't be good on their own... as if light can't exist without darkness." He glanced up, his faced etched with pain. "What if your vicars preached the truth: unless people are forced to believe the same, they'll eventually focus on their differences, and some poor soul like me ends up making carts of war."

I shifted in my seat and squared my shoulders to him. "What do *you* think I should do?"

His eyes narrowed to slits, but through them, a stream of warmth wafted my way.

I waited, letting it envelope me.

He reached out and covered my hand with his. "You and Nathaniel have found a way to view the world anew, different from the beliefs into which you were born. You envision a better way and, with the best intentions, you try to pass that hope on to others. The world you aspire to is extraordinary, but people are uncomfortable with the extraordinary. They prefer the familiar, to know what to expect, and so the possibility of change frightens them. I'm only a craftsman with no more wisdom to impart, but I believe this: you have been blessed with what the earth mother calls the gift of insight. I hope you use it well."

***

I dragged my gift of insight through the village like a prisoner's chains, more curse than blessing.

Perhaps Devorah might help. She'd studied at the feet of the earth mother since childhood, and now, with Kara's mentoring, she'd touched the souls of those in pain.

The healers scurried about in their red tunics with the white star upon their chests, caring for troopers still recovering from the battle, or stocking medicines and bandages in case the fighting resumed.

I asked them for Kara's apprentice.

"Gone off to learn another craft," one said.

Devorah's leanings trended more toward the gentler arts, and I'd be unlikely to find her among the coopers or woodworkers, skills more like Jacob's domain. So I searched the potter and basket maker, and the needle worker who stitched fine quilts, but to no avail.

Then I remembered my young friend, the shoemaker's daughter.

I found the two of them huddled over a workbench, tapping away at a half-soled shoe with hammer and awl.

Both glanced up when I entered, and paused their work.

"Good morning," Lizbeth said. "I'm surprised to see you here with such a weighty decision hanging over you."

Devorah approached and embraced me. "You look awful, like you haven't sleep in weeks."

Lizbeth set aside her tools. "She's been up all night, I bet, and who can blame her with the burden she bears."

I regarded her, a woman now and honored as an elder by her townsfolks, but still I recalled our first meeting, with her so much younger and grieving for her father. Though underage, she'd endured a teaching because of us — our first victim. In our search for truth, more victims had followed.

"Will the fighting resume?" she said.

"I don't know. A leader can only lead if those they lead will follow." My gaze wandered up to the rows of boots on the shelf, and I inhaled the steady scent of freshly tanned leather. "The troops are flush with their most recent victory, and now want revenge. They've become hardened to the horrors of war and lost sight of the need for peace." I turned back to her. "What do *you* think we should do?"

She came out from behind her workbench and formed a circle with me and Devorah. "What should we do? I find myself of two minds. I understand now what the vicars taught, that if change comes too fast, the darkness may return. We may have witnessed its beginnings. Yet nothing can take away what we've learned. If you destroy the keep, the progress will continue, though at a more modest pace, and the war will end." She raised her chin, as she did years before when she presented us with the final scroll. "But I'm also bound to honor my father. He and his ancestors kept faith for a thousand years to preserve the secret of the keep. Recovering its treasures was his fondest wish. How can I let them destroy it now? It seems worth fighting for."

As she spoke, Devorah shuffled from foot to foot, looking like she longed to be back on the slopes of her mountain home, gathering berries.

What is she thinking?

To find out, we needed time alone.

"Thank you, Lizbeth. I appreciate your thoughts and all you've done to help. May I interrupt Devorah's lesson and borrow her for a bit. I have a task for her to do."

I led Devorah to the outer bounds of the village, and we settled on the banks of the North River. Both of us stared at the water flowing by and listened to the splash of waves sloshing against the shore.

After a moment, she glared at me. "You have no task for me. What is it you want?"

"Your wisdom."

Her lips thinned into a pale line. "In the folly of this world, I have no wisdom to share."

"Then your opinion. You apprenticed to the earth mother, a leader in waiting. What would *she* do in my place?"

Devorah stood and made a small circle through the river grass, before returning and hovering over me. "Saving the keep is a noble thought, but Lizbeth hasn't felt the pain of the wounded as I have. That which has transpired here is what the earth mother warned of—the evil of machines. She would destroy them all, if it would bring peace."

"My thoughts as well. I pray I can convince the troops to follow."

Her lips curled upwards into a weak smile. "You pray to your light, and I'll pray to my earth. Perhaps between them, our prayers will be answered."

I laughed for the first time that day. "If only I could make peace without losing my new friends. I'll miss you if you have to go."

"I'll miss you as well, though for an end to the violence, it's a price I'm willing to pay."

I scrambled to my feet, and we embraced. When we separated, I grasped her by the arms and stared at her, until both our eyes misted.

My voice cracked as I spoke. "I'm sorry to have dragged you into such a mess. I hope you've found some value in this voyage."

She brushed a strand of hair from her eyes and blinked back tears. "Despite it all, I'm glad I came. I learned skills I can bring back home to improve the lives of my people, but most valuable, I learned to mend. Kara has promised to make me a mending machine of my own when we return, a blessing I'm sure the earth mother will allow. Then I'll add healer to my skills, and those sick or injured like Zachariah will never have to trek up the mountain again."

***

One task remained before the plan could proceed. No matter how realistic the illusion, the ruse would fail without the support of the troops' leader.

I found Caleb drilling his men, as always planning for the worst.

When he spotted me, he mumbled a few words to his aide, stepped away from his would-be warriors, and approached. "What news?"

"I need fresh air, to be away from the crowd, but I'm afraid of an ambush. Will you come with me?"

He nodded and hefted his axe. "Shall I bring others?"

"No, you and I alone."

We followed the side path to the small clearing where Thomas had taught me the magic of his flute, and I settled on the same bench.

Caleb loomed over me and spread his huge hands. "You brought me here for more than fresh air. Tell me what you want to say."

In a rush of words, I explained my plan. When I finished, I fixed on those eyes, which had seen so much sorrow and pain. "It's our only way out. Will you support us?"

He joined me on the log and laid his axe at his feet, staring as if wondering at its power. Here sat one of the few who'd straddled both worlds, a learned scientist who'd turned against progress, a rebel whose anger had moved him to try and destroy what remained of his former peers. Now, after mastering his impulse for violence on the far side of the sea, he'd stumbled into the seekers' war.

His lips twitched, and for a moment a cold smile showed like a ripple on the surface of the water. "After my dear Rachel died, I longed for something beyond the pursuit of science and knowledge. I didn't care what. Any god would do — the light, the earth. It didn't matter. But nothing explained what had happened, and none of it eased my pain. When I left the machine masters' city, the people of the earth embraced me more than any god, so I made a leap and accepted their faith. Though I believed it nothing more than superstition, their faith gave me comfort. Who am I to deny that comfort to others?"

He stood, unfolding himself to his full height, picked up his axe, and started to walk away, but before exiting the clearing, he turned.

"Perform your magic. I'll support your ruse, and the ignorant fools will follow."

***

When I returned to the inn to partake in the midday meal, Nathaniel was waiting with a pile of fresh notes in his lap, and we soon agreed on a plan.

Next, we went over the script with Kara — outlining who would appear and what words they would speak.

As she reviewed it, I searched for any hint of hesitation.

At last, she nodded, though the doubt lines in her forehead persisted. "These memories should be easy to find, and I can insert the speech you want. Words are words and sounds are sounds."

Then she gathered our notes and went off to commune with the dreamers.

Nathaniel and I poked at our food as the minutes ticked away.

If Kara failed, the only option was war.

An agonizing hour later, she came back clutching the bonnet in her hand. Her lips spread into a smile. "Success."

"Can we see what it looks like?" Nathaniel said.

Kara fluffed her hair where the sensors had matted it down. "We'd need the projectors, which we left hidden in the bush, ready for tonight. If we try to use them while others are about, we'd ruin the illusion."

She assured us we needed no test, that the images, words, and sounds were nothing but numbers. Once she received the algorithms from the dreamers, all should function as planned.

With so much at stake, Nathaniel refused to accept the magic on faith. "There must be some way to preview it?"

169

She sighed and shook her head. "Not unless we sneak the projectors back to the inn."

His shoulders slumped. "Then we're to risk all on the hope your numbers are correct."

She glared at him. "My numbers *are* correct, but if it will put you more at ease, Orah can commune with the dreamers, and they'll play out the scene in her mind."

***

The three of us gathered in the chamber with the black cube. Since Nathaniel lacked a way to communicate, I promised to tell him if I approved of what I saw.

Kara and I donned our bonnets, and though it made no sense, we held hands and closed our eyes. For an instant, I felt like the troopers in the village square, zealots praying to the cube.

At once images flashed through my mind, a scene from my past. The speech Nathaniel and I had scripted emerged in a voice I remembered so well.

Kara ended our session, and I opened my eyes to find Nathaniel staring, his lips parted with an unasked question. I smiled, no words needed for friends since birth.

The worry on his face eased, and he blew out a long stream of air.

The ruse would work, swaying the children of light as they'd once been swayed by the sun icon.

Yet one concern remained.

Years before, I'd described my thoughts on coming-of-age—that as adults, we needed to have no illusions.

Yet now, as leaders of our people, what we'd present them for their own good was not only an illusion... but a lie.

Chapter 28

Resurrection

I asked Caleb to pass the word to the troop leaders and through them down to the squads—everyone must attend a meeting on the training field after dark.

A murmur spread through Riverbend and swelled to an uproar, like the excited thoughts of the dreamers, but a sound everyone could hear.

Workers set up torches surrounding the field, and the bearers placed the black cube at the center, decorated with more than the usual array of flowers. The yellow of daffodils, the white of day lilies, and the blood red of roses reflected off its glassy surface. The faithful came to stare at the bits of lightning flashing inside, with many leaving offerings—a coin or a scrawled note or a scrap of clothing—while others mumbled a prayer to their would-be greater god.

Thomas cloistered in a secluded spot outside the village, practicing his new composition with his musicians.

Nathaniel, Kara, and I rehearsed where to stand and in which direction to face, memorizing the part each of us would play.

When satisfied the preparations were complete, Nathaniel and I retreated to our bedchamber at the inn to rest after the long night, but neither of us slept. We kept peeking past the curtain, gaping at the sun as it plodded its way across the sky.

At last, the yellow ball flamed red and began its slow drift toward the horizon. Along with Kara, we donned the silver tunics from the

171

machine masters' city—for the first time since arriving from the distant shore—and headed to the training field, but we paused at the tree line to remain hidden.

The bearers lit the torches, and their flames flickered off the faces of the expectant troops.

Once the light dimmed, Thomas and his musicians, dressed in white robes normally reserved for temple ritual, took their place on either side of the cube.

At the first strains of music, Kara and I put on our white bonnets and fiddled with them until they seated just right. Then the three of us locked arms, Kara on Nathaniel's left and me on the right. At the agreed sequence of notes, we started down the path.

The throng hushed as we paraded past, gliding to the beat of the music. When we stopped in front of the cube, gasps escaped from gaping mouths as our presence caused the lightning to seethe and swirl, sending sparks reflecting off our tunics.

For an eternal moment, we waited while Thomas and the musicians finished their piece, a tune more solemn than the one that kept the troops marching, but less hopeful than what he'd composed on our way to the keep.

When the lingering hint of the last note had faded, Nathaniel raised his arms to the heavens, and the crowd quieted, a congregation well trained by a lifetime of attending the blessing of the light.

He spoke as if he'd studied in the seminary. "Followers of the seekers of truth, children of the true light, we come before you today in our time of trial to seek guidance from the dreamers—a secret rite only we three have witnessed. Now you will see their power. Listen and heed their words." He stepped aside.

The air above the cube shimmered, and my former enemy appeared—the deposed temple leader who had made his peace with the people, the one we'd recently rescued from prison so he might die a free man. His image from my memory floated over our heads, hovering beside a stone altar bearing the sun icon.

He raised his arms as if mimicking Nathaniel, bony fingers pointing to the sky, and spoke with the booming temple voice, now amplified by Kara's magic. "Children of the light, I stand before you by the grace of those glorious souls symbolized by this black cube, those whose spirits live on and can never be destroyed. The dreamers have sent me here to impart this message. Both light and darkness dwell in our hearts, but if you will it, the light can conquer the darkness. Today, you are being tested. The temptation of the darkness has corrupted the usurper, and you have fought him bravely. Through the courage of your leaders, he has yielded, cowed by your strength, and offered the freedom you sought.

"Now the choice looms: accept the concessions you've won, or fight for more." His voice rose as it had that morning when calling for our stoning. "To fight for more is madness. Therein lies the path to the darkness."

The image turned to the altar, grasped the sun icon in both hands and raised it high over his head. "Choose the path to the true light instead. Choose the way of peace."

The sun icon began to glow, much as I imagined as a little girl during the seasonal blessings, and grew in size until it towered over us all—a nice effect Kara had proposed—and murmurs of awe filled the square. The arch vicar repeated his plea once more, his final words echoing through the village and dissipating in the breeze.

Then the scene flickered and winked out like the lights guarding the machine masters' city.

On cue, the musicians resumed their play, but different now, a lilting tune of hope with chords rising and falling in waves. Thomas had outdone himself, lifting the spirits of the assembled with a sound that might have been played as the dreamers trod up the mountain in their white gowns on the day of ascension.

After a climax of complex trills and harmonies, the musicians set down their instruments—all but Thomas, who continued to play his flute, though more muted now.

At this signal, Zachariah came to the fore, and lifted his angelic voice into the song Nathaniel and I had composed.

> *The seekers sought to find the keep*
> *Where the past did lie*
> *They hoped to reach beyond themselves*
> *They tried to touch the sky*
>
> ~~~
>
> *And then they sailed across the sea*
> *A place so very far*
> *They met the people of the earth*
> *And dreamers from the stars*
>
> ~~~
>
> *They brought back many miracles*

To make a better world
But found the scourge of evil
And the darkness flag unfurled
~~~

Too much freedom, vicars cried,
From the Temple never stray
Too much change corrupts the soul
The light's the only way
~~~

The seekers led the people
To strive for what is right
They vanquished vicars and their men
Despite a bitter fight
~~~

Now praise our martyrs, those who died
To bring a freer life
Take the peace as offered
And accept an end to strife
~~~

Praise the martyrs, heroes all
Reject the warlike drum
And for the children of the light
Better times will come

After the boy had finished his song, and the strains of his voice had silenced in the night, I turned to gauge the reaction.

All eyes remained fixed on the cube, where the dreamers still thought and planned. Like me, none of them could fathom the mystery of their existence. Yet now the troops would listen and obey, their intent revealed by the firelight from the torches flickering off their moist cheeks.

Chapter 29

Remorse

After the ceremony, Nathaniel and I milled about with a crowd that refused to leave. One after another, they came forward and brushed their fingertips to the cube, mumbling phrases like "bless you, dreamers" or "hail to the guardians of the true light."

Jacob cornered me and whispered in my ear. "A wise decision. No more war carts."

Lizbeth approached and kissed me on both cheeks. "A difficult choice. I'll miss the keep, but peace will prevail."

Devorah came by, a tear in her eye. She plucked a daisy from the display in front of the black cube and handed it to me. "The earth mother would be proud,"

The old prior limped up and made a respectful bow. "I'll mourn the loss of the keep... so many wonders yet to be found... and my passions push me to continue the fight, to take revenge on my enemy, but I yield to the wisdom of the dreamers."

As we tried to escape the throng, Caleb drew us aside. A squad of his most loyal men, those who'd followed him from the far side of the sea, blocked the others from coming near, creating a pocket in the crowd.

He lowered his voice so no one else could hear. "A good show, a fantasy for fools. Now, with your permission, I'll send a messenger to the usurper, saying we've agreed to his terms."

Neither Nathaniel nor I responded, the words sticking in our throats. We both nodded instead.

Caleb started to go, but turned back, a cruel smirk on his lips. "As your people would say, to the darkness with the truth. We'll agree to peace, and stop the bloodshed — the only thing that matters. As for me, I've had my fill of your vicars and deacons, and your children of the light as well. I look forward to returning home to the people of the earth. Since my Rachel died, I prefer a simpler way."

As he stomped off, I checked with Nathaniel, seeking his approval for what we'd done, but the moon now filtered through a hazy sky and I struggled to read his mood.

He stared off to the side before speaking, so part of his face lay in shadow and his smile seemed cut in half. "Caleb is right. Our quest for truth has ended. Time for us to go home."

***

The throng of admirers persisted, clustering around and showering us with praise. After a while, their words lost meaning and slipped past me like the evening breeze. How I longed to escape, to be somewhere else, away and alone.

A sharp toot startled me back to the present.

Thomas bustled through the crowd and wedged his way toward us, blocking out the surrounding host. He held up one hand and waved his flute in the other. "The seekers are exhausted from communing with the dreamers, like using the mending machine. They need to rest."

Those who'd hoped to get one last peek at us, to touch us or beg us to bless their children, grumbled a bit but gave way, and Thomas led Nathaniel and me from the training field.

"I have a surprise for you," he said as he hustled us away. "A different kind of ceremony to commemorate this day."

We followed him to the outskirts of the village and to a narrow trail through the woods, until we reached a small clearing, a place I'd never been. What I found there made me blink twice and wipe the mist from my eyes.

Suddenly, I was back in Little Pond and a child again — better than dreamer magic. Before me stood a replica of the NOT tree, not quite as tall and likely not constructed to last, but a wood frame nevertheless, cloaked with balsam boughs.

As I inhaled their fragrance, I turned to Thomas, my eyes as wide as they were when he appeared from nowhere to free us from the vicars' prison. "But how...?"

"I enlisted Jacob and his craftsmen. It took them only a few hours, and they were happy to get away from making the tools of war." He glanced away, down to his boot tops, but I could tell in the moonlight he was blushing. "I thought you'd need something to lift your spirits."

I rushed to embrace him. "Oh, Thomas, you know us so well."

When we separated, he pointed to the entrance of the shelter. "Wait. There's more." He motioned for us to enter.

Once we were seated cross-legged on the ground inside, he took out three candles from his tunic pocket and lit them. Their glow drove away the shadows, revealing two backpacks and a keg. From the first, he took out a silk cloth, which he spread on the ground between us, and three plates and mugs. From the second, he withdrew a loaf of freshly baked bread, still warm, a half-dozen apples, and four kinds of cheese.

I sniffed at the keg, steaming in the cool night air. "It can't be."

Thomas's lips widened into his customary grin, which had warmed my heart so often since childhood. "Yes, wassail. The drink's unknown here in Riverbend, but they had all the ingredients. I needed to experiment a bit, but you'll see it tastes like ours back home. I may have started a new tradition for them."

In the candlelight, he poured each of us a cup and raised his. "To peace."

I took a sip and smiled, but my smile quickly faded to a frown.

He glared at me. "Now what's wrong?"

"We used to toast to truth, to making a better world."

"Isn't peace a better world than war?"

"Yes... no... I don't know anymore. We started out seeking truth and now we've settled for peace and order. How is that so different from those well-meaning vicars who founded the Temple of Light?"

We all fell silent, each focusing on the nearest candle and getting lost in its flickering flame.

Nathaniel fidgeted where he sat and shifted closer to me. He pressed my cheek with his fingertips until I faced him.

"A paradox," he said.

"What's that?

"A strange word I learned in the keep. It means an idea that seems self-contradictory or absurd but expresses a possible truth. Hasn't our whole quest been a paradox? We sought a better world but started a war. We searched for the light only to slip down the slope to the darkness."

I looked back at my candle. "And we ended our quest for truth with a lie."

Thomas grabbed our mugs, and refilled them with wassail. "Here you two go again, worrying too much. It's all too complicated for me. What more can I do to make you smile?"

I stared up to the peak of our reborn NOT tree and followed a thread of smoke snaking out the opening to the sky—like our youthful aspirations floating away. I recalled another evening on a mountain path overlooking a lake, the three of us sitting around a fire, brimming with belief that we would make a better world.

I turned to Thomas. "You composed a beautiful tune for the ceremony, one that moved the troops and helped bring peace. You and your musicians were sublime, but now, do you remember a different melody, the one you played that night overlooking the lake on our way to the keep?"

He withdrew the flute and waved it in the air. "I... think so. There wasn't much to it, just a few notes repeated, from a time when I knew far less about music."

"That's what we need now, a tune from a simpler past, before teachings and prisons, before the keep and the keepmasters, before machine masters and the people of the earth, before the usurper and wars. Will you play it for us?"

He dipped his head in a small bow. "As you wish."

Thomas took a sip of wassail and raised the flute to his lips, then closed his eyes while his fingers danced over the holes as if searching for the notes. After a moment, he began to play, faltering at first, but with each passing note more confident, until he poured his soul into the instrument and transported me to a more hopeful time.

The song filled our newly built NOT tree, and for those few moments, I pretended that innocence had returned.

Chapter 30

Discord

The first response came two days later in the form of the caped envoy of the usurper sweeping into our village, accompanied by an honor guard of burly deacons. He bore a stack of more than fifty pages covered with what I once called temple lettering before I learned about printing in the keep. He proclaimed that we should review the terms and send back our comments as fast as possible, so we could complete our negotiation and sign the truce within two weeks.

Once he departed, Nathaniel and I retreated to our bedchamber to read through the document, slogging through the dense details one page at a time.

After the fifth page, Nathaniel's shoulders slumped and he blew out a stream of air. "What nonsense. It seems to be what we agreed to, but I can't be sure. What if they've hidden traps in all this clutter?"

When I handed him the sixth page, he tossed it on the bed.

I picked up the page and gathered the rest together. "We need help. Neither of us is skilled in deceit and betrayal."

I summoned Caleb.

He flipped though the stack of papers. "Here's what I'd advise. Put the old prior in charge. He's a learned man accustomed to their ways, and he has reason to distrust them. Let him pick one elder from each of the ten largest villages, a way to build support among the people for the truce, and more eyes will make for fewer mistakes. Ask them to take notes. When they've finished, you can review the results and compose a response."

Nathaniel agreed at once, relieved to be free of the burden. When I hesitated to hand over the papers, he snatched them from me and followed Caleb out the door.

I sat on the bed, hands folded in my lap, and stared at the floor.

What leaders we are. First we lie, and then we become so flustered by details that we sluff off our responsibility to others.

I shook off the mood and went for a stroll in the nearby countryside to clear my head.

Much like Little Pond, the hills surrounding Riverbend were dotted with apple orchards. This time of the year, most of the fruit had been picked, but I went there anyway, hoping to discover a late season prize.

As I glanced up, searching the branches for glimmers of red, the patter of footsteps sounded from behind me, running steps but light-footed, more like a dancer than an attacker.

I spun around, and beamed as Zachariah approached. Seeing the boy always lightened my spirits. "Good morning. Have you come to pick apples with me?"

He scrunched up his nose. "What are apples?"

"I forgot. You don't have any on your side of the world. Apples are fruit that grows in these trees." I gestured to a few, still green and not ready for picking.

Zachariah marveled at them. "They're big and shiny. Can we eat them like berries?"

"Yes, of course, but it's a bit past the season and most of the ripe ones have been picked. You need to find a red one still on the tree."

He scanned around and pointed high up. "I found one. May I eat it?"

"Yes, if you could reach it."

I wished Nathaniel were here to boost him up, as he used to boost Thomas when we were so much younger, before everything changed.

"I'd hoist you on my shoulders, but I'm not tall enough, and you've grown too big for me."

A gleam came into his eye as he surveyed the gnarly tree, starting with the lower branches and tracking higher up, much the way Thomas had studied the stone tower on the way to the keep.

"I can climb it," he said.

An image came into my mind of Zachariah flying off the carousel and breaking his arm. "No, you won't. I'd hate to have to mend you again."

He grinned at me, now ten years old and mischievous like Thomas had been at the same age. Before I could stop him, he scrambled up, pausing only to select the next branch, which hardly bent under his weight.

Near the top, he plucked the apple and tossed it down to me. "Now don't eat it till I come down. I get the first bite."

I polished the fruit on the sleeve of my tunic until it sparkled in the sunlight. Then the two of us settled on a nearby log and alternated bites, each crisp and juicy—like the apples of my youth.

When we finished, Zachariah wiped the juice from his chin and turned to me. "Why are you so sad? Thomas made music for you, and I sang the pretty words you wrote. Now we'll have peace, and people will stop hurting each other."

I shook my head. "It's complicated. You wouldn't understand."

He stood and made a small circle around the orchard as if searching for another apple. When he returned, he hovered over me with hands on hips. "Is it because you used holos to fool them?"

My mouth dropped open, and I gaped at him. "You know?"

"Uh-huh. I lived in the city until I was six. I remember holos from the food synthesizers and from my lessons before they sent me down the mountain. I can't imagine how they work, but I still recognize them."

I motioned for him to sit by me and wrapped an arm around him. "You won't tell anyone, will you?"

He snuggled closer, but kept his eyes focused on the ground. "I stayed silent for three years after my parents left, until you told me my mother's words. I'm an expert on staying silent." He looked up at me with eyes too big for his head. "You know I'd do anything you ask, but why did you need holos to make peace?"

I sighed. "Sometimes, you need to invent a story to convince others to do the right thing. Our people had begun to spin myths about the dreamers, claiming they had the power of gods. The only way they'd give up on total victory was if the dreamers told them to." I paused to make sure I had his attention. "You *do* know the dreamers aren't gods. They're nothing more than the thoughts of people like your parents stored in a machine. While they're smart enough to strike down our enemies, they're wise as well and prefer peace. Since they can't speak to the living without our help, we made up a story to show their intentions."

I rested a hand on each of his shoulders and stared into his eyes. "Do you understand?"

He nodded. "You're what the earth mother calls a prophet, someone who makes up stories to reveal the truth, like the one where she called you and Nathaniel a prince and princess with magical powers."

I crumpled my brow.

He's a child. Why do I need so badly for him to understand?

"I'm no princess, Zachariah, and Nathaniel is no prince. We're ordinary people in an extraordinary circumstance, trying to do the best we can. There's no magic to it."

His eyes drifted down and to the corners, following a wooly caterpillar as it crawled across the log.

I tightened my grip and pulled him closer. "Let me hear you say it."

He shook his head, still staring at the caterpillar, as if expecting any second for it to enter its cocoon and sprout wings. "No magic. Not really. Not a prince and princess either." He glanced up, and his smile sent a glow streaming through the orchard. "More like heroes."

I leaned in and kissed him on the forehead.

He wrinkled his nose, making a crease between his brows. "Still, the earth mother says we need to tell stories, to fill in the things we'll never understand, like how this caterpillar will someday turn into a butterfly, or why my parents became lost in the dream. So I'll keep telling my story about the prince and the princess to anyone who will listen, about the magic they used to bring peace, and if I tell it well, those who come after me will remember you forever."

***

I hovered in the air above a meeting place like the hall of winds, but much larger. High up on the back wall, the circular window still loomed, but four times the size, its fragments of colored glass now pieced together to form a more complex picture. On the right side, a golden sphere shone with rays of yellow spiraling from its center, and on the left, a blue globe floated through the air, our world as viewed from the keepmasters' ship that sailed to the stars.

In the center stood a host of people clustered together, their eyes raised to the heavens. Though I recognized no faces, I identified them by their dress: machine masters in their silver tunics; people of the earth in their brown and gray rags; my own children of the light in black; deacons with the star upon their chests; and vicars with their not-quite-square hats, but with a more benign expression on their faces.

At the base of the back wall, the banner hung as before. On it, four horsemen rode through the sky, their steeds caught in full gallop with steam bursting from their nostrils and their eyes ablaze: the first with a flaming sword; the second, a caped creature with a skull for a head; the next, a cloaked fiend whose features were hidden by a cowl; and the last a woman with serpents for hair.

Only the words scribbled at the bottom had changed. They now read: Pray for peace.

The same flagstone altar stood in front, but what had been nothing more than a crude table for the earth mother to lean upon was now embellished. A silk cloth covered the stones and bore on it two objects: an enormous sun icon, and a miniature black cube.

In the pews sat people like none I'd ever met. The men wore trousers with cuffs at the ankles and glossy collared shirts with white scarfs tied around their necks. The women were dressed in brightly-colored garments hanging from their shoulders, and hats like Kara's bonnet, but with more elaborate designs. All waited with backs straight and hands folded, staring at the front.

A tall man in a white robe, who might have descended from the mentor, strode to the back of the altar, bearing an impressive book bound in embossed leather. He plopped the book down with a thud, opened it to a place saved by a purple ribbon, and began reading in a voice not much different from a vicar at the blessing of the light.

"In the dimness of time, when the darkness ruled, there came a prophet and a dreamer of dreams, and showed us the way to the light. Let us praise the true light."

The assembled repeated the phrase in the same dull tone I recalled from other blessings, from the people of the earth and the machine masters, and from my own children of the light.

As they spoke, this would-be vicar beamed at them, a serene smile on his face. Once they quieted, he shifted to a new page, marked by a green ribbon instead, and glanced up. "Now please open your scripture to chapter fifty-seven."

The window on the back wall was situated so the afternoon rays streamed through it in slanting columns, warming the faces of the congregants and making rainbow flecks of light dance across the man's cheeks.

He waited for the bump of books and the rustle of pages to quiet before beginning. "Today's reading will be one of my favorites, the Truce of Riverbend from the book of Orah."

***

I startled awake so fast I feared rousing Nathaniel, but he grunted once, rolled over on his side, and fell back asleep.

There'd be no sleep for me. I stared wide-eyed at the darkened ceiling, my hands clenched beneath the covers. As the blood coursed thick and heavy through my veins, and each pulse pounded in my ears, a vision from the keep came to me. In my idle hours, I'd ask the helpers to see images from their age of enlightenment, so I could better understand their world. One of my favorite requests was to ask what it had been like to travel in their flying machines.

The screen would flicker and show me the view through an oval window. I'd stare out from more than ten thousand paces in the air, looking upon the bluest of skies, with only the stray cloud wafting beneath me like a puff of cotton.

I'd ask the helper for a glimpse of the land below, expecting to find terrain like Little Pond as seen from the granite mountains, with its green trees and rolling hills, but in places I saw only brown—no trees, no water, no people.

"Why the desolation?" I said.

"Not all the Earth is livable. After the cataclysm, some locations have become so harsh, even the hardiest plants and lowliest creatures struggle to survive."

I wondered now: are these my choices—the future ceremony of my dream, or the world a barren wasteland where no one can live?

I padded over to the small desk, lit a candle and opened my log. As I waited with pen in hand, gathering my thoughts, I let the silence envelop me. Yet after a while, my pen hovered unmoving over the page.

Why do the words that flowed in the past refuse to come to me now? Why does this stark white paper frighten me so?

I remembered my dream and realized what I feared. What if this log became like the book of light, words to be recited mindlessly by generations hence, or worse, to be accepted without thought?

As I stared at the blank page in the candlelight, my choice became as clear as the morning star in a crisp fall sky.

Now is my true test of courage, more than facing the stoning or entering the dream alone. Now is my time of trial.

Rather than write a new entry, I ripped out pages, a dozen or more, and set the log aside.

I'd pen a fresh script, different from before, a greater challenge for Kara and the dreamers, a grand story like the videos of heroes I'd watched on screens in the keep.

Now the words flowed. As I wrote faster and faster, filling page after page, my spirit soared.

My people wanted myths. I'd give them more than they could imagine, so many and so powerful, the myths would transform into truth.

After I finished, I crawled back into bed, my mind at ease. Only one worry remained.

As my eyes drifted closed, I whispered aloud, "Will Nathaniel agree?"

***

After Nathaniel awoke, I gave him a few minutes to splash water on his face and groom his hair and beard. Then I sat him down as I paced the room and laid out my latest plan.

He released a pent-up sigh and shook his head. "Haven't we done enough? Why for once can't you leave the world to fend for itself?"

I shrugged, and struggled to curl my lips upward into a smile. "Like the earth mother said, it's in our nature to strive, to try to make a more perfect world."

He closed his eyes and covered them with his fingertips and spoke to me from the darkness within. "Strive, yes, but she also said striving should have limits."

"But we're the seekers of truth. How can we accept driving away our friends and destroying these founts of knowledge that should become the foundation of our future?"

He opened his eyes and stared at me, a frightening stare, more the look of a stranger than a friend. "I was always the one with notions, while you stayed grounded. You were the one who kept me from flying off into dangerous adventures like we were playing our NOT tree games. Now we've switched places, it seems. I'm older and more tired, with scars within and without." He rubbed the place in his side where the battle wound still showed a mark. "I'm less willing to take chances."

I stepped closer and rested a hand on his cheek. "We've faced so many hardships and risked so much. Why stop partway when our goal is within reach?"

A stab of something like despair seemed to strike him, and his voice rose. "When is it enough? When is it someone else's turn? If the people don't want what we're offering, we can't force it on them. Their lives will be better because of what we've done, with more freedom than before. They're supposed to be creatures who strive. Time for *them* to prove their worth."

I fell back a step and glared at him. "Yes, we're creatures who strive, some with a passion that can destroy others, but we're also creatures who think. How can we leave them believing a lie?"

He stood and grasped me by the arms, his eyes pleading. "The last keepmaster said we should have more to life than our mission, that we should live hour to hour and day to day, and care for the ones we love. Time to heed that advice. You and I have sacrificed a lot to make a better world, a world worth bringing a child into. I'm ready to go back to Little Pond and make a life of our own."

I breathed two breaths in and two breaths out, giving me time to respond. As children, we'd sought answers to every question we'd ever had. Now it seemed only the questions remained, and these had multiplied, more confusing than ever. Perhaps Nathaniel was right. We should abandon our search for truth, and enjoy our days together, however long they may last.

Yet we'd come too far to give up now. How could I make him understand?

"You once said if we found any chance to save what's been lost, we have to take it. For the past four years, we've been swimming in future dreams, never seeing the reality of today. The result: a world worse than we imagined. Now we have this last chance to fulfill those dreams. How can we do anything less than grasp it with both hands?"

He pulled me closer until our foreheads touched. "You're right. You followed me when all hope seemed lost, and I've followed you as well, but this time, I see no chance. Show me a glimmer of hope—just a glimmer—and I'll follow you one more time."

Chapter 31

Decision

A week passed. The old prior had made three trips to the usurper's camp bearing our responses. Each time, he returned with more of the usurper's corrections, though their depth and nature dwindled in importance until little remained but nits.

Yet our enemy kept insisting on changes, and the negotiations dragged on.

After we'd received the latest feedback, and Caleb and the grumbling elders had left the meeting room, the prior lingered. He waited with head bowed and eyes focused on his shoe tops, as if struggling with a choice: suppress the words smoldering within, or grant them speech.

I closed the door to the chamber, hoping the absence of others would put him at ease. When he remained uncertain, I urged him on. "Good prior, you've been a help to us more than once now, and have earned the right to speak your mind. No vicars or deacons lurk here."

He declined to face us, this once proud man who'd been broken by those he formerly served. Speaking to authority pained him, and he labored to muster the courage to give his words sound. "There's... something you should know. For thirty-five years, I've worked with the brothers of the gray friars, and with vicars and deacons too. I call many of them friends. Most are good people with noble intentions, but all were taught to think one way and obey without question. The years in the keep have changed many, and the days of destruction even more."

Nathaniel took a step toward him and rocked on the balls of his feet. "What are you trying to tell us?"

The prior looked up at last, and his eyes widened as if seeing us for the first time. "The usurper is losing support. Many believe he's brought unnecessary disaster upon the Temple, doing more damage than the seekers ever did."

"And what do you expect us to do with this information?"

He rubbed the stubble on his chin. "Did you ever see a boulder on the side of a hill, so massive it appeared to have rested there for ages, and there you believed it would stay until the end of time?"

Nathaniel glanced at me, and we both nodded.

"Yet one day a rainstorm loosens a pebble beneath it, and it begins to wobble and then roll. Before long, the boulder tumbles headlong down the slope, changing the entire landscape with it."

I joined Nathaniel and grasped him by the arm. Like me, his muscles had tensed. "Do you mean...?"

The old prior's eyes burned. "Now is the time. Dislodge the pebble, and you may yet achieve your goal."

***

First comes the possible, and then the decision to act.

I summoned Kara to the meeting room and locked the door behind her.

"What now?" she said. "Do you need dreamer advice on drafting the truce?"

Nathaniel rechecked the lock and lowered his voice. "How fast can your conjured images move and change?"

Kara's brows rose. "How fast? Faster than the mind can comprehend. The images are nothing but numbers computed by the most powerful thinking machine ever made, beamed by projectors as points of light."

I stepped toward her, trying to temper my excitement. "How many can you project at once?"

"So long as they're based on memories stored in the archive, as many as you can imagine."

"What about size?" Nathaniel said. "You made the sun icon grow and glow. Can you do the same with people?"

Kara brushed away a shock of hair from her eyes as she shifted back and forth between us. "You still don't understand. The numbers don't distinguish between icons or people or dragons. Size is a matter of degree."

"The dragon," I said. "How did you make it roar?"

She laughed. "That turned out to be easier than I thought. To simulate its roar, I borrowed the rush of a waterfall and amplified it."

"Can you make other sounds?" Nathaniel said.

"Anything from the archive. Sounds are numbers too."

I squeezed Nathaniel's hand and whispered a prayer to the light, but the miracles I sought were based on science. If we failed, such insights might take a thousand years to relearn—*if* we ever rediscovered them at all.

I took a deep breath and described my plan.

When I finished, Kara nodded. "More complex a problem than before. More interesting too. I'll need extra time, but if you give me a few days, I can do it."

"So what we ask is possible, but will the dreamers cooperate this one last time?"

Kara's lips curled into a grin. "The mentor always claimed they had a sense of whimsy. As much as bits of electronic impulses can love, the dreamers will love this plan."

***

After Kara left, Nathaniel shuffled to the window and stared at the people bustling on the street below. His mind churned, much like it had when we stood in the keep's observatory, watching the ship on the screen launch to the stars.

Like that day, I struggled to read his mood, not because he'd become opaque but because his thoughts were in turmoil.

I slipped beneath his gaze and rested a hand on his cheek so he'd face me. "We have our glimmer, and now Kara says the science supports the plan. Will you do it?"

His lips spread thin and pale, but a hint of a twinkle showed in his eyes. "What if they stone us for lying to them?"

I shrugged. "We faced stoning before."

The vein in his temple pulsed, and his jaw twitched and set.

Then, the room brightened as if the shadow of a cloud had passed from the sun.

The muscles in his face relaxed, and he let out a laugh. "Somewhere between the keep and the dreamers, you've gone mad, and I've gone mad with you. Go ahead and hatch this plot of yours. Maybe they'll stone us, but maybe we'll change the world at last. And if your plan should fail, we'll fly off to the light with our heads held high, vanishing together like two shooting stars in the night."

Chapter 32

The Seekers of Truth

We answered the next stack of papers from the usurper with no changes, but rather with a terse response:

No more word games. We accept the text as is on one condition: we choose the time and place for the signing.

The ceremony would occur after dusk in one week. The location would be the broad no-man's land behind the rock face, an area spacious enough to hold a large host, including both armies. We insisted the historic truce be witnessed by all and encouraged our enemy to bring as many clergy, friars, and deacons as possible.

Since our craftsmen possessed the skills to do the event justice, we and we alone would set up the site—to avoid conflict, the vicars and their men would be banned from coming in advance. In exchange, we'd allow temple officials to arrive an hour early to review the setup and oversee access, stationing guards as they wished to check all attendees who entered. No weapons would be allowed.

Had we properly gauged the vicars' mood?

Every detail of the truce smacked of a single purpose: the Temple had controlled our people for a thousand years, and no doubt hoped for a thousand more. As long as they retained their titles and the tithe from the people, and their decorated sashes and capes and the crown of gold, they would believe they'd won. More than likely they considered it a matter of time before they reasserted control over the people.

With their leaders so focused on the long term, we hoped they'd concede some small authority to us for one night—control of the site—a seemingly worthwhile tradeoff.

But one night was all we needed.

***

For two agonizing days, we waited, until at last, a one-word response arrived: *agreed*.

Part one: success. We would control the time and place of the meeting. Now we had five days left to prepare.

As Nathaniel and I labored over the script, a story more expansive than any we'd attempted before, I gained a new appreciation for the effort that went into producing the videos in the keep.

After we finished each segment, we reviewed it with Kara, who would cloister herself with the dreamers to search for appropriate memories, extract the relevant algorithms, and add her own creative touch.

Finally, the day arrived. To be safe, the three of us moved the projectors to the site well before dawn, though the vicars had agreed to keep their distance until dusk. Jacob and his craftsmen had built a platform upon which the signing ceremony would take place, tall enough so everyone in attendance would be able to see. Now we added dirt mounds on either side, apparently to create a barrier to protect the leaders from their people.

In these mounds, we hid Kara's projectors, and before each we piled a decorative pyramid of stones.

We spent the remainder of the day practicing our roles and praying to any god who would listen.

As the sun settled below the treetops and crept its way toward the horizon, we signaled to let the temple inspectors in. I held my breath as they sniffed about, but as expected, they searched mostly for weapons. At last, they seemed satisfied, and ordered the guards to admit the crowd into the protected area.

Our troops, along with villagers from Riverbend and surrounding towns, entered from the south and west, each arriving empty-handed and waiting annoyed as deacons patted them down.

The temple army marched in from the north, where for the moment, the keep still lay. A column of gray friars followed, with red skull caps and crimson sashes across their chest, most looking glum at the prospect of losing their newfound playground. Next came the clergy, vicars and monsignors, bishops and arch bishops, each garbed more splendidly than those who went before.

And last, the usurper himself, self-proclaimed grand vicar, the human embodiment of the light on this earth, his silver-laced cape exaggerating his slight shoulders, and the smugness of presumed victory plastered on his face. The truce seemed to have left him confident his rule would survive.

It took more than an hour for everyone to be checked out and file in. When all had settled into their designated spots, Nathaniel and I climbed onto the platform from one side, and the usurper and his envoy from the other. The envoy unfurled an elaborate scroll, the ceremonial document to be signed.

I nodded to Kara, no more than a barely perceptible tilt of the head.

She needed no black cube, as the dreamers had done their work, and she required no bonnet, having pre-programmed the projectors. She needed only a tiny switch hidden in the palm of her hand.

She responded to my nod with a head tilt of her own.

The air above us shimmered, and a circular chamber appeared, similar to the vicars' teaching chamber but with some notable changes. In place of the vaulted stone arches, a false sky arced overhead, supported by the muscular figures of seven giants. At the front, the high desk of the vicars loomed, tenfold taller than that which had once terrified me in Temple City.

Behind the desk hung the tapestry depicting the battle of light and darkness, but with two differences: its increased dimensions matched that of the desk, and the images upon it had come alive. Storm clouds scudded across the sky, bolts of lightning flashed and thunder boomed, and the host of praying vicars, rather than holding their ground, cringed in fear.

The viewing throng fell back a step as the scene came into focus, their gasps hissing through the night air.

The usurper looked up as well, but with the knowing smirk of a fellow conjurer of magic. His smirk vanished, however, when he recognized the pitiful figure in the center of the chamber, hunched by the lid of the teaching cell.

Kara and the dreamers had plucked from my memory a perfect image of the Little Pond vicar who long ago had dragged me and Thomas off to our teachings. He appeared as he had on that day, with a scrawny beard, and no red stripes on his hat, lacking the outlandish embellishments of a grand vicar. In a clever calculation of mathematics, Kara had rendered him tiny compared to those sitting in judgment upon him, a child quivering before giants.

The young usurper's holo image stared up wide-eyed at the panel of judges, gaping like his real-life counterpart.

Who were these judges?

In the center hovered the spirit of the deceased arch vicar, glaring down at the traitor who'd ordered his death. To his left sat Kara's grandfather, the mentor, towering over his colleagues, and to his right, still dressed in rags, the earth mother.

The arch vicar pointed a bony finger at the usurper. His dark eyes burned and his brows billowed over them like smoke.

"You!" His words resounded to the farthest reaches of the throng, his thundering voice now amplified by Kara's craft. "You stand accused of crimes against the light. The Temple relies on its rules, and you have violated many—blasphemy, praising the darkness, and inciting others to follow. What do you say in your defense?"

The projected usurper answered, not in the temple voice, but in the nasal whine I learned to loathe during our three-day trek to the teaching. "Perhaps I overstepped, but my intent was pure. What crime in being too zealous in preventing a return to the darkness?"

"Yet that's what you did—use our zealousness to grab and maintain power—and in so doing you brought us to the brink of the darkness. Here is the list of your crimes: snatching the title of grand vicar by force without being elected by the council; forcing your way from the middling rank of bishop and bypassing the required years of learning; pilfering the tools of the keep to resurrect the horrors of war, reconstructing weapons not seen for a thousand years, causing carnage, pain and death; imprisoning, torturing and killing innocents...." He leaned in, the blood draining from his face to make him appear more like a ghost, another of Kara's effects. "...and murdering me. Thank the light, the dreamers have granted me this final chance at justice."

"But I—"

The arch vicar slammed the flat of his hand upon the desk to silence him and turned to his left.

The mentor pressed down with both hands and winced in pain as he rose to standing, unfolding himself to an impressive height. His long face tensed, and the bits of lightning that comprised his incredible mind flashed in his blue eyes.

"I am the mentor, leader of the machine masters who created the black cube. We bestowed it with power far beyond what resides in your keep, including the ability to save lives or destroy worlds, but we conferred upon it wisdom as well. Now you come before us demanding we dismantle the keep and shatter the cube, repositories of the accumulated knowledge of our forbearers. Why? What is it about knowledge that terrifies you so? Do you rely so much on ignorance to rule, or false magic to delude your people? You want magic? I'll show you what your so-called magic has wrought."

He waved his hand at the tapestry behind him. The cloth rippled and blurred as if driven by a sudden gust, and the battle of light and darkness transformed. The four horsemen from the hall of winds appeared, and these now took on life, galloping out from the tapestry and growing in size, accompanied by the sound of a raging wind.

As they flew out over the frightened throng, the mentor declared in a somber tone, "Desolation, despair, destruction, and death."

The arch vicar stood as well and raised both arms above his head, waving toward the riders and crying out to the crowd. "Is this what you want for yourselves and your children?"

The phantom horsemen rode off into the night and vanished. The roar that accompanied them diminished and died, leaving a vacuum of sound.

The arch vicar's brows drooped at the corners and the smoldering abandoned his eyes, replaced by sadness. His voice quieted, not much more than a whisper, though thanks to Kara's magic he could be heard by all. "Do not destroy the keep. Its walls have been sanctified by those who have given their lives to save the knowledge of their day. The darkness lies not there, but in your own hearts."

He turned to the mentor, whose lids hooded his eyes as he shook his head. "Do not destroy the 'arc of the dreamers,' because the minds of those who strove to make a better world still dwell within."

Then both took their seats and nodded toward the third member of the panel.

The earth mother rose, slighter and more frail than the others, but with her craggy features and square jaw, a powerful presence no less. She scanned the throng to her left and right, as if trying to gaze into each set of eyes.

At last, she spoke in her gravelly voice, more befitting a man. "Both the earth and the light are sacred, as is the human mind, for we are neither the children of darkness nor the children of light. We are the stuff of stars. Time for us to aspire to more. Time for the light of reason to shine."

She waved a hand at the tapestry, which rippled once more, and on the blank space the horsemen had left behind, a phrase appeared in flames:

> The greatest truth must be... that in every child is the potential for greatness.

The words escaped the confines of the cloth and flew out overhead, growing in size and circling like the dragon had once circled me. They danced to the sound of Thomas's flute, the lilting tune he'd played on our way to the keep.

The earth mother grew in stature, and her voice, through Kara's craft, grew as well. She pointed at the usurper. "If the greatest truth must be that in every child is the potential for greatness, the greatest sin must be to deny that potential, and so, you—" Her arm stretched toward him, her enormous finger reaching close as if to poke him in the chest. "—must be the greatest sinner."

Despite knowing the false magic behind the image, the usurper fell back a step, lost his footing, and tumbled off the platform into the awaiting arms of his followers.

His envoy jumped down to rescue him, the silver cape slipping off his shoulder, revealing a frailer man. As he helped his superior scramble to his feet, and the two tried to climb back up, many hands restrained them, fellow clergy and friars holding them back.

The human embodiment of the light on this earth had lost the faith of his flock.

By happenstance, at that moment, fiction mimicked reality—the teaching cell cover in the holo slid open and the young usurper tumbled inside. His cries died out as the lid closed, casting him into a darkness deep enough to haunt one's dreams.

The scene faded—the grand chamber, the sky supported by giants, the outsized judgment desk, and the bare tapestry behind it—all scattered into bits of light, each winking on and off like a firefly before vanishing.

No one remained on the platform but Nathaniel and me.

How insignificant we must seem after such a grand show.

A confusion spread through the crowd, murmurs of doubt, cries of anger, expressions of awe, sentiments too complex to read.

All eyes fixed on us, two poor souls huddling alone and exposed. We were mortal now, but for Kara's remaining magic—a bright light that shined upon us, and the science that amplified our voices.

Nathaniel strode to the edge of the platform. "You know us, the seekers of truth."

I joined him. "The ones who led you to this point."

"Don't be afraid," Nathaniel said. "Like so much of what you've been taught, all is illusion."

I raised my chin and lifted up on my toes, trying to appear taller than I was, hoping to speak louder than the beating of my heart. "But here is what's real. *You* possess the power, and the time has come for *you* to judge."

I turned to Nathaniel, unable to face the crowd, relying on his strength.

Now is our moment of truth.

The pulse on his temple throbbed and his chin jutted out, but the words we'd agreed to never wavered. "We are frail and flawed beings like you. In the name of peace, we deceived you. There's no magic but that which lives in your minds and hearts. Now our fate is up to you." He waved his arm, gesturing below to the pyramid of stones at the base of the platform. "Stone us if you must, or choose peace and a better world."

We stepped back and waited. A few vicars grabbed rocks from the pile, as did a handful of deacons as well.

Before a rock could be thrown, Thomas hopped onto the platform, a move we'd never rehearsed, and the three of us locked arms—as we did on that chill morning in Little Pond so long ago.

Then a row of gray friars appeared, led by the old prior, and set a wall between us and those who bore stones, with the glare from the projectors shining off the tops of their skull caps.

Next Caleb and his men came forward, with no axes or weapons now, to block the way.

Jacob, Devorah, and Kara followed.

Others joined in, our people first by the dozens, and then by the hundreds, and vicars and deacons too.

Last of all, slipping between legs and squeezing past elbows, the slight figure of Zachariah scrambled onto the platform and grasped my hand.

He glanced up at me with eyes too big for his head. "Potential for greatness? I like the sound of that." His lips curled into a grin, and he winked at me. "But I'll still tell your story forever."

Epilogue

A year had passed since our grand show on the former battlefield outside Riverbend, and so far at least, the peace had held.

After a week-long trial attended by many, a panel of judges, consisting of the old prior, three bishops, and five elders from the children of light, found the usurper guilty. Yet the new order had banned teachings, stonings, or any other form of harsh punishment, so they struggled to come up with a sentence. Following four days of deliberation, they condemned the would-be grand vicar to be locked up at night, but allowed to work during the day in the Temple City kitchens — a penance Thomas found amusing to no end.

Most of those who'd served our cause returned home to resume their former lives, though many relished sitting around a fireplace and telling exaggerated tales of how they'd overthrown the vicars. Others used their newfound freedom to change their preordained lot, and we all discovered that the pursuit of potential took many paths. Craftsmen switched to farming, and farmers to crafts. Some sold their farms, moved to the larger towns and became merchants. An odd few like Thomas took up musical instruments or experimented with new approaches to art. With no more temple restrictions, ground-breaking fashions and forms began to appear daily.

With an end to secret rituals, and knowledge open to all, the gray friars discarded their sashes and skull caps, and disbanded. A relieved few, no longer bound by the oaths of their youth, returned to their villages to raise families and work for the betterment of their neighbors, but many stayed in the keep, blending in with the scholars and relishing the chance to choose what to learn.

The once bitter enemies, Caleb and Kara, had made their peace through their endeavors on our side of the world and sailed home as allies, sworn to bridge the gap between technos and greenies. Most of those who'd accompanied them across the sea returned as well.

Jacob took back detailed diagrams of devices to simplify the lives of his people.

Devorah bore with her bags of exotic spices and intriguing flavors of tea, and patterns from which to make bright-colored clothing and festive quilts. Most of all, she carried with her a commitment from Kara to build a new mending machine, one that would reside with the greenies and allow her to take up her place as the village healer.

Only one traveler from our original crew stayed behind—Zachariah. After so many silent years, and with neither parents nor home to lure him back, the boy had asked to stay with Nathaniel and me. We quickly agreed.

And so, the three of us trekked back to Little Pond, no longer seeking truth but a quieter life instead.

At last, my roving mind and wandering spirit found a chance to rest. I spent my days roaming about the village and reacquainting with old friends, and teaching Zachariah how to work the loom. He, in turn, continued my learning of the flute, although given my limited ability, with less successful results.

Elder Robert and elder John invited Nathaniel and I to join them on the council and help run Little Pond, but we declined, insisting we were too young for such a role. Instead, Nathaniel's father helped us stake out a plot on the former site of the NOT tree, and we began construction of a modest cottage, which one day would become our new home.

In between, Nathaniel and I went for long walks and pondered all we'd wrought. I'd stare at him as he gazed at the horizon with the sunlight reflecting off his face. A thin crease had formed on his forehead, the start of a worry line, a well-earned badge of honor from all those times he'd wrinkled his brow since coming of age.

Kara had committed to return as soon as possible, so we might begin trade between our peoples, exchanging those goods fitting to each of our talents. First she needed to build a fleet of new boats, so that once such commerce started, we could maintain a steady flow.

"In four months," she'd said, "look to the west for the high masts poking their tops above the horizon.

We waited through the chill winter, but as soon as the snow melted, we lit the candle atop the watchtower and posted a lookout, with messengers positioned at intervals to herald their arrival.

At last, the first sparkles appeared as the silver sails in the distance caught the sun's rays. A sequence of crow caws echoed back to the village, and all those able raced to the west and scrambled over the mountain pass to the shore.

Within hours, the boat had settled into the shallows of the bay at the base of the granite mountains. My neighbors gawked as the crew unloaded new inventions, designed by the children of the machine masters. In exchange, we bartered crafts and tools, and plants and grains unknown on their side of the world.

Now, the rare week passes without a new boat arriving, laden with the fruits of the tree of knowledge. We began to trade people too. Our young craftsmen, artists, and farmers, those without families to tie them down, sought their fortune on the distant shore, where land was plentiful and their expertise would be rare and valued. One by one, some of the older techno children came to us as well, taking up residence in the keep to mentor the scholars and provide a more cordial instruction than those stilted recordings on the screens.

Each boat's departure became cause for celebration, a new kind of festival. People flocked from villages far and wide to make the pilgrimage over the mountains and watch it set sail. No longer the edge of the world, Little Pond grew into a booming port, with a road built from the village to the sea to ease the passage of freight.

Long after the boat had departed and the crowd dispersed, Nathaniel and I would climb to the peak of the watchtower and wait until the topmost sail dwindled to a speck on the horizon and disappeared.

When nothing was left to see, he'd head for the stairs, but I would linger, staring through the archway that housed the giant candle, and gaping at the vastness of the ocean. Here lay a new world to explore, and I'd think about all the creatures living beneath the waves.

With the advent of spring, my twenty-third birthday arrived, a day I'd often worried I'd never live to see. Six tumultuous years had passed since my coming-of-age. To celebrate, I started a new tradition — with each passing year, I promised to gather those I held most dear and head for a feast at the grist mill, a place with special meaning for me.

As Nathaniel, Thomas, Zachariah, and I sauntered down the moss-strewn path, the sound of splashing water filled the air, and I paused to take in the scene. The setting seemed smaller now, less imposing than the one in Riverbend, a town now celebrated by all as the birthplace of peace and enlightenment, where the people had erected a large obelisk that overshadowed the wheel.

As if to join in our party, the world came alive with the welcoming chirp of birds. Sprouting leaves and newly budding flowers brightened our way.

We spread a blanket on the ground by the stream, opened our basket, and laid out before us cheese and smoked ham, and freshly baked bread with a variety of jams.

After we'd partaken our fill, I turned to Zachariah and pointed toward the wheel. "When I was little, even at your age, I'd never dare peek behind to where the shadows lie."

"Why not?"

Nathaniel laughed. "Because she imagined demons of the darkness living there."

The boy's eyes widened. "Do they?"

Thomas grinned at the boy. "We never found out. She was too afraid to look, and so terrified she'd never let us go near. Why don't you go check it out?"

As I slapped Thomas on the arm and glared at him, Zachariah scrambled to his feet and inched toward the stream, but not too close. He braced one hand along the mossy wall bracketing the wheel, bent low, and peered into the shadows behind.

Thomas crept up behind him, pretending to peek as well. "Well, what do you see?"

Zachariah skipped back to us. "I don't see anything. It's too dark."

"So what do you suspect lives there?" I said.

He shrugged. "Maybe rats and bats, or most likely nothing at all. Maybe the wheel is like the carousel back home, another symbol of the earth mother's circle of life, always cycling between darkness and light."

"So no demons?"

He beamed at us, a beautiful trusting smile. "I don't think so, but even if there were, I wouldn't be afraid, because I'm here with the best musician in the world, and a prince and princess. Your magic would be more powerful than theirs."

Thomas nodded in appreciation, took out his flute, and began playing a tune that seemed to harmonize with the flow of the stream.

As he played, I recalled my vision of the future in a place like the hall of winds. I had considered destroying my log because of that dream, but decided against it. The story of our efforts to make a better world deserved a kinder fate than to be burned in a Little Pond fireplace.

Yet now this boy gawked at me through the tangled locks of hair the wind blew across his face, stubbornly persisting in speaking of magic.

The light of reason indeed.

Nathaniel must have read my thoughts. He grasped my hand and, with the slightest tilt of his head, calmed me without words, his eyes alone insisting all would be well.

I wasn't as sure.

Perhaps Zachariah spoke more truth than he knew — that for all our efforts, we'd merely managed to spin the wheel a half turn and emerge for a brief while into the light.

I prayed we'd find the wisdom to end the cycle and never return to the shadows.

The boy came and nestled beside me, and I wrapped an arm around him and squeezed. For the moment, his future seemed bright; for now, the light of reason reigned.

But for how long?

Had we driven the water wheel out into the sunlight, only to have the darkness in our souls rise up again one day, or had we finally learned to master our demons?

As I admired the sparkles flashing off the water, I recalled the words of the earth mother: *"We are the stuff of stars."*

Perhaps, but stars shine only when surrounded by night. Maybe someday, we'd cast off the darkness that lurked in our souls and shine with our own light, always and forevermore.

THE END

Acknowledgements

From start to finish, a novel is an enormous amount of effort and would not be possible without a great team. It starts with my beta readers, including the members of my writing group, The Steeple Scholars from the Cape Cod Writers Center, and continues with Lane Diamond, Dave King, and John Anthony Allen. It finishes with the wonderful formatting and cover art of Mallory Rock. Through it all, the encouragement of others kept me going, my friends and family, including my dear wife, who has put up with my writing aspiration through the good and bad years. Finally, I want to acknowledge my readers, who are, after all, the reason I write, and especially for prodding me to make the first book into a trilogy. So many of you wanted to know what happened to my characters, that I was compelled to give them life once more. Orah and Nathaniel are grateful.

About the Author

The urge to write first struck when working on a newsletter at a youth encampment in the woods of northern Maine. It may have been the night when lightning flashed at sunset followed by northern lights rippling after dark. Or maybe it was the newsletter's editor, a girl with eyes the color of the ocean. But I was inspired to write about the blurry line between reality and the fantastic.

Using two fingers and lots of white-out, I religiously typed five pages a day throughout college and well into my twenties. Then life intervened. I paused to raise two sons and pursue a career, in the process becoming a well-known entrepreneur in the software industry, founding several successful companies. When I found time again to daydream, the urge to write returned.

My wife and I split our time between Cape Cod, Florida and anywhere else that catches our fancy. I no longer limits myself to five pages a day and am thankful every keystroke for the invention of the word processor.

You can find me at my website www.DavidLitwack.com, where I blog about writing and post updates on my current works. I'm also on Twitter @DavidLitwack and Facebook Facebook.com/david.litwack.author. If you'd like quarterly updates with news about my books, my works in progress, and my thoughts on the universe, please sign up for my newsletter.

More from David Litwack

THE DAUGHTER OF THE SEA AND THE SKY

This literary, speculative novel examining the clash of religion and reason is now available.

~~~~~

After centuries of religiously motivated war, the world has been split in two. Now the Blessed Lands are ruled by pure faith, while in the Republic, reason is the guiding light-two different realms, kept apart and at peace by a treaty and an ocean.

Children of the Republic, Helena and Jason were inseparable in their youth, until fate sent them down different paths. Grief and duty sidetracked Helena's plans, and Jason came to detest the hollowness of his ambitions.

These two damaged souls are reunited when a tiny boat from the Blessed Lands crashes onto the rocks near Helena's home after an impossible journey across the forbidden ocean. On board is a single passenger, a nine-year-old girl named Kailani, who calls herself *The Daughter of the Sea and the Sky*. A new and perilous purpose binds Jason and Helena together again, as they vow to protect the lost innocent from the wrath of the authorities, no matter the risk to their future and freedom.

But is the mysterious child simply a troubled little girl longing to return home? Or is she a powerful prophet sent to unravel the fabric of a godless Republic, as the outlaw leader of an illegal religious sect would have them believe? Whatever the answer, it will change them all forever... and perhaps their world as well.

~~~~~

More from Evolved Publishing:

CHILDREN'S PICTURE BOOKS

THE BIRD BRAIN BOOKS by Emlyn Chand:
> *Courtney Saves Christmas*
> *Davey the Detective*
> *Honey the Hero*
> *Izzy the Inventor*
> *Larry the Lonely*
> *Polly Wants to be a Pirate*
> *Poppy the Proud*
> *Ricky the Runt*
> *Ruby to the Rescue*
> *Sammy Steals the Show*
> *Tommy Goes Trick-or-Treating*
> *Vicky Finds a Valentine*

Silent Words by Chantal Fournier

Maddie's Monsters by Jonathan Gould

Thomas and the Tiger-Turtle by Jonathan Gould

EMLYN AND THE GREMLIN by Steff F. Kneff:
> *Emlyn and the Gremlin*
> *Emlyn and the Gremlin and the Barbeque Disaster*
> *Emlyn and the Gremlin and the Mean Old Cat*
> *Emlyn and the Gremlin and the Seaside Mishap*
> *Emlyn and the Gremlin and the Teenage Babysitter*

I'd Rather Be Riding My Bike by Eric Pinder

SULLY P. SNOOFERPOOT'S AMAZING INVENTIONS by Aaron Shaw Ph.D.:
> *Sully P. Snooferpoot's Amazing New Christmas Pot*
> *Sully P. Snooferpoot's Amazing New Dayswitcher*
> *Sully P. Snooferpoot's Amazing New Forcefield*
> *Sully P. Snooferpoot's Amazing New Key*
> *Sully P. Snooferpoot's Amazing New Shadow*

Ninja and Bunny's Great Adventure by Kara S. Tyler

VALENTINA'S SPOOKY ADVENTURES by Majanka Verstraete:
> *Valentina and the Haunted Mansion*
> *Valentina and the Masked Mummy*
> *Valentina and the Whackadoodle Witch*

HISTORICAL FICTION

SHINING LIGHT'S SAGA by Ruby Standing Deer:
Circles (Book 1)
Spirals (Book 2)
Stones (Book 3)

LITERARY FICTION

The Daughter of the Sea and the Sky by David Litwack
THE DESERT by Angela Scott:
Desert Rice (Book 1)
Desert Flower (Book 2)

LOWER GRADE (Chapter Books)

THE PET SHOP SOCIETY by Emlyn Chand:
Maddie and the Purrfect Crime
Mike and the Dog-Gone Labradoodle
Tyler and the Blabber-Mouth Birds
TALES FROM UPON A. TIME by Falcon Storm:
Natalie the Not-So-Nasty
The Persnickety Princess
WEIRDVILLE by Majanka Verstraete:
Drowning in Fear
Fright Train
Grave Error
House of Horrors
The Clumsy Magician
The Doll Maker
THE BALDERDASH SAGA by J.W.Zulauf:
The Underground Princess (Book 1)
The Prince's Plight (Book 2)
The Shaman's Salvation (Book 3)
THE BALDERDASH SAGA SHORT STORIES by J.W.Zulauf:
Hurlock the Warrior King
Roland the Pirate Knight
Scarlet the Kindhearted Princess

MEMOIR

And Then It Rained by Megan Morrison
Girl Enlightened by Megan Morrison

MIDDLE GRADE

FRENDYL KRUNE by Kira A. McFadden:
Frendyl Krune and the Blood of the Sun (Book 1)
Frendyl Krune and the Snake Across the Sea (Book 2)
Frendyl Krune and the Stone Princess (Book 3)
Frendyl Krune and the Nightmare in the North (Book 4)
NOAH ZARC by D. Robert Pease:
Mammoth Trouble (Book 1)
Cataclysm (Book 2)
Declaration (Book 3)
Omnibus (Special 3-in-1 Edition)

SCI-FI / FANTASY

RED DEATH by Jeff Altabef:
Red Death (Book 1)
The Ghost King (Book 2)
THE PANHELION CHRONICLES by Marlin Desault:
Shroud of Eden (Book 1)
The Vanquished of Eden (Book 2)
THE SEEKERS by David Litwack:
The Children of Darkness (Book 1)
The Stuff of Stars (Book 2)
The Light of Reason (Book 3)
THE AMULI CHRONICLES: SOULBOUND by Kira A. McFadden:
The Soulbound Curse (Book 1)
The Soulless King (Book 2)
The Throne of Souls (Book 3)
Shadow Swarm by D. Robert Pease
Two Moons of Sera by P.K. Tyler

SHORT STORY ANTHOLOGIES

FROM THE EDITORS AT EVOLVED PUBLISHING:
Evolution: Vol. 1 (A Short Story Collection)
Evolution: Vol. 2 (A Short Story Collection)

YOUNG ADULT

CHOSEN by Jeff Altabef and Erynn Altabef:
Wind Catcher (Book 1)
Brink of Dawn (Book 2)
Scorched Souls (Book 3)

THE KIN CHRONICLES by Michael Dadich:
The Silver Sphere (Book 1)
The Sinister Kin (Book 2)
UPLOADED by James W. Hughes:
Uploaded (Book 1)
Undone (Book 2)
Uprising (Book 3)
DIRT AND STARS by Kevin Killiany:
Down to Dirt (Book 1)
Living on Dirt (Book 2)
STORMBOURNE CHRONICLES by Karissa Laurel:
Heir of Thunder (Book 1)
THE DARLA DECKER DIARIES by Jessica McHugh:
Darla Decker Hates to Wait (Book 1)
Darla Decker Takes the Cake (Book 2)
Darla Decker Shakes the State (Book 3)
Darla Decker Plays it Straight (Book 4)
Darla Decker Breaks the Case (Book 5)
JOEY COLA by D. Robert Pease:
Dream Warriors (Book 1)
Cleopatra Rising (Book 2)
Third Reality (Book 3)
Anyone? by Angela Scott
THE ZOMBIE WEST TRILOGY by Angela Scott:
Wanted: Dead or Undead (Book 1)
Survivor Roundup (Book 2)
Dead Plains (Book 3)
The Zombie West Trilogy – Special Omnibus Edition 1-3

CPSIA information can be obtained
at www.ICGtesting.com
Printed in the USA
LVOW13s1510070617

537271LV00002B/111/P